SWEET

COLLECTION

including

Out of Place
(No. 22)

Claim to Fame
(No. 23)

Jumping to Conclusions
(No. 24)

Standing Out
(No. 25)

Written by
Jamie Suzanne

Created by
FRANCINE PASCAL

BANTAM BOOKS
TORONTO · NEW YORK · LONDON · SYDNEY · AUCKLAND

SWEET VALLEY TWINS

Out of Place

Written by
Jamie Suzanne

Created by
FRANCINE PASCAL

BANTAM BOOKS
TORONTO · NEW YORK · LONDON · SYDNEY · AUCKLAND

To Mia Pascal Johannson

One

◇

"Hurry up, Lizzie, we're going to be late!" Jessica Wakefield called impatiently to her twin sister, Elizabeth. It was a sunny Monday morning in Sweet Valley and Jessica could hardly wait to get to school.

"What's your rush, Jess?" Elizabeth asked, closing the front door behind her and running to catch up. "School doesn't start for twenty minutes. Since when have you ever wanted to get there early?"

"Today's special." Jessica picked up her pace a little. "Janet Howell asked me to meet her at the fountain this morning."

"Oh." Elizabeth nodded. Now she understood her sister's hurry. Janet Howell was one of the most popular eighth graders at Sweet Valley Middle School. She was also the powerful president of the Unicorn Club, an exclusive club of which Jessica was a member. Jessica and Janet had recently had a big argument about the Hawaiian luau party that they were planning. The argument was so big, Jessica had almost been forced to resign from the club. Although the party ultimately went off without a hitch, Jessica was more determined than ever to stay on Janet's good side now. And that meant showing up for their meeting at the fountain on time.

Walking side by side the twins looked like mirror images. Both girls had long, silky, blond hair. Their eyes were the sparkling blue-green of the Pacific Ocean. Everything about them looked the same, right down to the dimple in their left cheek. But that was where the similarities ended. Elizabeth was four minutes older, and even though it wasn't much of a time difference, she often felt like she was four years older. She was certainly more serious, and much more responsible than her impulsive sister.

Elizabeth was conscientious about everything she did. She worked hard in school, loved to read, and devoted a lot of her free time to writing for *The Sweet Valley Sixers*, the official sixth grade newspaper she had helped found.

In contrast, Jessica was entirely caught up in activities involving the Boosters, Sweet Valley Middle School's cheering squad, and the Unicorn Club. Although Elizabeth thought the Unicorns were mostly snobs, Jessica was convinced they were a group of very special girls. She enjoyed the meetings where they sat and gossiped for hours about nothing but boys, soap operas, and clothing. And, since all the members had to wear something purple every day, it was the perfect opportunity to plan their outfits.

"Hey, slow down, you two!" Ellen Riteman, one of Jessica's friends and a fellow Unicorn, came up beside them. "Today's the day Mrs. Waldron's niece is coming to school."

"For a visit?" Elizabeth asked.

"No, I heard she's coming to stay. Can you believe it?" Ellen rolled her eyes. "Just what this town needs."

"Hey, maybe I could interview her for the next issue of *The Sweet Valley Sixers,*" Elizabeth said. She was always on the lookout for interesting new stories.

Ellen narrowed her blue eyes. "Why would you want to interview a hillbilly?"

"How do you know she's a hillbilly?" Elizabeth asked.

"Because." Ellen let out an exasperated sigh. "She's from someplace in the Smoky Mountains called Stony Gap." She giggled and added, "Can you imagine a place being called Stony Gap?"

"Yes, I can," Elizabeth replied. "That's where Mrs. Waldron's from and *she's* not a hillbilly."

"Want to bet?" Ellen put her hands on her hips.

Mrs. Waldron was one of Elizabeth's favorite teachers. She didn't like to hear anyone speak unkindly about her. "Ellen, you're just holding it against her because you got a C in science last term."

"Well, it *was* unfair," Ellen complained, as the girls approached the school grounds.

"Maybe if you'd studied a little harder—" Elizabeth began but Jessica interrupted her.

"Oh, come on, Lizzie. Don't lecture."

Obviously Ellen had had enough. At the front steps of the school, she said a hasty goodbye to the twins and ran to join Bruce Patman and a couple of other seventh graders.

"I've got to go, too," Jessica said as she hurried off. "Janet's waiting for me." As Jessica neared the fountain, she spotted Janet in a purple sweater and matching plaid skirt, tapping her foot impatiently.

"Where have you been?" was Janet's only comment when Jessica finally got within earshot.

Elizabeth kept an eye out all morning for the new girl, but by the time social studies class rolled around her attention had shifted to a more important matter—her social studies report. She was anxious to see her grade.

Slipping into her desk near the front of the room, Elizabeth waited eagerly for class to start.

When the bell rang, Mrs. Arnette, who was nicknamed "The Hairnet," stood up and faced the class. "I read your history reports over the weekend," she announced, "and I am greatly disappointed."

She peered meaningfully over her wire-rim glasses and began to return the papers.

"In fact," Mrs. Arnette continued, "I could safely say that some of you never even read the assigned chapters—"

"Yoo-hoo! Excuse me!" a loud voice twanged from just inside the doorway. Mrs. Arnette stopped in mid-sentence and spun around to glare at the intruder.

Standing at the door was a tall, thin girl, with dark brown eyes and thick, red, braids. She was wearing a puff-sleeved green dress with a full, billowing skirt. On her feet were thick green knee socks and worn brown leather shoes.

"I'm sorry to just bust in like this," the girl said, "but I'm looking for my aunt Barbara."

"It's her," Ellen Riteman announced loudly from the back of the room. "The hillbilly!"

Ignoring Ellen's comment, Mrs. Arnette went on. "Now see here, young lady, this is a classroom!"

"Well, heck, I know that!" the girl said. "My aunt Barbara Waldron teaches science here. I'm Ginny Lu Culpepper. Y'see, Aunt Barbara was supposed to meet me at the bus depot," Ginny Lu explained, "but we got in early, so I decided to come straight here."

Ellen Riteman chose just that moment to get up and sharpen her pencil. Keeping her back turned to Ginny Lu and Mrs. Arnette, she crossed her eyes and did a bucktoothed impression of Ginny Lu which made the rest of the class burst into laughter.

Ginny Lu turned around and noticed Ellen at the sharpener. She leaned forward and whispered loudly, "I think they're all laughing at you 'cause your slip's showing."

Ellen looked quickly down at her dress and her face turned a bright pink. A white strip of lace showed just beneath her skirt. Someone in the back row let out a loud guffaw and even Elizabeth found herself stifling a giggle.

Mrs. Arnette clapped her hands together sharply. "Class! Silence!" Then she turned to face Ginny Lu.

"Young lady, don't they teach you manners where you come from?"

"Yes, ma'am," Ginny Lu mumbled.

"I'm sure your aunt would be appalled by your behavior and I certainly won't stand for it! Now march yourself down to the principal's office," Mrs. Arnette commanded, "and straighten this mess out."

Ginny Lu turned to leave. "I'm sorry, ma'am," she whispered just before slipping out into the hall. The door clicked shut and a buzz of chatter went around the room.

"It serves that hillbilly right for trying to embarrass me!" Elizabeth heard Ellen say.

When class ended, Elizabeth hurried down the hall hoping to find Ginny Lu and introduce herself. As she rounded the corner toward the principal's office, she was practically run over by Jessica, who grabbed her arm and pulled her toward an alcove.

"Elizabeth, I have to talk to you." Jessica's face was red and she was out of breath. "I ran all the way from P.E. Boy, am I in trouble!"

"Jess, what's the matter? Tell me what happened."

Jessica looked up and down the hallway and then whispered, "You know Dad's lucky tennis racket?"

"The metal one he keeps in the front closet?"

"Yes, that one. Well . . ." Jessica swallowed hard. "It's gone."

"You mean stolen?" Elizabeth's eyes widened.

"No. I lent it to Janet Howell."

"Jessica, how could you! You know that's Dad's prize possession. He said we were never to use it."

Jessica shrugged. "I know that, but Janet was in trouble. She had a tennis date yesterday with Derek Willoughby, a really cute ninth grader. She forgot her racket and since the tennis courts are so close to our house . . ."

"She asked if she could borrow one and you lent her Dad's favorite racket."

Jessica nodded guiltily.

"Well, ask for it back."

"That could be a problem," Jessica said hesitantly. "Janet's brother ran over it with the lawn mower."

"Oh, no. Jessica, that's awful!"

"I know!"

Elizabeth looked confused. "She should replace it then."

"She did." Jessica had been holding a bag in one hand. She reached into it and pulled out a slightly warped wooden racket. "I told Janet that it was just an old racket that Dad had lying around. I had no idea this was going to happen. Oh, Lizzie, what am I going to do?"

Their father, who was usually warm and funny, had no sense of humor when it came to his tennis racket.

Elizabeth put her arm around her sister. "Jess, I think you're going to have to buy Dad a new racket exactly like the old one before he finds out about this."

Jessica's chin quivered. "That's the bad part. I found out that Dad's racket cost fifty dollars!"

"Fifty dollars!" Elizabeth repeated. "That's awful!"

Jessica nodded miserably.

"Do you have any money at all?" Elizabeth already knew the answer to that question.

"No," Jessica answered. "I bought those new Johnny Buck tapes last week and that lavender sweater the week before."

"Well, the one good thing is, Dad has a business trip this weekend so he won't be playing tennis."

"That gives me two weeks."

"And anything can happen in two weeks!" Elizabeth put her arm around her sister. "Don't be discouraged, Jess. I'll help you figure something out."

"Thanks, Lizzie." Jessica hugged her twin tightly. "You're the best."

Elizabeth watched her sister trudge away and got a sinking feeling in her stomach. *How is she going to get out of this one?* she asked herself.

Two

◇

After school ended for the day, Mrs. Waldron drove Ginny Lu back to her new home. Ginny Lu stared glumly out the window of her aunt's station wagon. The day couldn't have gone worse for her.

She could still hear Mrs. Arnette's angry voice sending her to the principal's office. The shrill laughter of the others as she turned to leave the classroom still rang in her head. She let out a tired sigh and sank back against the seat.

"Penny for your thoughts," her aunt said, glancing over at Ginny Lu.

"Boy, Aunt Barbara, today was one of the worst days of my entire life," Ginny Lu declared. "And that Mrs. Arnette is the meanest teacher I've ever met!"

"That bad, huh?" Mrs. Waldron nodded with sympathy and patted Ginny Lu on the knee. "I know it's not going to be easy getting used to this big school. You just have to give it a chance. Besides, that old house of mine is just too big for one person. It'll be nice to have some company again."

Ginny Lu nodded. Her uncle Pete had died several years ago and she figured her aunt must be pretty lonely.

"It's important to give you some of the advantages your mother and I never had," her aunt continued.

Ginny Lu smiled at her aunt and noticed for the first time how much she looked like her mother. The only difference was the way they wore their hair. Her aunt's was short and stylish while her mother's hung long and straight. But they had the same sparkling blue eyes and warm, open smile.

"And we'll start tomorrow by buying you some new clothes," her aunt announced.

"Oh, Aunt Barbara, that would be great!"

The car turned the corner and pulled into the circular driveway in front of a big white stucco house with a red tile roof. Ginny Lu sat straight up in the seat and stared. "Is this whole place your house?"

Mrs. Waldron nodded, her eyes twinkling. "It sure is. The whole thing. Now, come on in and take a look at your room."

When Ginny Lu stepped into her new bedroom she gasped loudly. "It looks like one of those fancy doll houses in the mail-order catalogs."

The room had been done completely in blue and white. Even the wallpaper was patterned with tiny blue-and-white roses. Ginny Lu ran around the room, inspecting every nook and cranny.

"Is this really my very own room?" She had to blink to hold back her tears.

Mrs. Waldron grinned and nodded. Ginny Lu wrapped her arms around her aunt, hugging her as tightly as she could.

"Aunt Barbara, it's so beautiful!" She shook her head in amazement.

"I'm just glad I could do this for you." Mrs. Waldron smoothed her hand over Ginny Lu's hair. "I hope you won't miss home too much. Your mother and I agreed that you could call her once a week."

The hopeful look on Ginny Lu's face made Mrs. Waldron burst out laughing. "OK, you can call her right now."

Ginny Lu let out a loud whoop. "I'd better call her before I wake up and find out this is all just a dream."

* * *

That night Jessica and Elizabeth met in the kitchen for a conference before dinner.

"What have you decided to do?" Elizabeth asked, leaning against the kitchen counter.

Jessica made sure that no one was nearby. Then she whispered, "I'm going to ask Dad for an advance on my allowance."

"You mean you're going to tell him about the tennis racket?"

Jessica's eyes widened. "Are you kidding? Of course not. I'm going to tell him it's for a sweater."

"But will that be enough money to buy a new racket?"

"No." Jessica shook her head. "But it will cover the down payment."

"Hey, you two," Mrs. Wakefield said as she entered the kitchen followed by Steven and Mr. Wakefield. "Time to set the table."

"That's what we were just about to do, Mom." Jessica moved quickly to the silverware drawer. "Is there anything else you need?"

Elizabeth covered the grin on her face with her hand. Jessica was already turning on the charm.

Steven, their fourteen-year-old brother, raised an eyebrow. "Jessica must want something," he announced. "She's being too nice."

* * *

Jessica was attentive to her father all during dinner. "Here you go, Daddy," she said as she placed a huge piece of crumbcake and a steaming cup of coffee in front of him at the end of the meal.

Steven rolled his eyes. Jessica never called their father "Daddy" unless she was about to ask him for something.

"Oh, I almost forgot," Jessica said, as she sat back down at the big oaken table. "I found the most incredible sweater today."

She paused just long enough to wait for Mr. Wakefield's reaction. He smiled pleasantly but said nothing.

"And I thought I should get it because I've been needing one."

"You just bought that violet one with the unicorn on it a few weeks ago," Mrs. Wakefield said.

"Yeah," Steven agreed. "Why do you need another one?"

Jessica shot her brother a withering look, then smiled back at her parents innocently. "Oh, that sweater. It's such a confining color."

Mr. Wakefield reached for his coffee cup. "That's why we give you an allowance." He took a long sip. "Just so you can buy these special things for yourself."

"But I already spent my allowance."

"Well, you'll just have to save up some more until you have enough."

"There isn't time for that!" Her parents both looked up and Jessica quickly corrected herself. "I mean, it's on sale and, well . . . it probably won't be there for long."

"I'm sorry, Jessica." Her father shook his head. "The reason we give you kids an allowance is so you can learn how to budget yourselves."

Mrs. Wakefield nodded. "You should follow your sister's example. How long have you been saving for those riding boots, Elizabeth?"

Elizabeth deliberately avoided her twin's eyes and murmured, "Three months."

A big tear had begun to roll down Jessica's cheek but the news of Elizabeth's savings made her eyes brighten. Hastily she wiped the tear away.

Elizabeth saw the change in her sister and knew exactly what was coming next. There was no way she was going to give in this time.

Jessica waited until the dishes were rinsed and loaded. Then she turned to her sister. "Lizzie, would you do me a teensy favor?"

Elizabeth gathered her courage. It was never easy to say no to Jessica. She could be very persuasive.

Elizabeth looked her sister squarely in the eye. "Forget it, Jess. I've waited too long for these boots. I'm not giving you my savings."

"I'm not asking you to give it to me. I just need a little loan."

"A loan means you pay me back, you know," Elizabeth retorted.

"I know that. Pretty please? You *have* to help me. I'll be in such big trouble if Dad finds out."

Elizabeth felt herself start to weaken. "When did you say you were ordering the racket?"

"Tomorrow."

"Well . . . Maybe I can lend you enough for the down payment," Elizabeth said. "But that's all."

"I knew you'd help me. You're wonderful!" Jessica threw her arms around her sister.

"But remember, you still have to pay me back *and* earn the rest of the money to pick up the racket."

"That's two weeks away." Jessica dismissed the problem with a wave of her hand. "I'll think of something by then." She turned and dashed for the door.

Elizabeth leaned against the counter and sighed. She had a sinking feeling she would never see that money again. And, she thought with a smile, wasn't it just like Jessica to run off and leave her to finish cleaning up.

Three

◇

"Wow, Aunt Barbara, I've never seen so many mirrors in one place!"

Ginny Lu Culpepper stood in the middle of the gallery at the Sweet Valley Mall on Tuesday afternoon. The escalators leading to the second floor were circled by tall pillars covered with mirrors. Light bounced off the glass in a dazzling display.

"It looks like a magical kingdom!"

Mrs. Waldron laughed and gently guided her niece through the crowd of shoppers. They stopped in front of a small dress shop with silver mannequins in the window.

"This is Valley Fashions," her aunt announced.

"It seems to be pretty popular with the girls at school."

"That's right," a voice said from behind them. "It's the only place to shop."

Ginny Lu spun around and saw a vaguely familiar dark-haired girl standing by the window.

"Are you shopping for yourself, Mrs. Waldron?" the girl asked politely.

"Goodness, no!" Ginny Lu's aunt replied with a chuckle. "I decided to help my niece pick out a few new things for school. Ellen Riteman, I'd like you to meet Ginny Lu Culpepper."

"We've met," Ellen said curtly.

"Oh?" Mrs. Waldron said.

"Yesterday," Ellen explained, her eyes fixed steadily on Ginny Lu. "In Mrs. Arnette's class."

"Oh, that's right." Ginny Lu snapped her fingers. "You're the one whose slip was showing."

Ellen frowned. "Yes. Thanks for pointing that out to me."

"Aw, it was nothing." Ginny Lu looked down at her feet and then back at Ellen with a big grin. "Just trying to help."

"Mrs. Waldron, I've got an idea," Ellen said suddenly. "Why don't I help Ginny Lu shop? I'm sure I can find her an outfit that's just right for her."

"Well, that's awfully nice of you, Ellen. I'm

pretty old-fashioned when it comes to what you girls are wearing these days." Mrs. Waldron looked at Ginny Lu. "I have some errands I can run while you two girls shop."

"Just leave it to me," Ellen said, "and when you come back, Ginny Lu can model for you."

"How's that sound to you, Ginny Lu?" her aunt asked.

Ginny Lu could only nod excitedly. Maybe things were going to work out after all. Ellen was going to help her find the perfect outfit for Sweet Valley. Now she'd be sure to fit in!

"OK, honey." Her aunt gave her arm a squeeze. "See you in twenty minutes!"

"Come on, then!" Ellen pushed open the glass door to Valley Fashions and led Ginny Lu inside.

"They sure don't have stores like this in Stony Gap," Ginny Lu said, as Ellen led her toward the back of the store.

"I'm sure they don't," Ellen echoed heartily. She stopped at a rack marked CLOSEOUTS and began flipping through it. "Now, the secret to dressing well is finding clothes that reflect your personality."

"Oh, boy," Ginny Lu mumbled. "I wouldn't know where to begin."

"That's why I'm going to help you." Ellen looked her straight in the eye. "Just like you helped me yesterday." She thrust some hangers into Ginny Lu's arms. "Here, try these on."

"Gee, some of these are a little wild." Ginny Lu pointed to a pair of tights with a leopard-skin pattern. "I don't think they're me at all!"

"Don't be silly," Ellen said confidently. "You're in California now. We do things differently here."

A tinny laugh rippled across from the front of the shop. "Ellen Riteman, what are you *doing* with those clothes? Going to a costume party?"

Ginny Lu looked up and saw a pretty girl with long brown hair looking at them, trying to hold back her laughter.

"Lila, what a surprise!" Ellen exclaimed. "What perfect timing!"

"A costume party?" Ginny Lu stammered. "I—I don't understand."

"Oh, Lila is always joking around. Aren't you?"

Before Lila could reply, Ellen said, "Lila, I'm helping Mrs. Waldron's niece find the perfect outfit to wear to school tomorrow."

"Oh." Lila's eyes grew wide and she giggled. "Let me help!" She dropped the bags she was carrying and immediately began pulling clothes off the rack and handing them to Ginny Lu.

Ginny Lu couldn't believe her good luck. She stood in the middle of the boutique while both girls ran around the store collecting outfits for her to try on.

"OK, Ginny Lu," Ellen finally announced, ushering her toward the corner dressing room. "I think we've got everything."

Ellen pushed back the curtain, shoved Ginny Lu into the tiny room, and hung up two skirts, socks, tights, a couple of sweaters, two blouses and some accessories.

"Now, be sure and put these on," Lila ordered as she handed Ginny Lu a pair of earrings that had bunches of bright yellow plastic bananas dangling from a silver chain.

"Hurry and get dressed before your aunt comes back!" Ellen said, drawing the curtain shut.

"I can't wait to see what I look like!" Ginny Lu cried excitedly.

From the other side of the curtain Lila and Ellen chorused, "Neither can we!"

Ginny Lu put on the first outfit the girls had assembled for her. Then she took a look at herself in the full-length mirror. The leopard-skin tights had blue-and-white striped knee socks pulled up over them and the orange leather miniskirt made her knees look even knobbier than usual.

"Gosh, people in Sweet Valley sure have a crazy idea of what looks good!" she remarked to her reflection. The huge green sweater they had told her to put on was at least three sizes too big but Ellen had said that everyone wore them that way. She knotted the long pink scarf around her neck and put on the earrings.

"Ginny Lu? How's it going?" It was her aunt calling from outside the dressing room. "Where's Ellen? I thought she was going to help you."

"She should be out there somewhere," Ginny Lu replied, slipping into a pair of snakeskin-pattern tennis shoes. "Another girl named Lila was helping me, too. Isn't she there?"

"Lila Fowler?" Mrs. Waldron remarked. "My, my."

Ginny Lu could tell her aunt was impressed. She knew she had been worried about her fitting in. Ginny Lu took one last look at her reflection and threw open the dressing room door.

"Well, how do I look?"

Mrs. Waldron gasped and covered her mouth with her hand.

"Oh, no!" The saleslady standing beside her looked appalled. "How dreadful!"

Ginny Lu felt confused. "What do you mean? Don't I look OK?"

"That sweater is ten times your size," her aunt began.

"I know, but—"

"And those colors clash horribly," the saleslady said. "Is your niece colorblind?"

"No, she is not," her aunt retorted. "It's just . . . well, she's from—she's new to town."

Ginny Lu could tell she had embarrassed her aunt. "I don't get it," she muttered. "They told me this is what everyone's wearing."

Her aunt looked very unhappy. "Ginny Lu, have you ever seen anyone dressed like this?"

"No, but—"

"I'm afraid those two have played a joke on you," Mrs. Waldron said gently.

"No, they wouldn't!" Ginny Lu protested. "They're my new friends!"

Suddenly a burst of laughter exploded behind her. Reflected in the mirror Ginny Lu could see Ellen, Lila, and a few other girls pointing at her through the shop window. Their mocking laughter echoed through the shop. Ginny Lu stared at her reflection in the three-way mirror. Her feet felt like lead as she stood there, staring at herself. She squeezed her eyes shut and wished that she could disappear.

Mrs. Waldron turned sharply and strode to the front of the shop. Lila and Ellen were still howling and patting each other on the back when Mrs. Waldron's voice silenced them.

"How could you girls be so cruel? What gives you the right to laugh at someone, just because they're different from you? You should all be ashamed of yourselves!"

No one said a word. Ellen and Lila stood still and stared at the ground.

When Ginny Lu stepped back out of the changing room with her old clothes on, she noticed that her aunt and the girls were all still there. She was tempted to run right back into the dressing room, but instead, she tilted her chin up proudly and marched out of the store. Her aunt joined her and, side by side, they walked down the long corridor to the exit of the mall.

Once they had gotten into the car, Mrs. Waldron turned to Ginny Lu, her eyes glistening with tears. "It never occurred to me that the children would take it out on you because I'm a teacher."

"It's not you, Aunt Barbara. It's me. I just don't fit in. I'm different than they are."

Mrs. Waldron gazed at her niece for a moment, then started the car. They drove the whole way home in silence.

Four
◇

"May I have your attention, please?" The voice of Mr. Clark, the principal, boomed over the P.A. system on Wednesday morning. "Excuse me, teachers, for interrupting your classes, but I have a brief announcement to make."

All the students in Mrs. Arnette's class sat up to listen.

"Mrs. Cunningham, the art teacher from Rourke Middle School, is visiting us today. As you know, the Tenth Annual Arts and Crafts Fair is to be held a week from this Saturday. Mrs. Cunningham helped to organize the fair last year and is here to answer any questions you might have about entering. The proceeds from the fair, as you know, will go toward building improvements in honor of the twenty-fifth anniversary of our school. Students, please stop by the lunchroom to ask her questions about the fair. Thank you."

Ginny Lu listened to the sound click off on the speaker and said out loud, "I'd like to enter that fair. What do you have to do to get in?"

Mrs. Arnette peered over her glasses and said, "You have to have a skill or talent."

"Well, I guess that leaves you out," a voice whispered from the back.

Ginny Lu spun around and glared at Ellen Riteman.

Mrs. Arnette didn't hear Ellen and continued. "Every year the middle schools around Sweet Valley take turns sponsoring the fair and students from all participating schools operate booths and display their artwork. Will anyone here be entering?" Mrs. Arnette asked the class.

"Ginny Lu could enter and model hillbilly fashions," Ellen whispered loudly.

Charlie Cashman, who sat directly behind Ginny Lu, chimed in. "Yeah, she could show off the latest in overalls and corncob pipes."

Ginny Lu was not only hurt, but angry. She bit her lip and listened to the kids around her snicker.

Then she heard Ellen say, "You should have seen our little backwoods girl at the mall yesterday!"

That did it. Ginny Lu spun around in her seat and said loudly, "Ellen Riteman, you be quiet!"

"What did you say?" Mrs. Arnette's smile disappeared as she focused her steely gray eyes on Ginny Lu.

Ginny Lu slumped in her seat. Before she could answer, Mrs. Arnette said, "Young lady, at this school we do not shout. If you have something to say, you raise your hand. Is that understood?"

Ginny Lu nodded and stared as hard as she could at the eraser on the end of her pencil. All of a sudden the classroom was so quiet she could hear the clock at the front of the room ticking loudly. How come she was always the one Mrs. Arnette caught talking?

"Now," Mrs. Arnette said, "let's turn back to page one hundred twenty-three of our social studies books. Winston, will you read for us?"

As Winston Egbert started to read, Ginny Lu squeezed her eyes shut and prayed for the hour to end quickly.

That afternoon in the cafeteria, Elizabeth paid the cashier for her lunch and then made a face at the meal on her plate. "Zucchini casserole—ugh," she muttered.

She moved away from the counter and scanned the lunchroom. Finally, she spotted her best friend, Amy Sutton, having an animated discussion with Nora Mercandy. She wound her way across the room to join them.

"Hi, Elizabeth," Amy said. "I'm glad you're here. Nora just got this great idea for the next issue of *The Sweet Valley Sixers*. It's about the Arts and Crafts Fair." She nudged Nora. "You tell her."

Nora tucked a strand of long dark hair behind one ear and grinned. "I thought it would be really cool if we had pictures of all of the contestants posing with their entries on the front page. Then inside—"

"We would have a ballot," Amy interrupted excitedly. "So the kids could vote for their choices. You know, 'Most Original,' et cetera."

"We could call it 'The Student's Choice.' What do you think?"

Amy and Nora folded their hands on the table and looked expectantly at Elizabeth. Elizabeth munched on a slice of carrot from her salad, mulling the idea over.

"Well?" Amy prodded her.

"It *would* be kind of interesting to see what the students like best, as opposed to the judges. I think it's a terrific idea!"

Elizabeth reached in her bag and pulled out her notepad. "But we need to get started on it right away. First, we need to talk to Mr. Bowman and have him OK it. Then we have to figure out a way to reproduce the photographs since we usually don't have pictures in the newspaper. Maybe Mr. Bowman will have some ideas."

Mr. Bowman was an English teacher as well as the faculty supervisor for the sixth grade paper. He usually was enthusiastic about his staff's suggestions for articles or special issues.

"I'll go talk to him now," Nora said, pushing her tray aside. "I can't find anything edible on this plate so I might as well use the lunch period for something worthwhile."

Elizabeth turned to Amy. "Mr. Clark announced that Mrs. Cunningham is meeting with people during lunch. Why don't you go tell her about our idea?"

Amy nodded and held up her own notebook. "I was just going to suggest that."

Just then Elizabeth caught sight of a thin, red-headed girl weaving through the tables toward the far side of the room. She remembered the incident in Mrs. Arnette's class and frowned.

Amy saw her, too, and said, "That poor girl. It must be awful to be new and have people make fun of you."

Nora nodded. "You're not kidding. Remember what happened to me when I was new?" Then she looked over her shoulder and said, "She sure has changed since she first arrived here. She was so smiley and friendly then. Now she hardly looks at anybody."

"Well, can you blame her?" Elizabeth said, setting her notepad down. "After that mean trick Ellen and Lila played on her at the mall yesterday, I'm surprised she even came to school."

"Those two can be pretty cruel," Nora said sadly.

Elizabeth remembered how mean Lila and Janet Howell had been to Nora when she was new at school. They had spread the rumor that she was a witch just because she lived in an old house.

"I'm going to go ask Ginny Lu to join us," Elizabeth said, pushing her chair back from the table. "I'm sure she could use a few friends."

"Amy and I have to get going on our assignments," Nora said.

"Oh, that's right. Well, I'll see you guys later then."

Elizabeth waved goodbye to her friends and then looked around for Ginny Lu. Just as she stood up to go get her, Jessica appeared.

"You can't leave now, Elizabeth. I just got here."

"I'll be right back," Elizabeth said. "I'm going to see if Ginny Lu wants to join—"

"Aren't you going to eat your casserole?" Jessica interrupted, sliding into the chair next to her. "It smells delicious."

Elizabeth looked at her sister in astonishment. "Jessica, you can't stand zucchini!"

"Well, I'm starved," Jessica replied. "So anything looks good to me."

"Why don't you buy yourself lunch?"

Jessica folded her arms across her chest and sighed. "I can't. I have to save my money for the racket."

"Oh, Jessica," Elizabeth said, sitting back down and picking up her fork. "You're not going to make me feel bad about eating my lunch, are you? If you're so hungry, spend the lunch money Mom gave you and earn the racket money some other way."

"I'm not trying to make you feel bad," Jessica said simply.

"Well, good," Elizabeth said bluntly. "The whole

problem is your own fault and you're just going to have to work it out by yourself."

Jessica nodded sadly. "You're right."

"OK, then," Elizabeth said. "So if you want to starve yourself to save money, go ahead."

There was a long pause. Finally Elizabeth took a bite of her salad.

"I just thought you'd like to know," Jessica said, "that in order for me to buy Dad his new racket, I'll have to save my lunch money for the rest of the year." Her lower lip trembled dangerously. "I may never eat lunch again."

At the sight of a single tear streaming down Jessica's cheek, Elizabeth dropped the fork on the table and threw her hands in the air. She always gave in when her sister started to cry. "You win, Jessica. You can have a bite!" Then she added, "but just one!"

"Thanks, Lizzie," Jessica said, her eyes glowing. She slid her sister's tray in front of her. "You're the greatest!"

Elizabeth sighed and rested her chin on her hand. Within seconds Jessica had devoured her entire lunch—casserole and all.

Ginny Lu picked at her lunch with her fork but she wasn't very hungry. She had tried to eat but every time she looked up, she'd catch someone staring at her. They'd turn away quickly and then she would hear whispers and giggles.

"I can't take this anymore," she muttered under her breath. She stood up and shoved the tray through the return window. Then she walked briskly toward the exit trying not to look at anyone.

Just as she opened the door, a paper airplane swooped by her head and hit the wall with a flat thunk. Ginny Lu spun around to see who had thrown it and was hit square in the face with another one. She shrieked and ran into the hall. The doors swung closed behind her and a ripple of laughter echoed in her ears.

Ginny Lu decided that it would be safest to hide out in the girls' room. *Why do they hate me?* she asked her reflection in the bathroom mirror. She made a face at herself. *Because you're ugly, you don't dress right, and your hair is awful.* She angrily tugged at her braid, then turned away from the mirror and went into one of the stalls.

Suddenly the door burst open and Ginny Lu heard several girls come bustling in. They stood in front of the mirrors over the sinks, chattering away as they combed their hair. Ginny Lu recognized a voice that made her heart stop.

"Oh, Janet, I wish you'd been there! She looked so funny in the store!"

It was Ellen Riteman. Then Lila Fowler chimed in.

"She stood there like a skinny clown and asked, 'Doesn't this-here outfit look goo-ud?'"

Then Janet added, "It's too bad Ginny Lu wasn't here for our luau party. We could have told her to come dressed as a palm tree and she probably would have."

Ginny Lu winced as the girls imitated her accent. She heard Ellen and another girl burst into gales of laughter.

"Didn't she know she was being set up?" the other voice asked.

"No, of course not," Ellen replied. "She's just a hillbilly!"

A wave of humiliation rolled over Ginny Lu, followed by hurt, and then boiling anger. She wanted to leap out and scream at them all but she bit her lip. She knew she would only make things worse for herself.

The bell rang. Ginny Lu listened from inside the stall as the girls walked out the door and clattered down the hall, their voices echoing behind them.

Ginny Lu didn't move. She stood quietly until a perfect stillness returned to the corridors of the school. She tiptoed out into the hall. At the end of the corridor the double glass doors glistened in the afternoon sun.

I've got to get out of here! she thought to herself. Taking a deep breath, she tore down the hall and burst through the exit doors.

Then she ran harder than she had ever run before. She didn't know where she was going. All she wanted to do was get as far away from Sweet Valley Middle School as possible.

Five

◇

Ginny Lu pounded down the sidewalk past rows and rows of trim suburban houses. She hardly noticed that the neighborhood was changing around her.

The modest homes grew into mansions with neatly manicured lawns that seemed to stretch on forever. Then the sidewalk beneath her feet turned into the shoulder of the road and the houses grew fewer and farther apart.

She ran up over a short rise and a warm gust of wind carried a familiar scent that stopped her in her tracks. It was a wonderful smell, rich and earthy, like

Tennessee, the Smoky Mountains, and her family's farm.

Ginny Lu followed the aroma to a lush group of palm trees. A white fence lined a meadow full of green grass. Next to the fence a large wooden sign hung on twin posts. It read "Carson Stables."

"Horses!"

For the first time that day Ginny Lu smiled. She ran to the fence and hopped up on the first plank, drinking in the view with delight. In the middle of it all were several wooden buildings, painted red.

Ginny Lu let out a hoot that echoed off the buildings. She hopped off the fence and skipped up the winding lane all the way to the stable. She leaned back against the building, closed her eyes and took a deep breath. The air was thick with the smell of hay, saddles, and horses.

She walked dreamy-eyed down the long line of stalls, pausing at each one to whisper greetings to the horses. When she reached the last stall, Ginny Lu peeked inside.

There, standing half in shadow, was the prettiest white mare she had ever seen. Its big brown eyes blinked soulfully and as the little mare stepped out of the shadows, Ginny Lu realized with delight that the horse was pregnant.

"Come here, girl," she whispered, clucking

gently to the beautiful white Arabian. "Aren't you just the prettiest little mama-to-be."

The mare's ears pricked up at the sound of Ginny Lu's voice. She stepped over to the stable door and gently nuzzled the girl's cheek. Her muzzle was as soft as velvet. Ginny Lu scratched her behind one soft ear and ran her hand over the mare's sleek mane. Engraved on a little brass plate along her halter was the name Snow White.

"It's perfect," Ginny Lu said with a sigh. She reached both arms up and hugged Snow White around the neck. "I wish I could stay here with you for ever and ever."

Elizabeth decided to ride her bike to Carson Stables after school. That way she'd have enough time to visit the horses and chat with Ted, the stable boy, before her lesson.

She raced into the kitchen and stuffed a paper bag full of carrots from the refrigerator. Then she tucked a few sugar cubes into her pocket and checked her backpack for her riding equipment.

"Riding hat, gloves, sturdy shoes—all there." As she zipped up the pack, Elizabeth thought wistfully of the riding boots that would soon be hers. She looped her arms through the pack, pushed open the front door and got her bicycle out of the garage.

It was a brilliant sunny afternoon. Elizabeth checked her watch, climbed on her bike, and took off. When she reached Carson Stables, she leaned her bike against the porch of the front office, paused long enough to catch her breath, then skipped over to the tack room.

"Ted?"

There was no reply as she stepped onto the broad wooden planks of the big room. The walls were lined with saddles, halters, and bridles of all types and sizes.

"Ted? You around?" she called again.

When she still got no answer, Elizabeth trotted across the dusty road between the tack room and the stables. She paused and listened to the stirrings and rustlings of the horses in their stalls.

"There you go, Calypso," she cooed to the dappled gray as she held up a piece of carrot. She moved down the line of stalls and each horse came forward to greet her like an old friend.

Suddenly Elizabeth cocked her head. Someone was singing in a sweet, clear voice. And it was coming from Snow White's stall. Elizabeth tiptoed to the stable door and listened to the song.

Go to sleep, my little baby.
When you wake, you will see

All the pretty little horses.
Dapples and grays, pintos and bays,
All the pretty little horses.

As quietly as she could, Elizabeth peered around the door. Unfortunately, the white mare saw her and skittered backwards in the stall.

"Who's there?" Ginny Lu cried, leaping to her feet.

Elizabeth stepped forward. "It's me, Elizabeth Wakefield. I'm in one of your classes at school. Mrs. Arnette's."

"Oh." Ginny Lu peered out timidly from the shadows. "I recognize you. You're in my math class, too."

"No, that must be my sister, Jessica."

"Gosh. You look exactly alike."

"That's because we're identical twins."

"That must be fun," Ginny Lu said, inching her way into the light. "I mean, playing jokes on people and stuff."

"Sometimes it is. And sometimes it's a problem. Especially if you have a sister who's as mischievous as mine!"

Ginny Lu flashed a big smile and Elizabeth thought that she looked quite pretty. Then she noticed what looked like a tiny wooden doll peeking out from the pocket of Ginny Lu's dress.

"That's neat. Where'd you get it?" Elizabeth asked, pointing at the doll.

"I whittled it," Ginny Lu replied. "Back home, I carve wooden dolls for the younger kids to play with. Then they dress 'em in scraps of material or whatever they can find." She held it up for Elizabeth to see.

"That's fantastic!" Elizabeth took the little figure and examined it. The body was carved simply but the eyes, nose, and lips were all clearly outlined in the wood. Even the strands of hair.

"You really like it?" Ginny Lu asked shyly.

"Of course I do," Elizabeth said. "I'm amazed that you could carve it all out of a single piece of wood."

"You can have it." Ginny Lu looked down at the ground and smiled.

"Why, thank you!"

Ginny Lu shrugged. "It just takes a little practice. I'm sure you could learn to do it in no time if you wanted to."

"Yes, but it wouldn't be as nice as this."

"My granddaddy taught me so I've had years of practice. Whittling is my favorite hobby." Ginny Lu put her hand over her mouth and whispered, "Or, I should say, second favorite." She stroked Snow White's neck. "Horses are my absolute number one favorite thing."

"Mine, too." Elizabeth patted the mare's nose. "I wish I had one."

"You don't have a horse?"

"No, I take riding lessons here and Ted—he's the stable boy and a great rider—Ted lets me ride his chestnut, Thunder."

"Boy, you're lucky." Ginny Lu buried her head into the white mare's neck. "I'd sure love it if Snow White's owner would let me ride her sometime." She looked back at Elizabeth and added, "After she's had her foal, of course. I wonder who her owner is."

Elizabeth hesitated. She didn't have the heart to tell Ginny Lu that Snow White belonged to her worst enemy in Sweet Valley.

She didn't have to. Just then a shrill voice cut through the air.

"Get away from my horse this instant!"

Ellen Riteman was standing at the door of the stall, her eyes flashing with anger.

"Snow White is . . . is *your* horse?" Ginny Lu asked in disbelief.

"Of course she's mine!" Ellen stamped her foot

on the ground. "And I am ordering you to get out of her stall this instant!"

"Ellen, why are you being so mean?" Elizabeth demanded. "Ginny Lu was just petting her."

Ellen ignored Elizabeth and stepped by her into the stall. "Come here, Snow White," she commanded shrilly.

The white mare's eyes widened with alarm. She darted backwards away from her mistress.

"Don't you disobey me!" Ellen yelled. "Bad girl!"

Snow White whinnied nervously, her nostrils flaring, and she beat against the stall with one of her hooves. In a flash Ginny Lu came between Ellen and the horse.

"It's all right, girl," Ginny Lu said. "Steady, now. No one's going to hurt you." She reached up and stroked the mare's neck and the horse calmed down.

"Good girl." Ginny Lu turned and walked slowly to the stall door. She unlatched the handle, taking care not to make any abrupt moves.

Ellen grabbed the edge of the lower door and swung it open wide. The sudden movement scared Snow White again and she reared up on her back legs.

"Easy, girl, easy," Ginny Lu said.

"I'll calm my own horse, if you don't mind," Ellen said.

"Well, everything you're doing seems to be scaring her," Ginny Lu said. "You have to keep a nice steady voice with animals and try not to make too many quick moves or—"

"This is my horse and I'll do what I want!" Ellen shouted. Elizabeth could tell that Ellen was getting embarrassed.

Ellen put her hands on her hips and faced Ginny Lu. "What are you doing here, anyway? This is a private club. Members only."

"Ginny Lu is here as my guest," Elizabeth said quickly. "She has every right to be here and I don't appreciate how you're treating her."

"Oh, you don't, eh?"

"No. You're not being very nice."

Ellen couldn't think of anything to say. She looked back and forth between the two girls, her face twisted with frustration and anger. "We'll just see about that!" Then she turned on her heel and marched off toward the office.

"Don't mind her," Elizabeth said, after Ellen had rounded the corner. "She's just upset. She loves her horse but she's been having trouble with her ever since Snow White got pregnant."

"Just the same," Ginny Lu muttered, "I think

I'll try and stay out of her way for a while." She looked over at Elizabeth and smiled. "Thanks for sticking up for me."

"Any time."

Ginny Lu looked back at Snow White and whistled softly. The mare's ears flipped up to attention and she ambled over to the stall door. Ginny Lu rubbed her face against the mare's neck and whispered, "Sure going to miss seeing you."

As Ginny Lu started to walk away, Elizabeth ran up beside her.

"Listen, maybe you'd like to come out here with me when I don't have my riding lesson. Then you could meet Ted and maybe ride Thunder."

Elizabeth lowered her voice and added, "And if you just happened to be near Snow White's stall and just happened to pet her, who'd ever know?"

A broad smile crossed Ginny Lu's freckled face. "Boy, I'd like that a lot!"

"OK, then. It's a deal!"

Six

Crash!

Elizabeth flinched at the loud noise she heard as she walked through the front door. The sound was followed by a series of footsteps and then another loud crash. She sprinted up the stairs and followed the clamor to Jessica's bedroom. She found her sister standing in the middle of her room holding a large cardboard box filled with books. She dropped the carton on the floor with a thud.

"Jessica! What are you doing?"

"Thinking." Jessica spun in a quick circle, surveying her room, then marched straight into the bathroom straight into Elizabeth's room.

Elizabeth followed but stopped short at her doorway. "Jessica, call the police!" she gasped. "We've been robbed!"

The beautiful blue- and cream-colored room that she worked so diligently to keep tidy was in a shambles. The bed and desk were covered with clothes. Every drawer of her bureau was open, and worst of all, her favorite photo of the greatest race horse of all time, Man O'War, was gone.

"Calm down, Elizabeth," Jessica said. "We haven't been robbed. I'm having a garage sale." As Jessica talked, she moved to Elizabeth's closet and proceeded to throw more clothes onto the bed. "You see, I figure it's the fastest way to earn some money."

Elizabeth finally recovered enough to shout, "Don't touch another thing in that closet!"

The strength of her sister's voice stopped Jessica dead in her tracks. "What's the matter?"

"What's the matter?" Elizabeth repeated. "Look at my room! It's a mess."

"Oh, if *that's* all you're worried about," Jessica replied, "I promise I'll clean it up."

She started to move back to the closet but Elizabeth grabbed her arm first.

"Jess, why are you tearing my room apart?"

"I told you. I'm having a garage sale."

"Not with my things, you're not." Elizabeth

snatched up one of the dresses on the bed and carefully smoothed out the wrinkles.

"But, Elizabeth, you know you have the best clothes."

"That's because I take care of them and hang them up." Elizabeth carefully put her dresses and skirts back on their hangers. "And I still want to wear them."

"Please, Lizzie, I *have* to buy that tennis racket." Jessica put on her most pitiful voice.

"Then sell your own clothes."

"I don't have anything!" Jessica wailed. "I already looked."

Elizabeth marched back into her sister's room and dove into the closet. "You've got lots of clothes. Like this! You haven't worn this in a year." She held up a pink sweatshirt.

Jessica grabbed it out of her hands. "I couldn't sell that! I sometimes wear it when I get cold at the beach. Besides, it has a hole in it."

"The perfect reason to sell it."

Jessica looked absolutely aghast at the thought. "I don't want people to think my clothes have holes in them!"

"Jessica, that's what garage sales are for. You sell what you can't use anymore. And *all* of my clothes are still in use."

Elizabeth picked up the cardboard box and marched back to her room. "And one more thing," she yelled over her shoulder. "Sell your own books!"

"Oh, come on, Elizabeth. You've got twice as many as I have. You'll never miss them."

Elizabeth stared at her sister, dumbfounded. How could she explain that each book was a special treasure? Some of them she had read ten times.

"Hey, you two," a voice called from the top of the stairs in the hall. "What's going on in there?"

"Come on in, Mom!" Jessica called cheerily. "I was just helping Elizabeth weed out her closet."

"I would have thought it was the other way around," Mrs. Wakefield commented with a laugh.

"Jessica's room is next." Elizabeth gave her sister a mischievous smile.

"That's good to hear." Their mother stepped back into the hall. "Dinner will be ready in five minutes, girls."

"OK, Mom," Elizabeth replied. "We'll be right down."

While Elizabeth hung up her clothes and rearranged her drawers Jessica watched in mournful silence. When she'd finally put everything back in its place, Jessica released one more pitiful sigh.

"I guess the garage sale is off."

"I guess so."

As Jessica trudged wearily back out of the room, Elizabeth heard her mutter, "Back to the drawing board."

Later that evening, after Elizabeth had finished her homework, she strolled downstairs for a late night snack. Her mother was sitting at the dining room table, turning something over and over in her hands.

"Elizabeth, is this yours?" Her mother held up the little wooden doll that Ginny Lu had given her.

"Yes, the new girl in our class gave it to me. Her name is Ginny Lu. It must have fallen out of my pack. Isn't it pretty?"

"It's exquisite." Mrs. Wakefield held the carved figure up to the light. "A lovely example of Appalachian folk art."

"Really?" Elizabeth picked up an apple and sat down opposite her mother.

"Whittling dolls like these is almost a lost art," her mother explained. "Along with friendship quilts and authentic cornhusk dolls. I have a few clients who are collectors."

Mrs. Wakefield worked part-time for an interior design firm in Sweet Valley and sometimes had to scour the countryside for just the right antique or piece for a client.

"Wait till I tell Ginny Lu. She'll be thrilled," Elizabeth said.

"Well, you tell her that she is a true artist," her mother said.

Elizabeth took a bite of her apple and chewed it for a moment. An idea was brewing in her head. The Arts and Crafts Fair was the very next week and Mr. Clark had said they were looking for unusual displays. What if Ginny Lu entered her dolls in the show? That would be a perfect opportunity for her to make some new friends and build her confidence.

"Mom, you're a genius!" Elizabeth said suddenly.

"Thank you. But what did I do?"

"It's what you said. About folk art." Elizabeth took the doll out of her mother's hand. "I'm going to make sure that Ginny Lu Culpepper enters the Arts and Crafts Fair at Sweet Valley Middle School. I bet she'll even win!" She winked at the little doll and whispered, "That'll show Ellen Riteman a thing or two!"

At school the next day, Elizabeth couldn't wait to find Ginny Lu. But she did not see her at all until Mrs. Arnette's social studies class. Elizabeth tore a page out of her loose-leaf binder and hastily scribbled a note:

Ginny Lu,
Let's eat lunch together. I have a terrific idea
that's going to make you famous!!!

She drew a picture of a horse's head and signed
the note, "E.W." Then she added:

P.S. Mrs. Arnette looks grumpier than
usual. Maybe her bun is too tight.

Elizabeth carefully folded the note, caught
Ginny Lu's eye and then pretended to drop her pencil. They both bent over at the same time and passed
the note. Mrs. Arnette turned around just as they sat
back up in their desks and she eyed them suspiciously.

As soon as the teacher turned back to the blackboard, Ginny Lu opened the note and read it. She
giggled out loud at the last part and then nodded a
quick "Yes!" to Elizabeth.

Later at lunch, Ginny Lu listened to Elizabeth's
proposal.

"I don't think it's such a great idea," she said
once Elizabeth had explained. "I mean, Ellen Riteman and her friends already make fun of me. Entering the fair might make things worse."

"No, it won't," Elizabeth insisted. "If you show your dolls in the Arts and Crafts Fair, people will get a chance to see how talented you are. And no one will make fun of you for that. Besides, I'll bet you'll win first prize!"

Ginny Lu blushed and looked down at her plate. "I suppose I could show them what Tennessee and the Smoky Mountains are like," Ginny Lu said. "Maybe even hang up a map and some pictures."

"You could do a whole display of the folk art and crafts from right around where you live."

"How 'bout some quilts. My mama's quilts win awards at the county fair all the time." She grinned proudly. "Aunt Barbara has one of her prize-winners."

"How about if you displayed other kinds of mountain crafts behind you and then let your special talent be whittling?" Elizabeth was growing more and more excited at the idea. "You know, you could even carve a doll as the judges walked around . . . kind of give a demonstration."

The idea was beginning to get Ginny Lu excited and her voice grew louder as she talked. Elizabeth noticed some kids at another table turn around and snicker but fortunately Ginny Lu didn't notice. "Oh, Elizabeth, my aunt would be so proud!" Ginny Lu clapped her hands together. "It might be just the thing to show her I can fit in."

"Hey, keep it down over there!"

Bruce Patman yelled over to them from two tables away. Then he mimicked Ginny Lu's accent so the whole cafeteria could hear. "You don't have to holler. We can hear you-all clear as day."

The sparkle disappeared from Ginny Lu's eyes and she stared down at her plate. Elizabeth could see that her cheeks were blazing pink with embarrassment.

"Bruce Patman, mind your own business," Elizabeth shouted back angrily. She picked up her tray and motioned to Ginny Lu. "Come on, let's go. We don't need to hang around these bores."

A grateful half-smile flickered across Ginny Lu's face. They dropped off their trays and then walked out of the cafeteria.

"Listen, Elizabeth," Ginny Lu said as the bell rang, "I'm still not sure this Arts and Crafts Fair is such a good idea—"

"Don't say no yet," Elizabeth broke in. "Come with me to the stables after school. We can talk about it more then."

Ginny Lu nodded. "Okay. But I don't think I'll change my mind."

"Just remember," Elizabeth said trying to prove a point, "guys like Bruce Patman don't have any special skills. You do."

"Now, hold on a minute!" Ginny Lu's eyes brightened. "If I remember right, Bruce makes a pretty good paper airplane."

Elizabeth burst out laughing, remembering how many times his paper planes had whizzed past her head in the hallway. "You're right about that, Ginny Lu!" Then she added, "But Bruce could never enter one in the fair."

Ginny Lu giggled and waved goodbye. "I'll think about it and see you later."

Seven

"PRIVATE PROPERTY—KEEP OUT"

Elizabeth read the newly painted sign on Snow White's stall out loud.

"I don't know what Ellen Riteman has against me," Ginny Lu said, shaking her head, "but she sure means business."

Elizabeth glanced around the empty stable, then whispered, "The sign says 'keep out,' but it doesn't say, 'don't feed the animals.'" She pulled a carrot out of her pack and handed it to Ginny Lu. "As long as you stay out of the stall, I guess you're OK."

"Thanks, Elizabeth." Ginny Lu took the carrot and held it over the stall door. She whistled softly into the dark shadows. "Come on, girl. I've got a special treat for you."

Snow White blinked her soft brown eyes and stepped up to the gate. The little mare shoved her muzzle playfully against Ginny Lu's shoulder, knocking her off balance.

"Whoa, girl, whoa!" Ginny Lu giggled with delight. "I would have come earlier but I promised my aunt I would try to stay in school for a full day."

Snow White let out a whinny and nudged her on the arm, trying to get at the carrot.

"Ooh, you're pushy today!" Ginny Lu laughed and opened her hand with the carrot. "There. Now you can have it."

Snow White ate the carrot and then prodded Ginny Lu's pockets with her nose, searching for another.

Elizabeth watched quietly, marveling at how good Ginny Lu was with horses. Around animals she became a different person, confident and sure of herself.

"I hate to rush you," Elizabeth said, "but my lesson starts in fifteen minutes and I need time to saddle Thunder and walk him to the ring."

Ginny Lu nodded. "Sure thing." She wrapped

her arms around the white mare's neck and whispered, " 'Bye, Snow White."

Moments later they were standing in Thunder's stall. While Ginny Lu fed the chestnut carrots and sugar cubes, Elizabeth slipped his bridle over his head. Then they walked him over to the tack room to get his saddle. Much to their dismay, Ellen Riteman was there.

"Just ignore her when we walk by," Elizabeth whispered to Ginny Lu. Both girls kept their eyes straight ahead as they passed. When they reached the tack room, Elizabeth handed the reins to Ginny Lu. "Hold Thunder while I get his saddle," Elizabeth said, hurrying into the building. Out of the corner of her eye, she noticed Ellen and her friends clustered in a circle, whispering.

Elizabeth pulled Thunder's saddle and blanket off their perch and ran back outside. Just as she was about to swing the saddle onto Thunder's back, Ginny Lu screamed, "Hold it! Don't put that on him, it's broken!"

Elizabeth dropped the saddle in midair. "What's wrong?"

"The saddle horn's fallen off!"

Hoots of laughter rang out behind her and Ginny Lu spun around. "What's so funny?"

Ellen Riteman was laughing so hard she could

barely get her words out. "Haven't you ever seen an English saddle before?"

Ginny Lu turned to Elizabeth, who whispered, "English saddles don't have saddle horns."

She hoped that Ginny Lu would calm down but it was too late. The fiery redhead put her hands on her hips and shouted, "Where I come from, we don't need saddles. We ride bareback. Saddles are for babies!"

Ellen stopped laughing and glared at Ginny Lu. "Babies, huh? We'll see about that."

Ellen pushed past Ginny Lu and ran into the tack room. When she reappeared she was carrying a western saddle. "We'll find out who's a baby around here!"

Ellen and her friends walked over to the far practice ring where a black mustang was tied to the main post.

"Uh-oh," Elizabeth said with a groan. "She's saddling up Midnight!"

"Who's Midnight?"

"Her father's mustang. Ellen never rides him because he's too wild. Ted's the only person who can handle him."

Ellen stepped cautiously toward the coal-black horse. After a few misses, Ellen managed to throw the saddle over his back. Then she turned to face Ginny Lu.

"OK, Little Miss Hick from the sticks," Ellen shouted. "I challenge you to ride Midnight!"

"Ginny Lu," Elizabeth whispered hurriedly, "I wouldn't if I were you."

"Oh, don't worry about me," Ginny Lu said quietly. "Back home I break ponies all the time."

She started to walk toward the ring and Elizabeth grabbed her arm, "But he's not a pony!"

"What's the matter?" Ellen taunted from across the ring. "You scared?"

Her friends started to chant in unison, "Scaredy-cat, scaredy-cat, Ginny Lu's a scaredy-cat!"

"You hear that?" Ginny Lu hissed. "Nobody calls me that!"

Before Elizabeth could stop her, Ginny Lu ran to the fence, hopped over and approached the horse.

"Come on, boy," she crooned, keeping her eyes glued to the mustang. "I'm not going to hurt you. Just let little old Ginny Lu mount you."

"Let's see if Ginny Lu, here, knows which end of the horse is the front!" Ellen jeered from the rail.

"You're going to be sorry you said that!" Ginny Lu yelled back.

Midnight sensed the tension in the air and flattened his ears back. He skittered back and forth, throwing his head up in jerky movements.

Ginny Lu kept her distance, all the while talking in a soothing tone, but Elizabeth could hear the nervous quiver in her voice. Suddenly Elizabeth became frightened that Ginny Lu might get hurt and she rushed to talk to Ellen.

"Ellen, this is getting dangerous. Don't let her ride Midnight."

"Nobody's forcing her to ride him," Ellen said calmly. "If she wants to admit she's a scaredy-cat, that's fine with me."

"Never!" Ginny Lu shouted, which caused the black horse to thrash at the ground with his front hoof. "There, there, boy," she purred, softening her voice. "Let's not get excited."

Elizabeth looked around, hoping that one of the teachers might be approaching the ring. But there were no adults in sight.

I know. I'll get Ted! she thought suddenly. *He'll make them stop.*

Elizabeth ran as fast as she could toward the main office of the stables.

Ginny Lu watched her go and her heart sank. Now she was completely alone. Her stomach felt like she had swallowed a hundred butterflies and they were all trying to get out at once.

Keep calm, she said to herself. *Don't let the horse know you're scared. Try to put Ellen out of your mind.*

Midnight stood still, eyeing her cautiously. Ginny Lu took a deep breath and walked up beside the black mustang. She could feel sweat on the horse's hide as she put a calm hand on his shoulder. His sides were heaving as he breathed in and out, snorting nervously.

Slowly, she reached up under his chin and grabbed the reins of the bridle. He lifted his head but didn't resist her. She untied him from the fence and started to walk the black horse around the ring in a circle. She hoped this would show him who was the boss.

"What are you going to do, walk him till someone comes to save you?" Ellen called from the side.

"I can ride this horse with my eyes closed!" Ginny Lu blurted out. She was so angry that she didn't take the time to steady Midnight before mounting him. She just stuck her left foot in the stirrup and swung her leg up in the air.

"Ginny Lu, look out!"

Elizabeth's voice carried down from the hill just as the saddle slipped sideways. Midnight reared up on his hind legs. Ginny Lu dropped the reins and threw her arms around the horse's neck, clawing at his mane for a grip. The useless saddle slipped off his back and fell onto the dirt.

The horse began to gallop around the ring, trying to shake her off. Ginny Lu was jostled so much, she thought her teeth would shake loose. She tried to kick her legs across the horse's back but it was all she could do to hang on.

Over the pounding of hooves she could hear a strange male voice shouting, "Whoa, boy, whoa!" Suddenly the mustang came to an abrupt stop. Ginny Lu felt her body jerk forward over his head. Then the whole world turned upside down.

She hit the ground with a thunk. The impact knocked the breath out of her and she realized she couldn't move. The arena was completely silent except for the sound of Midnight's hooves, as he galloped away from her.

"Ginny Lu, are you hurt?"

Ginny Lu blinked at Elizabeth who was kneeling beside her. The painful jolt had brought tears to her eyes. Her chin quivered as she mumbled gruffly, "Just my pride."

Elizabeth helped her to her feet and Ginny Lu winced. "My pride and my tailbone," she added, rubbing it.

"Well, if it makes you feel any better," Elizabeth

said, holding her friend by the elbow, "you're the first one of us ever even to *try* to ride Midnight!"

"I could've, too, if that saddle had been buckled."

Elizabeth's eyes grew wide with horror. "You mean Ellen didn't cinch it?"

As if in answer, Ted's angry voice cut through the air. "Ellen Riteman, that was one of the most irresponsible things I have ever seen! That girl could have been seriously hurt. I'm going to make sure your father hears about this!"

As Ted strode out of the ring, Ellen hurried after him. "Don't tell him, Ted, please!"

"See, it's Ellen who's the big baby," Elizabeth whispered. "You don't need to prove a thing to her."

"Yes, I do," Ginny Lu said quietly. "I want her to know I'm as good as she is."

"Well, you're not going to prove that by breaking your neck."

"That's for sure." Ginny Lu kicked at the dirt. "But what else can I do?"

This was the chance Elizabeth had been waiting for. "Well, one way you can prove yourself is to enter the Arts and Crafts Fair."

Ginny Lu shook her head so hard, her braids lashed back and forth. "No way!"

Elizabeth shrugged. "I just thought that since Ellen was entering the contest . . . "

"She's entering?" Ginny Lu interrupted.

Elizabeth nodded. "She said she's going to enter her horse drawings."

"Horse drawings!" Ginny Lu repeated. "Why, I can do better than that!"

"Then why don't you?"

"Maybe I will." Ginny Lu put her hands on her hips. "Maybe I'll show Ellen and some of those kids that you don't mess around with a girl from Tennessee!"

"Right!" Elizabeth encouraged her.

"I *will* enter that contest," Ginny Lu announced. "And maybe I'll even win!"

"That's the spirit!"

Elizabeth was answered by a loud whinny from in front of the tack room.

"Come on!" she said. "Poor old Thunder has been tied up forever and he knows I've got another carrot for him."

Ginny Lu followed Elizabeth back to the tack room with a definite bounce in her step. Suddenly, beating Ellen Riteman was the most important thing in her life!

Eight

◇

"It's now or never," Jessica said, as she stood outside her brother's door on Saturday morning. She hated asking Steven for a favor but time was running out. She knew her father was going to be playing tennis soon and she desperately needed the money to replace his racket. Steven was her last hope.

Jessica put on her sweetest smile and tapped gently on his door.

"Who is it?" a voice mumbled from inside.

"It's Jess. Can I talk to you a second?"

"What's the password?"

"I'm serious, Steven." Jessica usually would

have played along with her brother, but today she didn't have the time. "I have to talk to you."

"So?"

"So, open your door!" She could feel her temper starting to go.

Steven put on his Dracula accent. "Nobody enters the chambers of Count Wakefield unless they speak the secret password!"

"Steven, I don't have time to play games. You open this door this minute!"

"Open it yourself," Steven drawled in his normal voice. "It's not locked."

Jessica burst through the door. Steven looked up, startled. He had his ten-speed bicycle turned upside down on newspapers and the gears were spread out over the floor. The greasy chain hung from his hands. "Jess, what's so important that you have to kick down my door?" he asked.

Jessica was about to reply sarcastically when she remembered her mission. She quietly worked her way across the room and sat on his bed. Taking a moment to regain her composure, she began the little speech she'd practiced all afternoon.

"Steven, I've been thinking—"

"That's something new!" He grinned at her.

"Very funny. Now that you're a star on the basketball team, I'll bet keeping up with your school-work is really hard for you."

"It sure is." Steven motioned for her to hand him the socket wrench.

Jessica gave it to him and then tried to find some place to wipe the grease that had gotten on her hand.

"And with all that basketball practice and home-work, it must be extra hard keeping up with your household chores."

"It's a pain." He nodded. "I'm already two weeks behind on cleaning the upstairs floors and this morning Dad asked me to clean out the garage."

Jessica's eyes sparkled. That was just what she wanted to hear.

"Well, I've got a little proposition to make that might just help you out."

Her brother stopped working and eyed her sus-piciously. Jessica added quickly, "And it will help me, too."

"That's more like the Jessica I know."

"Here it is," Jessica began. "I'll do your house-hold chores for you if you'll pay me your weekly allowance."

"Then what am I going to do for money?"

Jessica hadn't thought about that. She bit her lip thoughtfully. "Okay, you can keep part of your al-lowance. Ten percent."

"Half."

"Half?" she blurted out. "While I'm doing all the work?"

"If you really want to help me out—" Steven smiled mischievously, "—then that's the deal."

"Steven! Sometimes you make me so mad!" Jessica knew he had her and there was nothing she could do about it.

"I think you should get started right away," Steven declared. He pulled a broom and dustpan from under his bed and handed them to Jessica. "Mom said she needed the hall swept and dusted. Pronto."

Jessica grabbed the broom and briefly thought about using it on her brother's head.

"Temper, temper!" he cautioned with a sly grin, one hand held up in protest. "Or the deal is off.

"Oh, and Jessica?"

She turned to look at him from the doorway. "Yes?"

"Don't tell Mom and Dad about our little plan. I don't think they'd be too keen about it. We'll just pretend you're helping me out 'cause you like me so much."

"You make me sick!" Jessica slammed the door to block out his laughter but she could hear him all the way down the hall to her room.

* * *

By Friday, Jessica was ready to quit. But she forced herself to hold out until she had gotten Steven's money. That night after dinner Mrs. Wakefield gave them their allowances.

"I just want you to know how pleased we are with you three this week," Mrs. Wakefield said as they sat around the dining room table. "And," she added, "Steven, I am simply amazed. For once, you did everything we asked of you."

Steven flashed a smile that stretched from ear to ear.

"Of course, I know you couldn't have done it without your helper," she said, turning toward Jessica. "Jessica, your father and I both noticed how thoughtful you've been to your brother this week and we want you to know we appreciate it."

Mrs. Wakefield looked back at Steven and continued, "Steven, we hope you will be as considerate toward your sister."

"Sure, Mom," Steven replied solemnly.

"And for setting such a good example, Jessica, your father and I have decided to give you a little bonus with your allowance this week."

"What!" Steven almost leaped out of his seat. "That's not fair!"

"Steven, how can you say that?" Mrs. Wakefield

asked. "Jessica has worked so hard to help you."

"But—"

"I saw her out there, hauling boxes around the garage, while you were shooting baskets with your friends."

"But—"

"And taking out the garbage while you and Joe Howell played video games in the den," Mr. Wakefield added.

Steven sunk into a stony silence. Mrs. Wakefield looked at him sternly and said, "I think you owe Jessica an apology."

He started to object again but the look on his mother's face made Steven think better of it. When he turned to face his sister, Jessica was wearing her most angelic expression.

"I'm sorry, Jessica," he said between clenched teeth.

As Elizabeth watched the exchange between her sister and brother, a light went on in her head. *Of course!* she thought. *Jessica's been doing Steven's chores to get his allowance to pay for the tennis racket! And now she's doubly rewarded for it by Mom and Dad.*

Mr. and Mrs. Wakefield left the dining room and Jessica waited only a moment before she held out her hand. "OK, Steven, pay up!"

Steven shot her his most withering look. Grumbling the whole time, he counted out half of his allowance and dropped it into her hand. "I still don't think it's fair."

At that moment, the doorbell rang, interrupting their squabbling, and Elizabeth ran to answer it.

Someone stood on their front porch, balancing a big cardboard box in each arm. Elizabeth could barely make out the top of a red head.

"Hi," a voice drawled from behind the boxes. "It's me, Ginny Lu. I brought the dolls and stuff for the fair."

Elizabeth grabbed one of the boxes and held open the door for Ginny Lu. She led her up the stairs, pausing just long enough to call, "Mom, Ginny Lu is here."

"I'll be right there."

"I thought my mother might be able to give us some tips on setting up the display."

"Great idea!" said Ginny Lu. At Elizabeth's bedroom doorway, Ginny Lu stopped and whistled. "Boy, your room sure is pretty."

"Thank you." Elizabeth smiled and set the box on her bed. Then she reached for a yellow piece of paper she had laid on her desk.

"I picked up the rules for the contest from Mr. Clark's office. Each contestant gets a six-foot-wide booth with a table."

"That should be plenty of room to show Mama's quilt and her homemade preserves."

Both girls sat on the bed and examined the rules for the contest. Ginny Lu pointed to the last line on the page.

"It says we each get five minutes with the judges. What'll I say?"

"You can use that time for anything. I think you should demonstrate how you whittle these." Elizabeth reached into the cardboard box and carefully removed the dolls.

Each was dressed like a pioneer woman, in a long calico dress and matching bonnet, and stood about eight inches high. Ginny Lu had whittled each face and even carved delicate little hands for each of the dolls.

"These are beautiful, Ginny Lu. Each one is so different."

"Some of them I had already made in Stony Gap but these three I whittled here." She pointed to the ones carved from pine. "Aunt Barbara helped me make the dresses."

"Well, I think they are exquisite," Mrs. Wakefield declared from the doorway. "If I were a judge, you'd have my vote for first place!"

"Why, thank you, ma'am," Ginny Lu said with an excited giggle.

Elizabeth's mother held up one of the dolls and examined it closely. "You know, dolls like these are very rare. They can sell for, oh, twenty-five dollars apiece in craft stores."

Jessica, who was sweeping the hall outside her sister's room, froze at her mother's words.

"Twenty-five dollars!" she gasped. Her mind started clicking away like an adding machine. Selling just two of those dolls could pay for the tennis racket! If she could talk Ginny Lu into letting her show her dolls to some of the stores—why, they could be rich! Of course, she would have to convince Ginny Lu that she should be her partner. But that didn't worry Jessica. Once she turned on her famous charm, Ginny Lu Culpepper would be begging her to be her business manager.

Jessica marched straight down the hall to Steven's room. She knocked three times on his door and sang, "Yoo-hoo! Count Wakefield!"

A voice inside responded in a Dracula accent. "What's the password?"

Jessica opened the door and tossed the broom at her brother. "Do your own dirty work," she snapped.

Then she carefully shut Steven's door and giggled all the way back to her room.

Nine

◇

Saturday morning at exactly ten o'clock, the doors of the gym at Sweet Valley Middle School swung open and crowds of people began pouring inside.

A long banner announcing, "THE TENTH ANNUAL ARTS AND CRAFTS FAIR," fluttered gaily over their heads.

Ginny Lu had been assigned a booth in one of the corners of the room. Sizing up the situation, Elizabeth and Ginny Lu decided to take advantage of the joining walls and decorate the corner to look like an old-fashioned country kitchen.

They stocked the corner shelves with brightly labeled jars of Mrs. Culpepper's fruit preserves. On the other wall they hung her prizewinning quilt, with a sign beneath it that read, "Wedding Ring Pattern." An oak butter churn Mrs. Wakefield had borrowed from an antique store sat in front of the quilt.

"Is everything ready?" Ginny Lu asked, nervously eyeing the approaching crowd. She smoothed her gingham skirt and pulled at the hem of the hand-embroidered apron she wore.

"I think so." Elizabeth put the final touches on the booth's sign. Then she sat back and read proudly, "Folk Art from the Great Smoky Mountains. Ginny Lu Culpepper, Sixth Grade."

Ginny Lu sat on a wooden stool next to the churn, pulled out her jackknife and a piece of soft pine, and started whittling.

Elizabeth flicked on a cassette recorder hidden behind the table and a spirited mountain jig began to play softly. It gave the booth just the right touch.

"Well, you're all set," Elizabeth announced. "I'm going to check out the competition. I'll be back."

Elizabeth strolled up the aisle. There were the usual exhibits—macraméd hangings and planters, knit items, crocheted blankets and afghans, jewelry and stained-glass ornaments. Elizabeth hurried back. She couldn't wait to report to Ginny Lu.

"I just took a look at the other entries," she announced with a grin, "and yours is by far the most original!"

Ginny Lu's eyes shone. "I sure hope you're right!"

While they were talking, Charlie Cashman and Jerry McAllister appeared and stood off at a distance, watching Ginny Lu whittle. They stared at her hands, absolutely fascinated.

Finally Jerry McAllister, who considered himself a pretty good carpenter, spoke up.

"What are you making?"

"This is what's known as a whimmy diddle," she explained. Both boys laughed and Ginny Lu said, "I know it's a funny name but that's all I've ever heard it called."

"What's it do?" Charlie asked, stepping closer to the table.

"See this?" Ginny Lu held up a little hand-carved propeller with a tiny hole in the center. They both nodded.

"I'm going to attach this to the end of this stick with a finishing nail." She tacked the nail in with a hammer and spun the propeller to see that it turned freely. "Then, when I rub a stick over these notches, the propeller will spin by itself."

"No kidding?" Jerry said, joining Charlie to get

a closer look. A few other sixth graders stopped at Ginny Lu's booth, curious to see what was going on.

"Some people call it a gee-haw whimmy diddle," Ginny Lu went on, warming to her audience.

"Gee-haw?" Charlie repeated. "What's that mean?"

"Gee and haw are commands you give to a horse to make 'em go right or left." She held up the toy. "This is a gee-haw whimmy diddle because you can make the propeller go to the right or left, depending on how you hold the stick."

She demonstrated the whimmy diddle and little gasps of delight came from the crowd. Ginny Lu handed the toy to Charlie. "Here, you try it."

"Where'd you learn that?" Jerry asked, as Charlie rubbed the stick and laughed delightedly when the propeller started to spin.

"My granddaddy taught me," Ginny Lu said. "But everyone in Stony Gap knows how to make them."

"Could you teach us?" Charlie asked. A couple of other boys that had joined them chorused, "Yeah, me, too!"

"Sure. There really isn't much to it. While I'm at it, I could teach you how to make smoke grinders, which are like spinning tops."

"That would be cool!" Jerry said.

As Elizabeth watched Ginny Lu demonstrate the toys, she couldn't help feeling proud. The kids from Sweet Valley were discovering a whole new side to the redheaded girl from Tennessee.

The tape ran out and Elizabeth went to flip over the cassette. As she punched the start button she noticed the judges starting to make their rounds.

There were four judges, one from each of the competing middle schools. Mr. Sweeney, her art teacher, was representing Sweet Valley Middle School. At each display they examined the entries carefully and then chatted for a few minutes with the contestant.

The crowd around Ginny Lu was getting bigger by the second. More and more of the students were coming over to watch. Out of the corner of her eye, Elizabeth noticed Ellen Riteman and two of her friends leave their booths to join the crowd. At the same moment, the judges reached Ginny Lu's exhibit and began to take notes.

Elizabeth raised her hand and whispered, "Go!"

Ginny Lu took a deep breath and began to recite a poem she had rehearsed at Elizabeth's house the night before. They had decided that that would be the crowning touch for her exhibit. It was about a young boy and his father, who lived all alone in the mountains. Each night the father would take down his fiddle and play until dawn as he practiced for a big contest.

Ginny Lu's voice played with the rhythm of the poem. She made it sound like a fiddle going faster and faster.

He fiddled in the meadow, fiddled in the glen;
Fiddled over Piney Top and fiddled home again.

By this time some of the audience had begun to clap in time with the words. Elizabeth noted with delight that even the judges were tapping their toes. Then Elizabeth tuned back into Ginny Lu.

So he took his daddy's fiddle,
    and the young boy played and played,
And while the bow sawed back and forth,
    the coonhounds bayed and bayed!

A loud snickering erupted from the back of the audience. Elizabeth spun around to see Ellen Riteman and her friends trying to stifle their giggles behind their hands. Nearby Bruce Patman and Joe Howell let out a yowl like a hound dog.

Ginny Lu blushed and almost forgot her next

line. But she recovered and bravely kept on with her story. She told how the young boy won the contest for his father and brought the ribbon back home. When she came to the final verse, with its chorus about the coonhounds, Ginny Lu shut her eyes.

> He laid the bright blue ribbon,
>   on his daddy's fresh dug grave;
> Then taking up his bow in hand,
>   the young boy played and played;
> And while he made that fiddle sing—

Ginny Lu paused and looked grimly in Ellen's direction. She never said the last line. Ellen and her friends finished it for her.

> The coonhounds bayed and bayed!

Then, to Ginny Lu's horror, the rest of the crowd shouted the line again.

> And the coonhounds bayed and bayed!

Ginny Lu stumbled off the stool, catching her foot and nearly tripping. She searched frantically for a way out of the gym. Then spotting the exit sign, she shoved the table away from the wall, toppling her dolls, and ran as fast as she could.

She felt like she could hardly breathe. The total humiliation of it all pounded in her head like a freight train. The only sound she was aware of was her own voice crying, "Let me out of here!"

Ten

◇

Elizabeth was frantic. She'd spent the last hour looking all over the school grounds for Ginny Lu but her friend was nowhere to be found.

She was exhausted and her feet hurt. Just as she was about to give up, Elizabeth spotted her sister entering the gym and she rushed to join her.

"Jess, I'm so glad you're here! Have you seen Ginny Lu?"

Jessica shook her head. "No. That's why I came. I have some great news. Mom gave me a list of shops she thought would be interested in Ginny Lu's dolls and I went to see them this morning. The first shop wasn't interested, but the second said yes! They'll pay twenty-five dollars apiece for the dolls. Isn't that great!"

"Oh, Jess, that's terrific!" Elizabeth replied.

"I can't wait to tell Ginny Lu," Jessica said.

"If we could only find her."

"What do you mean?" For the first time since her arrival Jessica noticed her sister's gloomy look. "What's wrong, Elizabeth?"

"Ellen Riteman and a few other kids made fun of Ginny Lu during her poem."

"Oh, no! Did it ruin her chances for winning?"

Elizabeth shook her head. "I don't think so but it sure upset Ginny Lu. She disappeared before the judges could talk to her. Jess, I feel responsible. I'm the one who talked her into entering this contest."

She slumped down onto some bleachers and Jessica sat down beside her. "Don't worry, Lizzie. I'm sure she'll turn up."

"I hope you're right." Elizabeth forced herself to smile.

They were distracted by a crackling noise from the loudspeakers. A tall man in a blue blazer was standing by a microphone at the front of the room.

"Welcome, everyone. It's good to see such a large crowd here on this beautiful Saturday afternoon. I have to say, I think the handiwork displayed this year is the best we've ever had. Let's hear it for all the participants."

There was a loud round of applause from the crowd. Then the man explained the rules for judging. Jessica and Elizabeth listened as they continued to search the crowd for any sign of Ginny Lu.

"Where do you think she could have gone?" Jessica whispered.

"I checked all around the school grounds and in the bathrooms."

"Maybe she's with her aunt."

Elizabeth shook her head. "No, I talked to Mrs. Waldron a little while ago and she couldn't find her either."

The man on the stage held up an envelope and announced, "It looks like the judges have made their decisions."

Jessica stood up with her hands on her hips. "Boy, Ginny Lu must have felt really terrible. She didn't even wait around to hear the winners."

"Jess, I'm really worried about her." Elizabeth grasped her sister's arm and pulled herself to her feet. "I'm going to go look for her."

"Okay. I'll wait here in case she decides to come back."

"Great. I'll try her house first."

"And if she doesn't come back here, I'm going to Ellen Riteman's house," Jessica announced.

Elizabeth's eyes widened in surprise and Jessica explained, "I'm going to tell Ellen to be nice to Ginny Lu—or else!"

Elizabeth grinned and set off for the nearest exit.

"I'm going home and never, ever, coming back to this awful place again!"

Ginny Lu threw her suitcase on top of the bedspread and filled it with her few belongings. Then she carried it downstairs to the sitting room and sat down at her aunt's desk. She opened a drawer and pulled out a slip of paper and a pen. After a moment's thought, she wrote:

Dear Aunt Barbara,

You've probably heard how I placed last at the fair and made a laughingstock out of myself and our whole family. Well, I'm not going to embarrass you anymore. I'm going home.

By the time you get this, I will be on my way to Stony Gap. I'm sorry for all the trouble I've been. I guess I just can't fit in with the life out here. Thanks for everything.

Love, your niece,
Ginny Lu Culpepper

As she folded the note and propped it on the desk, Ginny Lu's eyes filled with tears. She realized that there were some things she was going to miss. She loved her Aunt Barbara and her home. She liked having a room all to herself. And even though Ellen Riteman and Lila Fowler had been so awful to her, Elizabeth Wakefield and her friends were kind.

But even so, she thought, she didn't fit in at Sweet Valley and she never would. The only real friend she had made was a horse.

Just thinking about the pretty Arabian mare made Ginny Lu's heart ache. In the quiet refuge of the stall she had often poured out her heart, telling the horse all about the loneliness and frustration she felt in Sweet Valley. When she looked into the mare's warm brown eyes, Ginny Lu knew for certain that Snow White was the only creature who really understood her. She couldn't leave town without saying goodbye to her only friend. Ellen Riteman or no Ellen Riteman, she had to see the little mare one more time.

She took one last look around the big friendly house and then closed the door behind her.

I'd better follow the side roads out to the stables, she thought, *just in case Aunt Barbara finds my note and comes looking for me.*

She picked up her suitcase and hurried toward Carson Stables for a final visit with Snow White.

When Mrs. Waldron answered Elizabeth's knock on her door, she was holding Ginny Lu's note in her hand. She looked as though she had been crying.

"Poor Ginny Lu. I just feel terrible. I promised her mother that I would take care of her—and look what happened!"

"It's not your fault, Mrs. Waldron. I'm sure we'll find her."

"I just don't know where to look," Mrs. Waldron said, walking to the phone in the hall. "I guess I'll call the highway patrol, and check the bus station and airport."

As Elizabeth watched Mrs. Waldron leaf through the phone book, she got an inspiration.

"Before you make those calls, Mrs. Waldron, I think there's one place we should look first."

"Where?"

"Carson Stables."

Mrs. Waldron gave her a confused look and Elizabeth explained, "You see, there's this pretty white mare that Ginny Lu is crazy about. And the horse is in foal and really won't let anyone but Ginny Lu get near her. Anyway, Ginny Lu is very attached to that horse. I think we should check there."

"Oh." Mrs. Waldron nodded her head. "Well, let's go see. I just hope we're not too late."

Eleven

◇

Ginny Lu leaned against the sign for Carson Stables and tried to catch her breath. She hid her suitcase behind one of the white fence posts, then hurried up the lane to the stables.

Because it was Saturday, most of the horses were out of their stalls. Both practice rings were filled with classes in progress. She could see groups of riders dotting the hillside.

Ginny Lu tiptoed down the row of stalls, keeping a careful watch for unexpected visitors. The last person she wanted to run into was Ellen Riteman.

A loud whinny cut through the air and a male

voice answered it. "Easy, girl, you're going to be all right. That a girl, easy!"

Ginny Lu's heart started to pound. It was Ted and his voice was coming from Snow White's stall. Something was wrong with the little mare! She ran to the open door and gasped in horror.

Snow White was facing the door, panting heavily. Ted stood just inside the door, doing his best to approach the mare. But every time he got close, her nostrils flared and the whites of her eyes showed. Her ears were lying flat against her head, a sure sign that she was afraid.

Then she noticed something was different. "Snow White's had her foal!"

Lying motionless in the hay a few feet from Snow White was a tiny brown colt, looking scruffy and very groggy.

"That's right," Ted said. "But she wasn't due for another couple of weeks."

"Is the colt all right?"

"I can't tell," Ted replied.

Ginny Lu leaned across the stable door. "Judging by the looks of that little fella, he should have been on his feet long ago. Why, his fur is already dry from where his mama cleaned him."

Ted nodded. "I found them about forty-five minutes ago and she had just given birth."

"Forty-five minutes ago?" A horrible fear gripped Ginny Lu. "That little horse is premature. If he doesn't start nursing soon, he'll die!"

"But Snow White won't let me get near him. If we don't help him stand up and get to his mother soon, I don't know what will happen." A note of panic had crept into Ted's voice.

Ginny Lu tried to keep her own voice calm as she asked, "Did you call a vet?"

"Dr. Keating's on an emergency. Her office said she'll get here as soon as she can. In the meantime, I called the Ritemans."

Just the thought of Ellen made Ginny Lu's stomach tighten in knots. Then a feeble whinny came from the little foal. He lifted his head weakly and looked right at Ginny Lu.

"He wants me to help him!" she cried out. Without a moment's hesitation, Ginny Lu pushed back the door and stepped into the stall.

"Be careful!" Ted warned. "She might hurt you."

"Aw, Snow White knows me," Ginny Lu said soothingly. "Don't you, girl?"

The mare's eyes flickered forward at the sound of Ginny Lu's voice. She watched Ginny Lu inch up beside her but didn't respond. "There, there."

Slowly Ginny Lu reached out her hand and gently rubbed the white mare's neck. The horse visibly relaxed. She snorted softly and pressed her head into Ginny Lu's hand.

"That's amazing," Ted said.

Ginny Lu scratched Snow White behind the ears and intently studied the tiny foal.

"I'm going to see if Snow White will let me get close to the foal," she whispered. She gave Snow White another reassuring pat and slowly eased onto her knees next to the colt.

"How do you know so much about horses?" Ted asked.

"I help my daddy all the time back home in Tennessee. We have a couple of horses, one old mule and, of course, I've watched a lot of animals being born."

She gently rubbed the little foal's head. "He looks OK, Ted. I just think he wasn't quite strong enough to get out in the world yet."

Snow White lowered her head next to Ginny Lu and nudged the little colt, encouraging him to stand.

"Your mama wants you to get up and I think you'd better do what she wants." Ginny Lu wrapped her arms around the foal and lifted him to his feet. His knees buckled immediately but she held him tight.

Suddenly, Ginny Lu was startled by an earsplitting shriek that came from the stable door.

"Get away from my horse!"

Ellen Riteman stood framed against the stall door. Her hair was mussed and her face bright red from running. Jessica was right behind her, out of breath, too.

"Ellen, you promised to be nice," Jessica managed to say.

"But I didn't promise to let her hurt my horse!" Ellen glared back at Ginny Lu. "Get out of there this instant!"

Snow White tossed her head nervously at all the commotion and Ginny Lu nearly dropped the colt.

"Calm down, Ellen." Ted put his hand on her arm. "She's not hurting your horse. Ginny Lu is the only person Snow White will let get near her colt."

"But what's she doing to him?" Ellen sounded like she was going to cry.

"She's trying to save his life."

"I think Dr. Keating should do that, not her."

"I called the vet and she'll be here soon—but we can't wait that long. That foal was premature and he's too weak to stand by himself. If he doesn't get to his mother, he could die."

"What?" Ellen turned completely white. "Oh, no!"

Ginny Lu spoke up, keeping her attention focused on the foal all the time. "Every second we waste, this little fella gets weaker and weaker. It's important he gets his mama's milk right now."

Ted nodded grimly. "She's right, Ellen."

"I don't know what to do!" Ellen looked back and forth between Ted and Ginny Lu. Finally she turned to Jessica for advice.

"You've got to trust Ginny Lu and Ted," Jessica said quietly. "I think they know more than we do."

Ellen hesitated. She ran her hand through her hair several times. Finally she nodded. "OK. But be careful!"

They held their breath as Ginny Lu carefully lifted and carried the colt over to his mother. When she set him down his legs wobbled and he nearly lost his balance but after a few tries and with help from Ginny Lu he managed to stay on his feet.

Ginny Lu kept one arm around him, to steady him, then gently guided his muzzle to his mother's side.

"All right!" Ted whispered, sounding relieved.

No one spoke as they watched the newborn foal with his mother. His tiny brush of a tail twitched eagerly as he nursed.

Jessica's eyes glowed. "He's beautiful!"

Ellen squeezed Jessica's hand and nodded. "Isn't he?"

*   *   *

By the time Elizabeth and Mrs. Waldron arrived, Dr. Keating had everything under control.

"You should be very proud of your niece, Mrs. Waldron," the veterinarian said, once they had all been introduced. "Her quick thinking probably saved this little foal's life."

"It was nothing," Ginny Lu mumbled. Elizabeth grinned as she saw her friend's face turn beet-red.

Suddenly Ellen Riteman, who hadn't said a word, piped up. "The doctor's right. Ginny Lu was the only one of us who knew what to do."

They all looked at Ellen in surprise. A wide smile crept across Ginny Lu's face. "Well, you were the one who let me help."

Ellen responded with a genuine grin. Then she dropped her head and said, "I think I, uh . . . owe you an apology for a couple of things. I haven't been very nice or fair to you. Maybe I can make it up somehow."

"You don't have to do that."

"Well, I just thought that, since Snow White likes you so much, and you helped with the birth, and all . . ." Ellen lifted her head and smiled at Ginny Lu. "Maybe you should name the colt."

The two girls looked at each other without speaking. "I'd like that," Ginny Lu finally said. "And I know just the perfect name for him—Sooner.

Because he decided he'd rather get here sooner than later. And now that he's here, he's decided he'd sooner stay."

Everyone laughed. Then Mrs. Waldron asked, "How about you, Ginny Lu? Which would you rather do? Go or stay?"

"What?" Jessica exclaimed. "You're not thinking of leaving, are you? You can't! I found a shop that wants to buy your dolls. And I have it all figured out. We'll each take half."

"Half?" Elizabeth repeated, raising one eyebrow.

Jessica caught her sister's glare and said guiltily, "OK, OK, ten percent. I can still buy the tennis racket and have money left over."

Ginny Lu looked from face to face, thoroughly confused. "Why would anyone want to buy my dolls?"

"Because they're beautiful," Elizabeth said.

Ginny Lu tugged at one of her braids and made a face. "I'll bet the judges at the fair didn't think so."

"Judges!" Jessica yelled, then quickly covered her mouth, not wanting to disturb Snow White and her foal. "I knew there was something I had to tell you!"

Everyone turned to look at Jessica. "I forgot to

tell you the most important news of all. You won, Ginny Lu!"

"I did?" Ginny Lu looked completely amazed.

"You won the biggest prize of all, 'Best of Show' at the entire Arts and Crafts Fair!"

Mrs. Waldron put her arms around her niece and hugged her tightly. "Congratulations, honey. You deserved it."

"Boy, I think I need to sit down." Ginny Lu looked as wobbly as the new foal. "So many good things are happening at once."

"You still haven't answered my question," her aunt persisted. "Are you going, or staying?"

This time Ellen spoke up. "You can't go now. Who's going to help me with Snow White and Sooner?"

"Besides," Elizabeth said softly, "I'd miss you a lot."

"Me, too!" Jessica echoed.

They looked at her expectantly, waiting for her answer. Ginny Lu smiled up at her aunt and then over at the Wakefield twins.

"Well, maybe I'll stick around. At least till Sooner is strong enough to gallop around with his mama."

She was answered by a loud whinny from inside the stall.

Jessica giggled. "Snow White thinks it's a good idea."

"And so do the rest of us," Elizabeth added.

Twelve

◇

On Monday morning Elizabeth dashed out of her classroom as soon as the bell rang. The whole school was buzzing with excitement. Mr. Clark had made an announcement over the public address system. A special assembly was to be held in the auditorium during third period.

"What do you think it's all about?" Amy Sutton asked, as she and Nora Mercandy came up beside Elizabeth.

"I wish I knew."

Nora looked both ways slyly and whispered, "I heard from Mrs. Knight in the office that they're planning a big celebration."

"What for?" Amy asked.

Nora shrugged. "Something about a school anniversary or something."

"That's right!" Elizabeth exclaimed. "I completely forgot. Remember, Mr. Clark told us about the anniversary once before, and Mr. Bowman suggested we make it the theme of the next issue of *The Sweet Valley Sixers*."

They were interrupted by Jessica's shouting from down the hall. "Guess what?" Jessica shouted again as she made her way closer to Elizabeth. "Ginny Lu dropped off her dolls at the folk art shop this morning. The man paid her in cash for all of them!"

"That's wonderful!" Elizabeth replied.

"She gave me my share just before first period." Jessica caught the questioning look in her twin's eye and added hastily, "Ten percent agent's fee. That's *all*."

Elizabeth lowered her voice and added, "So what about the . . . you-know-what?"

Jessica beamed at her. "I'm picking it up after school. It'll be in the closet before Dad gets home from work. And I can pay you back now, too, Lizzie."

"I don't understand," Amy interrupted. "What are you talking about?"

"It's a long story," Elizabeth replied.

Jessica smiled at her sister. "But one with a happy ending!"

Jessica left her twin and continued down the hall until she found Tamara Chase and some of the other Unicorns standing beside the water fountain. As Jessica approached, Lila stepped away from the others and pulled Jessica to the side of the building.

"Listen," she whispered intently. "I found out what the assembly is all about."

"How'd you—?"

"Never mind how," Lila interrupted. "Just listen."

Jessica nodded excitedly. She could tell that Lila was onto something big.

"Since this is the twenty-fifth anniversary of Sweet Valley Middle School," Lila said, "they're planning something really special to celebrate."

"What is it?"

Lila took a deep breath, then said, "A time capsule."

Jessica looked confused. "A what?"

"A time capsule," Lila repeated. "You take articles from today, like newspapers and records, bury them in the ground, and then people dig them up years from now."

"So?"

"So, there's going to be a contest. Whoever wins will get their pictures put in the time capsule, which won't be opened for twenty-five years."

"You mean, people will know all about the winners when they open the capsule again?"

Lila nodded. "They'll be famous forever."

"Wow!" Jessica's mind reeled at the thought of being famous way off in the future. "What are the rules?"

"I don't know. That's what the assembly's about," Lila replied.

"I have to win that contest," Jessica declared softly.

"*We* have to win," Lila corrected her. "This is a chance for the whole world to know, forever and ever, that the Unicorns were the smartest and most popular girls at school."

Jessica nodded solemnly. "Of course."

The bell rang and the two girls headed for the auditorium. As she stepped through the double doors, a determined smile crept over Jessica's face.

I'm going to win that contest, she thought. *No matter what it takes!*

SWEET VALLEY TWINS

Claim to Fame

Written by
Jamie Suzanne

Created by
FRANCINE PASCAL

A BANTAM BOOK®
TORONTO · NEW YORK · LONDON · SYDNEY · AUCKLAND

One

$\Diamond$

"Elizabeth! Over here!"

Elizabeth Wakefield turned and saw her good friend Julie Porter beckoning to her. She made her way through the group of students chatting in the hallway between classes. "Hi!" she greeted Julie. "What's up?"

Julie's huge brown eyes were bright with anticipation. "I just heard there's going to be an assembly this period."

"I know," Elizabeth said. "It's got something to do with the middle school's twenty-fifth anniversary."

"Do you know what they're planning?"

Elizabeth shook her head. "No. But I've heard rumors that something really special is going to be announced."

"That's what I heard, too," Julie said. "When I

went by the principal's office I heard the secretaries talking about the assembly. They were saying something about a contest."

"What kind of a contest?"

"I don't know," Julie admitted. "But it's going to be part of the anniversary celebration."

"I wonder what a contest has to do with an anniversary," Elizabeth mused.

Other kids at school seemed to have heard the rumor about the contest too. As the two girls made their way down the hall, Elizabeth noticed several groups of students talking excitedly. She spotted her twin sister, Jessica, talking to her best friend, Lila Fowler.

"Maybe they know what's going on," Elizabeth said to Julie. "Hey, Jess, did you hear anything about the assembly this morning?"

Jessica nodded and exchanged a glance with Lila. They looked unusually smug. It was obvious that they knew something no one else knew.

Just then, Amy Sutton, Elizabeth's best friend, walked over and joined them.

"Hi, Amy. We're trying to pry some information out of Jessica," Elizabeth said.

"It's no big deal," Lila announced, looking bored. "It's just about that dumb twenty-fifth anniversary business."

"We *knew* that," Julie told her. "But I heard it's about some kind of contest, too."

"Oh, really?" Lila studied her fingernails casually. "What sort of contest?"

"Well, I guess we'll just have to find out when we get there," Elizabeth said. She had a strong suspicion that both Lila and Jessica knew a lot more than they were saying. But it was typical of Lila to want to keep the secret. It made her feel important.

"Lila always tries to act so cool," Amy whispered to Elizabeth and Julie as the took their seats in their classroom. "*I* don't think a twenty-fifth anniversary is dumb."

"Neither do I," Elizabeth whispered back. "I think it's neat! But you know how Lila is. . . ."

"Snobby," Amy broke in. Elizabeth wasn't that fond of Lila either, but Lila *was* Jessica's friend, so she had to be careful about what she said.

"I don't know why your sister hangs out with her," Amy mumbled.

"Well, they're both Unicorns, and Unicorns stick together," Elizabeth replied. The Unicorn Club was made up of a group of snobby girls who thought they were as special and as beautiful as the mythical beast for which their club was named. Just then, their teacher, Ms. Wyler, entered the room and began taking roll. Elizabeth sat quietly at her desk thinking about her twin sister.

Of course, it wasn't really surprising that she and Jessica had such different friends. They looked exactly alike on the outside, with the same long, blond hair, blue-green eyes, and a dimple in their left cheeks. But apart from that, they were complete opposites.

Elizabeth knew people thought of her as the more serious twin. She liked having fun and doing things with her good friends, but she also loved reading, writing, and spending time alone, just thinking.

Jessica, on the other hand, always liked to be the center of attention. She spent most of her free time with fellow members of the Unicorn Club, talking about clothes, makeup, and boys.

Elizabeth wasn't very interested in the Unicorn Club. Personally, she thought that most of the members were snobs. But she tried to be polite to them since they were Jessica's friends. In spite of all their differences, Jessica and Elizabeth were still the closest of friends and Elizabeth would never do anything to hurt her twin.

Elizabeth was jolted back into the present by the announcement that came over the intercom.

"Attention, all classes. Please proceed to the auditorium for a special assembly."

Elizabeth, Amy, and Julie joined the line of students filing out of the room. "Wow, this is great! We get to miss part of our class," Amy said. "I wonder if we'll find out what Sweet Valley Middle School was like twenty-five years ago. It was called Sweet Valley Junior High then," Amy informed them.

"How did you know that?" Julie asked.

"One of my mother's friends went to school here when it first opened," Amy replied. "She was a cheerleader."

"It must have been so different!" Elizabeth exclaimed.

Amy grinned. "I've even seen pictures of her when she was my age."

"What did she look like then?"

Amy giggled. "She had her hair all puffed up. She said all the girls used to tease their hair to get it like that. They called it 'ratting.'"

Julie made a face. "Ugh. That sounds gross!"

The girls entered the auditorium and took seats near the front. When everyone was settled, the principal, Mr. Clark, cleared his throat and spoke into the microphone on the stage.

"Good morning, students. I've called this special assembly today to tell you about a very exciting upcoming event. As you all must know by now, this year is the twenty-fifth anniversary of the opening of Sweet Valley Middle School. And I'm sure you'll agree with me that this is a cause for celebration."

"That's your opinion," hissed a voice behind Elizabeth. "Who wants to celebrate a school opening?"

Elizabeth didn't have to turn around to know it was Bruce Patman speaking. He was a conceited seventh grader who was always saying obnoxious things like that.

"We're kicking off the festivities," Mr. Clark continued, "with a dance next Friday to raise money for new softball dugouts."

Amy groaned. "A dance! I thought we were going to have a contest."

"Oh, come on, Amy. A dance will be fun," Elizabeth said enthusiastically.

Across the auditorium, Jessica Wakefield could hardly contain herself. The mere mention of a dance and she was already planning what she was going to wear.

"In honor of our anniversary," Mr. Clark went on, "this dance will have a sixties theme. We invite you to wear sixties clothes, dance to sixties music, and get the feel of what this school was like twenty-five years ago."

"Wow, this is going to be great," Jessica squealed excitedly. Lila nodded and murmured, "I think all the Unicorns should wear purple miniskirts."

Jessica agreed enthusiastically. Purple was the Unicorn official color and each member tried to wear something purple every day. Miniskirts would be fabulous!

"And," Mr. Clark continued, "we've got something very special planned. Mrs. Arnette, would you tell the students about your idea?"

The social studies teacher made her way up the stairs to the stage and over to the microphone.

Lila turned to Jessica and rolled her eyes. "I guess the Hairnet's going to tell us about the contest."

Jessica giggled. They called Mrs. Arnette "the Hairnet" because she always wore one.

The usually serious-looking teacher was smiling as she took the microphone. "As Mr. Clark told you, new softball field dugouts are going to be built. When the ground is broken to start construction, we're going to bury a time capsule, to be opened twenty-five years from now."

A murmur went through the auditorium and Mrs. Arnette rapped the podium for silence.

"I'm sure you're all wondering what's going to be placed inside the time capsule. Well, boys and girls, that's up to you. To make the collection of items as interesting and as varied as possible, we're going to hold a contest."

Jessica and Lila looked at each other and grinned.

Mrs. Arnette continued. "All students who would like to participate can team up in groups of four. Each team must find three items that symbolize the sixties, preferably from this school. The closer to the early sixties the better. Two weeks from tomorrow, a panel of teachers will decide which team has the most outstanding collection. The winners will get their pictures in *The Sweet Valley News*. And that's not all." She paused for a moment. "They will also have their photos placed in the time capsule."

Jessica already knew about this from Lila, who

somehow had a way of finding things out before anyone else. She turned to Lila. "Just think! Twenty-five years from now people will be looking at those pictures!"

Lila's eyes were gleaming. "And I know whose photos they'll be looking at! Ours!"

It was clear that a lot of other kids were having the same thought. As Mr. Clark dismissed the assembly, students began huddling together in groups and talking excitedly.

Ellen Riteman and Tamara Chase joined Jessica and Lila in the aisle. "We have absolutely got to win this contest," Lila informed them.

"If we can get our pictures in the time capsule, the Unicorns will have lasting fame," Jessica said happily.

Lila nodded and said, "Twenty-five years from now, when people find our pictures in the time capsule, they'll know we were the most important people at this school!"

"You're absolutely right, Lila," Ellen agreed. "This could make the Unicorns world famous!"

Tamara looked around the room. "It won't be easy coming up with the best stuff," she noted.

"Then we're just going to have to work harder," Jessica said excitedly. "Right?"

"Right," Lila said. "We'll have to find the best, most interesting things from the sixties. And we'll have to work fast to find them before anyone else does. After all, the reputation of the Unicorns is at stake!"

"This contest is going to be a lot of fun," Elizabeth said to Amy and Julie as they walked back toward their classroom. "I'll bet people come up with all kinds of interesting things."

"What sort of things were special in the sixties?" Amy wondered.

"A lot of people were hippies," Julie noted. "I saw an old photo in a scrapbook of my father playing a guitar. He had long hair, bell-bottom jeans, and he was wearing love beads!"

"Love beads!" Elizabeth tried to picture Julie's father wearing a necklace. It was impossible.

"Maybe he still has them," Amy said. "He could give them to us for the time capsule!"

Mrs. Arnette approached them. "Are you girls talking about the time capsule?"

Elizabeth nodded. "We're going to sign up for the contest as soon as we get a fourth person for our team."

"Well, I believe I've got a fourth person for you," Mrs. Arnette said.

"Who's that, Mrs. Arnette?" Julie asked.

"George Henkel," the teacher said. "I think it would be very nice if you girls invited him to join your team."

Elizabeth barely knew George, even though

they had a few classes together. He never spoke in class, and he didn't seem to have any friends. At least, whenever Elizabeth saw him, he was alone.

Mrs. Arnette was still standing beside them, waiting for an answer. Elizabeth spoke first. "I guess we could ask him to join us," she said. "Is that okay with you guys?"

"Sure," Julie said uncertainly. Amy just murmured, "OK with me."

Elizabeth knew they didn't sound terribly enthusiastic about the idea, but Mrs. Arnette was looking at them with approval. "We'll go ask him right now," Elizabeth said.

"I've never even noticed him before," Julie confessed in a whisper as the girls walked back to class.

"I'll bet he won't even want to do this," Amy added. "He doesn't seem like the type who would be interested."

"We'll never know unless we ask," Elizabeth said.

George didn't look up as they approached him. Elizabeth coughed to get his attention. When he saw them, he looked startled.

"Uh, George, we need a fourth person on our team for the time capsule contest. Would you like to join us?" Elizabeth asked.

He stared at them, as if he wasn't sure he'd heard her correctly. "You want me on your team?"

The girls nodded.

"Why?"

Elizabeth bit her lip and tried to think quickly. "Well, we thought it would be good to have someone who was in a class with us," she began. "So we could get together easily."

It wasn't much of a reason, and she didn't think George would buy it. But he just shrugged. "OK."

"Good!" Elizabeth said brightly.

George didn't say anything else, and they all just stood there awkwardly. Then Elizabeth thought of something.

"George, there's a Howard Henkel who doesn't live far from my house. Are you any relation to him?"

George stared at the floor for a minute. Then he nodded. "He's my father."

Elizabeth tried very hard not to look as surprised as she was. Mr. Henkel was a strange, reclusive man who was confined to a wheelchair. Elizabeth sometimes ran errands for him. And she'd never seen George there.

Amy didn't bother to hide her surprise. "You live near the Wakefields?"

"No," George said quickly. "My father does. I live with my aunt and uncle."

"Where's your mother?" Amy asked bluntly.

"She's dead," George replied.

There was another moment of awkward silence. "I guess we'd better sit down before the bell rings,"

Julie said. "When are we all going to get together?"

"Tomorrow's Saturday. Why don't we meet downtown," Elizabeth suggested. "How about one o'clock, in front of the drugstore?"

"OK," George said. Julie and Amy agreed, too.

Taking her seat at the front of the room, Elizabeth couldn't resist glancing back at George. She still couldn't believe George was Mr. Henkel's son. She'd never even seen George in the neighborhood.

The bell rang, and Elizabeth tried to concentrate on class. But it wasn't easy. All through class, she wondered about George. Why did he live with his aunt and uncle? Why didn't he live with his father?

Two

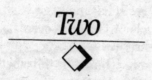

The next morning, Jessica lay in bed and thought about the time capsule. It would be buried for twenty-five years. The kids who would open it weren't even born yet!

She closed her eyes and tried to picture Sweet Valley Middle School twenty-five years into the future. In her imagination, students were opening the time capsule, and one of them pulled out a photograph of Jessica.

"What a beautiful girl," one student exclaimed. "She must have been really important to get her picture in the time capsule!"

"Jessica! Last chance for breakfast!" Her mother's voice broke into her fantasy. Jessica sighed before pulling herself out of bed and throwing on a robe.

"I was wondering if you planned to spend the

day in bed," Mrs. Wakefield commented as Jessica strolled into the kitchen.

Jessica grinned. "No way! I'm meeting Lila, Tamara, and Ellen at the mall."

Her brother, Steven, was at the table, working his way through a heaping bowl of cereal. "Didn't you guys just go to the mall last week?" he asked. "The stores probably haven't even had time to restock their shelves yet."

Jessica ignored him. "Is Elizabeth still sleeping?" she asked her mother.

Her mother handed her a glass of juice. "No, your sister was up and out ages ago. Do you want cereal or eggs?"

Jessica looked at her mother in dismay. Was Elizabeth already out hunting with her team?

"She's out helping Mr. Henkel," Mrs. Wakefield continued.

Jessica made a face as she sat down at the kitchen table. "He gives me the creeps. He just sits in that wheelchair and looks mean. Why does Elizabeth go over there anyway?"

"Because she cares about people." Mrs. Wakefield placed a bowl of cereal in front of Jessica. "And I wouldn't call him mean, Jessica." She paused thoughtfully. "I think he looks sad."

Jessica shrugged. She had other things on her mind right now.

"Mom, who do you know who went to Sweet Valley Middle School when it first opened?"

Her mother wrinkled her brow. "Let me think about that."

"Did you save anything from where you went to school? Like, maybe cheerleading pom-poms?"

Mrs. Wakefield laughed. "Good heavens, no."

Steven looked at her curiously. "What do you want old cheerleading pom-poms for? Can't the school afford to buy new ones?"

Jessica rolled her eyes. "It's for our time capsule, dummy. We're having a contest at school to see who can bring in the three best items representing Sweet Valley Middle School in the sixties. And I just thought Mom could give me some good ideas."

"Is Elizabeth entering the contest, too?" Mrs. Wakefield asked.

Jessica nodded. "But we're on different teams." The minute those words left her mouth, she wished she could take them back. Knowing they were on different sides was going to give Steven a great excuse to tease them. Not that he ever needed an excuse. Before he could say anything, she turned pleading eyes to her mother. "Can you think of any good ideas for collecting stuff?"

"Well maybe I'll go through some of my old things in the basement when I have a chance."

"Thanks." Hastily, Jessica gulped down the rest

of her juice and finished eating her cereal. "I better go get dressed. See ya later, Mom."

An hour later, Jessica was hurrying into Casey's Place, an ice cream parlor at the mall. Lila, Ellen, and Tamara were already there, waiting for her in a booth. Jessica slid in next to Lila. "Sorry I'm late," she said breathlessly.

"You haven't missed anything," Lila told her. "We're trying to think of special things that have something to do with the sixties. Do you have any ideas?"

Jessica thought. "We could find some pictures of people back then. I know my mother has an old scrapbook."

Lila shook her head. "That's not special enough. We need things that will really impress the judges. Anyone can bring in old photographs."

"What about old clothes?" Ellen suggested.

"Everyone will be looking for old clothes for the dance," Jessica told her. "And they might use them for their time capsule collections too."

"We need things that are more original," Lila said firmly. "We've got to come up with stuff no one else has. Everybody, *think!*"

They sat there in silence, thinking. But no one came up with any brilliant ideas. A waitress came up to their table.

"What can I get you girls?"

Jessica was on the verge of suggesting hot fudge

sundaes, but Lila jumped up suddenly. "Nothing," she said to the waitress, turning to the others. "We're wasting time just sitting here. Let's walk around the mall and see if we get any ideas. It's much too early for ice cream, anyway."

Jessica and the others followed her out of the ice cream parlor. Once in the mall, they began strolling past the stores and looking in the windows. Tamara paused in front of a jewelry store.

"I've seen pictures of people wearing peace symbols around their necks," Jessica remarked. She scanned the window display, but she didn't see anything that looked like a peace symbol.

"Ooh, let's go in the poster shop!" Ellen exclaimed.

Lila looked at her in exasperation. "We're not going to find what we need in there."

"I know," Ellen said, "but I want a new poster for my bedroom. Can't we just go in there for a minute?"

Lila sighed. "OK, but just for a minute."

They were on their way across the mall to the poster shop when Jessica stopped suddenly. "Look," she whispered to Lila. "It's Bruce Patman."

Bruce sauntered toward them carrying a bag and looking very pleased with himself.

"Hi Bruce," Jessica called out sweetly. Behind her, Ellen and Tamara were giggling. "What are you doing here?"

"I'm meeting some of the guys," Bruce said. "We're just going to hang out."

"We're trying to find things for the time capsule," Jessica told him. Lila poked her in the ribs.

"And we've already found some wonderful things," Lila added quickly. "But don't ask us what they are because we're not telling."

Bruce grinned. "I don't even want to know. I just got something pretty fantastic for my team. This alone ought to get our pictures in the time capsule." He held up the bag, and the girls looked at it curiously.

To Jessica's surprise, Bruce opened the bag. "And I don't mind showing you, either. 'Cause you'll never find anything like this." He stuck his hand in the bag and pulled out an oddly shaped metal figure.

Jessica stared at it. "What's that?"

Bruce smirked. "It's the hood ornament from a Corvette Stingray. That was one of the most popular cars in the sixties, and they don't even make them anymore."

Jessica's heart sank. She knew what Bruce was holding could be a winning item. "Where'd you get it?"

"It's from one of my father's first cars," Bruce said. "He's been saving it all these years."

"And he's going to let you bury it in the time capsule?" Lila asked.

Bruce's smirk faded a little and he didn't look quite so confident. "Well, I haven't actually asked him yet. I just took it from his desk to show the guys."

Jessica gave Lila a reassuring look. She was sure Mr. Patman wouldn't want Bruce putting his hood ornament somewhere where he couldn't see it again for twenty-five years.

"That's very nice, Bruce," Lila said. "But I think maybe you'd better ask your father before you start bragging about winning the contest." She turned abruptly and headed for the poster store. Jessica managed to flash one quick smile at Bruce before following her. Bruce might be a showoff, but he was still pretty cute.

"His father will never go for that," Jessica said confidently as they entered the poster store.

"I'm not so sure about that," Lila said with less confidence. "Bruce is used to getting everything he wants."

Jessica stifled a laugh. If anyone got what she wanted, it was Lila—she was an only child and her father was one of the wealthier men in Sweet Valley. All Lila had to do was mention something once and she got it.

Tamara and Ellen paused to admire a poster of a rock star, while Jessica and Lila wandered toward the back, gazing at all the other posters.

"Oh, Lila, look," Jessica sighed. "It's a poster

from *Gone With the Wind*. Remember when we checked out that video?"

Lila didn't answer. She stared at the poster, and then her eyes widened, as if something had just occurred to her. Quickly, she called to a salesperson. "Do you have any movie posters from the 1960s?"

"Why, yes, we do," the man replied. "Any movie in particular?"

"No," Lila said. "But I'm looking for something that was very popular and *very* sixties."

The man smiled and went over to a special poster rack. Jessica and Lila followed him and waited while he flipped through the rack.

"Here's one you girls might like," he said. "I was a teenager when this film came out, and I can assure you, it was very popular."

"*Bikini Beach Party,*" Jessica read from the poster. The picture showed a group of teenagers on the beach. "Lila, this is perfect!"

"It's rather expensive," the man warned them. "You see, it's an original, not a reproduction. This actual poster was used in a movie theater, right here in Sweet Valley. It's a collector's item, so it costs quite a bit more than our usual posters."

Lila casually pulled out her father's credit card and said, "We'll take it."

Jessica hugged herself in glee. "Lila, this is great! I'll bet no one else comes up with an original movie poster!"

Ellen and Tamara joined them, and Lila and Jessica told them about their find. They all agreed it would be a perfect contribution to the time capsule.

"That's one down, two to go," Ellen noted. "What else can we get?"

Lila cocked her head to one side. "You know, I keep thinking about Bruce's hood ornament. I wonder if my father saved anything like that."

"I asked my mother, too," Jessica said. "She's checking."

"Let's go back to my house and see if my father has anything," Lila suggested. The salesman returned with the rolled-up poster neatly wrapped in brown paper, and the girls took off.

On the way back to Lila's, the girls talked about other possible items for the capsule. "What does Elizabeth have?" Lila asked Jessica.

"I don't think her team has started looking yet," Jessica said.

"I'll bet they're out looking today," Lila remarked. "Maybe you should sneak into her room when she's not there and take a look around."

"OK," Jessica said slowly, but she felt a little funny about spying on her own sister. Lila seemed to read her thoughts.

"Remember," she pointed out, "you're doing this for the Unicorns."

"I know, I know," Jessica said quickly. "I'll see what I can find out."

When they arrived at Lila's big house, Mrs. Pervis, the Fowlers' housekeeper, let them in. "Where's my father?" Lila asked her.

"He's not home at the moment, dear," Mrs. Pervis told her, and Lila frowned. She turned to the others. "Let's go in the den. He keeps a lot of stuff in there. Maybe we'll find something."

"Would you girls like some sandwiches and sodas?" Mrs. Pervis asked them as they trailed into the den.

"Yes," Lila yelled over her shoulder.

Jessica couldn't believe that Lila didn't even say thank you. If Mrs. Wakefield offered refreshments and Jessica didn't bother to thank her, they'd never see those sandwiches!

The den was a big room filled with lots of fancy stereo equipment. "You can put some records on," Lila called to the others.

Jessica began looking through the huge record collection. She had never heard of most of the names, but she found one album that was familiar.

"*Meet the Beatles*," she read from the cover. "I know this record. It was their first album. They still play it on the radio all the time." When she slid the record out from the sleeve, she noticed it was pretty scratched up. "This must be really old."

Lila gasped and whirled around. "The Beatles! They were big in the sixties!"

"And this must be an original record!" Jessica

exclaimed. "Lila, this is fantastic! My father told me the Beatles were the number one group when he was younger."

"It's perfect for the time capsule," Ellen said happily. "Would your father mind if we took it?"

"He'll never even notice that it's gone," Lila replied. "OK, now we've got two terrific things. All we need is one more."

"Any ideas?" Lila asked.

"I can still check with my mother," Jessica said. "Of course, if she does find something, I'll have to fight Elizabeth for it."

"Maybe you can bribe Elizabeth," Ellen suggested. "You could offer to do all her chores for the next month."

Jessica looked at her in shock. "All her chores?" She couldn't imagine anything more horrible.

"Remember," Lila reminded her, "you're doing this for the Unicorns, Jess."

"I know, Lila, but even if I offered to do all her chores, Elizabeth wouldn't agree."

"Well," Lila continued, "I still think you should find out what Elizabeth's team is up to."

"I will," Jessica assured her. She made a promise to herself that she would. Nothing was going to stop Jessica from winning now.

Three

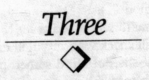

"There!" Elizabeth carefully wedged a bookend between two books and climbed down the small ladder. Then she stepped back to survey her work.

The new bookshelves reached almost to the ceiling, and practically every inch of them was covered with books. "It looks nice," she murmured.

"Very nice." Mr. Henkel gazed up at the shelves from his wheelchair and nodded in approval. "Thank you very much, Elizabeth. You're a big help."

"It was no problem," Elizabeth said cheerfully. "Who put the shelves up?"

Mr. Henkel gave a short, bitter laugh. "I have someone who comes in regularly to help out with the heavy work around the house."

A thought struck Elizabeth. "Mr. Henkel, how

are you going to get those books down from the upper shelves?"

Mr. Henkel pointed to a long pole with a clamp on one end leaning against the wall. "I use that."

"Oh." Elizabeth imagined Mr. Henkel struggling with the pole, trying to get a particular book off the shelf. And once again, she wondered why George didn't live here. Having someone around would certainly make life easier for Mr. Henkel, and there was plenty of room.

Of course, she couldn't ask him about that. She didn't want to seem nosy.

She looked at the shelves again. "You must read a lot," she noted.

Mr. Henkel grunted. "There's not much else I can do, is there."

It was more of a statement than a question, and Elizabeth didn't know what to say.

"Let me give you something for your work. . . ." Mr. Henkel began, breaking the uncomfortable silence.

Elizabeth shook her head vigorously. "No thanks, Mr. Henkel. I'm happy to help out." She couldn't remember how many times she'd said that to him. Every time she did something for Mr. Henkel he offered to pay her. And every time, she refused.

Mr. Henkel smiled slightly. "All right, Elizabeth." He sounded tired, and Elizabeth figured she'd better leave. She had to meet her team down-town anyway.

When Elizabeth turned to say goodbye to Mr. Henkel, she noticed that he was staring into space. Her heart ached for him.

Impulsively, she said, "Mr. Henkel, I know your son."

The man blinked and then looked at her. "What?"

"Your son, George. I know him. He's in some of my classes."

There was a moment of silence. "Oh," Mr. Henkel said finally. "Please close the door tightly be-hind you when you leave."

"OK," Elizabeth said. "Have a nice day, Mr. Henkel."

How strange, she thought, as she hurried downtown to meet the others. Mr. Henkel didn't even sound interested in his own son!

Julie and Amy were waiting for her in front of the pharmacy when she arrived downtown. "Hi," Elizabeth greeted them. "Where's George?"

"Here he comes now," Amy said. Elizabeth could see George walking slowly up the street. When he looked up and saw the girls, he quickened his pace.

"Am I late?" he asked when he reached them.

"No," Elizabeth assured him. "I just got here

myself." She paused and added, "I was helping your father put some books away. He just got some new shelves."

George didn't show any more emotion about his father than his father did about him. "Oh. Hey, I passed a secondhand shop on my way here. That might be a good place to start looking for things," George interrupted, changing the subject.

"Great idea," Julie said, and Elizabeth nodded in agreement. She was pleased to see George taking such an interest in the project. She was still curious about his relationship with his father, but she decided not to say anything more.

George led the group down the street and around the corner, to a little store called The Olde Junque Shoppe. Elizabeth had passed it before but she'd never looked at it closely. Now, peering in the small display window, she saw all kinds of interesting things.

"Look at that old-fashioned doll," she exclaimed. "It must be a hundred years old!"

"Wow. That does look old. I hope they have some newer stuff than that," Amy said. They went inside and Elizabeth looked around in fascination. Though it was a small shop, it was crammed full of the oddest assortment of things she'd ever seen.

"I'll look through these old magazines," Julie offered. "Maybe one of them is from the sixties." Just then, a gray-haired, jolly-looking woman emerged through curtains at the back of the shop.

"Can I help you?" she asked.

"Where do you have things from the 1960s?" Amy asked.

The woman laughed. "I'm afraid I'm not that organized! You'd better just browse and see what you can find."

Elizabeth was actually hoping she'd say that. She thought it would be more fun to poke around and discover something on their own than just to have something handed to them. Julie started going through the magazines, while the others explored the rest of the shop.

"Ooh, look over here!" Amy called out from the back. Elizabeth and George joined her. Amy was standing by a rack of clothes, and holding up a bright yellow, almost Day-Glo, minidress.

"I'll bet this is from the sixties," Amy said. "I've seen dresses like this in old pictures."

Elizabeth examined it. "But we can't know for sure if it was made in the sixties," she said. "I mean, there's no date on it or anything."

"Yeah, I don't think we should turn anything in for the time capsule unless we're sure it's authentic," George said.

Reluctantly, Amy agreed. "But I'll bet we can all find some clothes here to wear for the dance."

"I'm not planning to go to the dance," George said stiffly. Elizabeth wasn't surprised to hear that. She couldn't remember ever seeing George at a school function.

"I'm not crazy about dances either," Amy confided. "But I thought this one might be fun."

George just shrugged. "I'm going to look over there," he mumbled, and went toward the other side of the shop.

"He's kind of strange, isn't he?" Amy whispered to Elizabeth.

"I don't think he's strange, exactly," Elizabeth replied. She was thinking about the look in George's eyes. It was the same look she'd seen just that morning, in his father's eyes. "I'm going to check out that box over there."

She turned away from Amy and started going through a box of old books. Some of the covers were so faded she couldn't even read them, but one of them caught her eye. She could just make out the title beneath a thick layer of dust: *American Literature*. She opened it and almost yelped.

Stamped on the inside cover were the words "Sweet Valley Junior High." Under that was the handwritten signature of the student who had used the book. And next to the name, there was a date—exactly twenty-five years ago!

"Hey, everyone look!" Elizabeth held the book

in the air as George, Julie, and Amy came toward her. "This textbook is from the very first year Sweet Valley Junior High was opened!"

"Oh, wow!" Amy squealed. "That's perfect!"

"And it's not just some ordinary object from the sixties," Elizabeth said, her voice ringing with glee. "It's from *our* school!"

Even George seemed pleased.

As if on cue, the gray-haired woman emerged through the curtains again. "Have you kids found something?" she asked.

"This book," Elizabeth said, holding it out to her. "Can you tell us how much it costs?"

She held her breath as the woman leafed through it.

"Why, it's just an old textbook," the woman said. "I can let you have it for a dollar."

Amy let out a squeal and Julie clapped her hands. The woman looked at them in amused bewilderment. Quickly, Elizabeth explained their mission.

"What a marvelous idea," the woman commented.

"We're having a sixties dance, too," Julie told her. "Maybe we can find some clothes here to wear."

"I've got some more clothes in the back," the woman said. "Why don't you come back later this week and I'll show them to you?" Her twinkling eyes focused on George. "I may even have some old bell-bottom jeans for you."

George didn't say anything. He just reached in his pocket and pulled out a quarter. The girls each added a quarter, and the woman put the book in a paper bag.

"Where should we go next?" Elizabeth asked, clutching the bag tightly as they left the store.

"Let's go back to my place," Amy suggested. "We can ask my mother if she has any ideas."

"That's a good idea," Julie said. "It's not enough just to find things that are from the sixties. If we're going to win, we need to know what was special about the sixties."

Luckily, Amy's mother was happy to talk with them about the sixties. Over homemade cookies and milk, she shared her memories.

"It was an exciting time," she told them with a sentimental smile. "There were a lot of changes. Some were good. Some were terrible. I remember when President Kennedy was assassinated," Mrs. Sutton's face became somber. "That was a terrible time. In fact, I was just thinking about that the other day when I came across something. . . . " She got up and left the room. When she returned, she was carrying a photograph.

"It's President Kennedy," Elizabeth exclaimed. She recognized the photo from her history book. "And it's autographed!"

"I wrote him a letter when I was just about your age," Mrs. Sutton's smile returned. "And I got this."

The kids gazed at the photograph in awe. And then they looked at each other.

Amy said what they were all thinking. "This would be wonderful to put in the time capsule."

Mrs. Sutton looked thoughtful, and Elizabeth held her breath.

"Please Mom?" Amy pleaded.

Her mother nodded. "I think a time capsule is the perfect place for it. I'd like to know that twenty-five years from now, kids your age will still think about President Kennedy."

Amy threw her arms around her mother. "Now we've got two fantastic things. All we need is one more."

"But how are we ever going to find another item as terrific as the two we've got?" Julie asked.

"It's not going to be easy," Elizabeth said. "We've got to come up with some good ideas. I'll ask my parents, and Julie, you ask yours, and George—" she stopped suddenly, and blushed.

"I'll ask my aunt and uncle," George said.

"Fine," Elizabeth said quickly. "And we'll meet in class on Monday to compare ideas."

"If we have any," Amy said.

"Don't worry." Elizabeth spoke with more confidence than she actually felt. "We will!"

When Jessica got home that afternoon, a note on the refrigerator told her that her parents were out.

From upstairs, she could hear the muffled sound of music—that meant Steven was home, but his door was closed and he wouldn't hear her.

She crept lightly up the stairs and headed directly for Elizabeth's room. The door was open and the room was empty. She went inside and looked around.

This could be a waste of time, she thought. *Lizzie's team probably hasn't found anything yet. And even if they have, one of her teammates might be keeping the stuff.*

But she'd promised Lila she would look, and that's what she was here to do. Under the bed seemed like the logical place to start, so she knelt down and was just about to lift up the edge of the bedspread when she heard a voice.

"Jess! What are you doing?"

Jessica jumped up guiltily. "Oh! Uh, hi, Lizzie. I was just, uh, just looking for my—purple socks."

Elizabeth looked at her in puzzlement. "Under *my* bed?"

Jessica managed a weak smile. "Yeah, I thought maybe I took them off in here."

Elizabeth rolled her eyes and then grinned knowingly. "Tell the truth. You were trying to find out what my team has for the time capsule."

Jessica opened her eyes wide. "Oh, Lizzie," she said innocently, "you don't think I'd stoop that low, do you?"

Elizabeth laughed. "You can snoop all you want. We left our things at Amy's."

"Oh." So her team *had* found some items. She eyed her sister suspiciously. She was looking awfully pleased with herself. "How many things do you have?"

"Two," Elizabeth said happily. "And they're both pretty terrific."

Jessica sniffed. "Ha! I'll bet they're not as terrific as the stuff *we* found." She waited for Elizabeth to ask her what they were. But Elizabeth just smiled. "We'll see," was all she said.

"How's the contest going?" Steven was standing at the doorway, with his hands behind his back.

"My team's doing great," Jessica said quickly. "We've found two incredible things already."

"So has mine," Elizabeth added.

"But you need three, right?" Steven asked.

The girls nodded, and Steven grinned slyly. "Well, I just might have that third item right here." From behind his back, he brought forth a large book.

"What is it?" Jessica asked.

"A Sweet Valley Junior High yearbook. From the very first year the school opened."

Jessica let out a shriek. "Steven, that's fantastic! Give it to me!"

"Wait a minute," Elizabeth objected. "Why should he give it to you?"

"Because I asked for it first," Jessica replied. "C'mon, Steven, hand it over."

"Not so fast," Steven said. "I guess you could both use this, right?"

The girls nodded and Steven's grin broadened. "Then make me an offer."

Jessica thought rapidly. "I'll bake you a dozen brownies tonight. No, I'll bake two dozen. With nuts."

Steven turned to Elizabeth. "Care to top that?"

"I'll make your bed for the next two weeks," Elizabeth offered.

"Hey, that's not bad," Steven said thoughtfully.

"Wait," Jessica said frantically, "I'll make your bed for three weeks. *And* bake the brownies."

"Hmmm. This is getting better and better." He looked back at Elizabeth. "It's your turn."

Just then, Mrs. Wakefield appeared at the door. "Who's going to help me get dinner started?" Before any of them could speak, she noticed the book in Steven's hand. "What have you got there?"

With obvious reluctance, Steven handed it over.

"A Sweet Valley Junior High yearbook! Where did you find it?"

"It belongs to one of my friend's mothers," Steven muttered.

Jessica groaned silently. *So it wasn't even his to give away.* But she had to do something. She owed it to the Unicorns. "Steven," she wheedled, in her sweetest voice, "please, can I have it for the time capsule? My team only has two things, and we need one more. Pretty please."

"My team needs one more thing too," Elizabeth said firmly.

Mrs. Wakefield looked at Jessica, then at Elizabeth, and then at Steven. A slow smile spread across her face. "I think this yearbook is going right back to your friend's house. You have no right to auction off someone else's property. Besides, you'll make your sisters crazy."

Mrs. Wakefield closed the yearbook and tucked it under her arm. "Now let's all go and get dinner on the table." As she left the room, Jessica groaned. "Darn, I really wanted that yearbook."

"Me, too," Elizabeth sighed.

"Don't complain to me," Steven said. "*I* really wanted those brownies."

And in spite of everything, they all burst out laughing.

Four

◇

Elizabeth got to her social studies class early on Monday. Julie and Amy were already huddled with George at the back of the room. Elizabeth crossed her fingers and hoped that one of them had come up with a brilliant idea for the time capsule.

But as she approached, she could tell by their glum faces that no one had anything to offer. "I don't even know what to look for," Amy said mournfully.

"I saw this ad in a magazine," George remarked. "You can send away for a newspaper from any date."

"That's great, George. Maybe we can order one from an important date in the sixties," Julie proposed. Elizabeth and Amy looked at George hopefully.

"Yeah, except it costs twenty-five dollars," George informed them. Their faces fell. "And it takes three weeks to get it," he added. Their faces grew even longer. They had less than two weeks to come up with something fantastic.

But Elizabeth had a thought. "You know, they have old newspapers at the public library. Maybe if we looked at them we'd get some ideas for other items. Why don't we all go there after school today?"

Julie looked at her apologetically. "I can't. I've got a flute lesson."

"And I have to babysit," Amy said.

"I have to run an errand for my aunt," George said. "I'm sorry."

"That's OK," Elizabeth assured them. "We don't all have to do it. I'll go and I'll let you guys know tomorrow if I find anything."

All day at school, she heard rumors of the wonderful things other teams had found. It was hard to pay attention in class. Her mind kept wandering as she tried to think of something special her team could get. But it was no use. She could only hope she'd find the answer at the library. As soon as the final bell rang, Elizabeth ran out the doors and headed straight for the library.

Not wanting to waste any time, she went directly to the reference desk.

Mrs. Donaldson, the librarian, smiled at her. "Can I help you?"

"I want to look at some 1960s newspapers," Elizabeth told her.

"Come this way and I'll show you where they are," the librarian said. Elizabeth followed her to a room behind the reference desk.

There was a row of small desks, each with a screen. Elizabeth expected to see stacks and stacks of old yellowed newspapers. Instead, the room was lined with cabinets containing small boxes.

"What year would you like to look at first?" Mrs. Donaldson asked.

Elizabeth told her the year Sweet Valley Junior High first opened, and the librarian went to a cabinet. She took out one of the small boxes and handed it to Elizabeth. "Here you are."

Elizabeth stared at it blankly. Mrs. Donaldson must have noticed her bewildered expression, because she smiled kindly. "Have you ever used microfilm before?"

Elizabeth shook her head.

"We don't have the actual newspapers," the librarian explained. "The kind of paper used would disintegrate over time. And they would take up too much space. Instead, the newspapers are photographed on these rolls, and you use a microfilm reader to look at them. Do you know how to work this?"

With only a bit of instruction, Elizabeth learned how to operate the machine. In no time at all, she was exploring the pages, reading bits of stories and reports. It was amazing to read about events that had happened in Sweet Valley so long ago, long before she was even born.

Elizabeth found an article about the opening of Sweet Valley's brand-new junior high school, but decided a photocopied article just wouldn't be special enough.

After an hour, her eyes ached from staring at the screen. She'd gone through almost four months of newspapers and she still hadn't come up with any great ideas. She was just about ready to rewind the film when something caught her eye.

It was the sports page. And the headline read "Sweet Valley Wins State Junior High Football Championship." Entranced, Elizabeth began to read the article. *It must have been a thrilling game*, she thought. The score was tied until the last few minutes of the last quarter, when Sweet Valley got the ball, the quarterback threw it, and—

Elizabeth practically jumped out of her seat. She read the lines again and again to make sure her eyes weren't deceiving her. But there it was, in black and white.

" . . . and the winning touchdown was caught by Howard Henkel. The crowd went wild, and the team carried Henkel off the field on their shoulders. Later, Henkel was presented with the football as a memento of Sweet Valley Junior's first championship season."

Elizabeth fell back in her seat, amazed by her

discovery. Howard Henkel. That was Mr. Henkel, George's father. She was sure of that.

Mr. Henkel, that sad-looking man in a wheel-chair, had once led a football team to victory. How proud George must be!

And then she had a fantastic idea. What if Mr. Henkel still had that football? It would be the perfect addition to their collection. *Wait until the others heard about this!* Quickly, she rewound the film and replaced it in the box. She couldn't wait to get home and call Amy and Julie and George.

She was hurrying toward the exit when she was distracted by a book display. A sign over the books read NEW MYSTERIES. Elizabeth immediately thought of Mr. Henkel. She knew he liked mysteries so she picked out a couple and checked them out at the circulation desk. Then she practically flew all the way home.

When she arrived she ran upstairs, tossed her books on her bed, and went out to the phone in the hall. Rapidly, she dialed Amy's number.

"Did you find out anything at the library?" Amy asked.

"Did I! Wait till you hear!" Elizabeth told her about Mr. Henkel, and Amy got just as excited as she was.

"Do you think he kept the ball?" she asked.

"I'm going to call George right now and ask

him," Elizabeth said. "If his father has that ball, I'm sure he's shown it to George a million times."

"I'll call Julie and tell her the news," Amy said. "Elizabeth, if we get that football, we'll definitely win!"

"I know, I know," Elizabeth exclaimed. "I'll talk to you later." She hung up and looked for George's phone number in the Sweet Valley Middle School Directory.

A woman answered. "Hello?"

"May I speak to George, please? This is Elizabeth Wakefield."

A moment later, she heard George's soft voice. "Hi, Elizabeth."

"George, you won't believe what I found out at the library! Why didn't you tell us your father caught the winning touchdown pass at Sweet Valley Junior High? And they gave him the ball to keep! Does he still have it?"

There was a silence on the other end.

"George?"

Finally, he spoke. "I don't know what you're talking about."

"You didn't know your father was a football hero?" Elizabeth was bewildered. Wasn't that the kind of thing a father would share with his son?

"No."

And he didn't sound like he cared very much, either. Elizabeth didn't know what to say. She tried to collect her thoughts. "Well, could you ask him about the ball? If we could get it for the time capsule, George, we'd have the best three items."

Again, there was a silence before George spoke. And when he did, his voice was dull and lifeless. "No, I can't ask him."

He didn't offer any explanation and the tone in his voice told Elizabeth she shouldn't ask for one. But she couldn't help herself.

"Why not?"

"Because I never see my father," George replied flatly. "We don't even talk to each other."

Elizabeth was shocked. She'd never heard of such a thing—a father and his son not speaking?

But that's what George said. And that was all he was going to tell her. "Look, Elizabeth, I've got to go."

"But George," Elizabeth said in a rush, "he's your father! Why can't you—"

All she heard was a click on the other end of the line.

It took a moment for everything to sink in, then she hung up.

She went downstairs. Her father had just come home from work and he was sitting in the living room, reading the newspaper. He looked up as Elizabeth sat down next to him on the sofa.

"You look like you've got something on your mind."

"Dad, do you know Mr. Henkel very well?"

"Well, I wouldn't say we're close friends," Mr. Wakefield said. "But I've known him for quite a while."

"Was he always as quiet as he is now?" Elizabeth asked.

"Not at all," her father said. "In fact, he was a very likable guy and a terrific athlete. He planned to become a football coach."

"What happened? What made him change?"

Mr. Wakefield sighed. "He fought in Vietnam, and he was very badly wounded there. That's why he's in a wheelchair."

Elizabeth shuddered. "That's awful."

Her father nodded sadly. "And his wounds were more than physical. He came back a different man, bitter and angry at the world. His wife tried to help him, but he just wouldn't respond. Then she died when their son was still very young."

"George," Elizabeth murmured. "He's in my class at school."

"That's when his wife's sister took the baby," Mr. Wakefield continued.

"Dad, it's so tragic," Elizabeth cried. "They don't even speak to each other! I want to help them!"

Her father put his arm around her. "That's sweet of you, Elizabeth. And I know you mean well. But I really don't think there's anything any of us can do. You can be a friend to George, and you can be a friend to Mr. Henkel. But as far as their relationship goes, they'll have to work that out between themselves. Getting involved in other people's family problems isn't always a good idea."

"I know," Elizabeth said. "I should mind my own business."

"That's right."

Elizabeth wasn't even thinking about the football anymore. She was thinking about poor George. And poor Mr. Henkel. And even though she knew her father was right, she wished more than anything that there was something she could do to bring them together.

Five

"He doesn't talk to his father at all?" Amy's expression was one of surprise.

"That's what he said," Elizabeth replied, keeping her voice low. They were standing outside their homeroom, and she didn't want anyone to overhear their conversation.

"Then I guess there's no chance we'll get that football," Amy said mournfully.

"I suppose not," Elizabeth said. "We don't even know if he still has it. When I asked George on the phone last night, he got so upset he hung up on me."

"You're kidding!" Amy's eyebrows shot up. "That doesn't sound like something George would do."

"Shh," Elizabeth cautioned her. She could see George coming toward them.

"I'll let you guys talk privately," Amy whispered, and hurried into the classroom. As George approached, Elizabeth gave him her brightest, warmest smile. He didn't smile back—but at least he didn't look angry.

And he got right to the point. "Look, Elizabeth, I'm sorry about last night. I shouldn't have yelled at you like that. And I shouldn't have hung up on you."

"That's OK," Elizabeth reassured him. "It was my fault. I shouldn't have pestered you like that."

George looked down at the floor. "It's just that I don't like to talk about my father."

"I understand," Elizabeth said. They stood there awkwardly, not even looking at each other. George wore the same dejected expression she'd seen so often on Mr. Henkel's face.

"George," Elizabeth said impulsively, "why don't you come to the dance Friday night?"

George grimaced. "I don't like dances. And I don't know the kids here at school that well."

"You know us," Elizabeth insisted. "You could go with me and Julie and Amy. It would be nice if we could all go together as a team."

George hesitated.

"Please? We'd really like you to be with us."

George looked surprised. "You would?"

"Absolutely," Elizabeth declared. "We'll have

fun! And maybe we could find out what some of the other kids are collecting for the time capsule. It might give us some fresh ideas."

She could tell that George was wavering. Finally, he gave her a half-smile and said, "OK."

"Oh, George, I'm so glad!" Elizabeth said happily. "Let's all go back to that little shop this week and see if we can find some clothes. And just think! You'll probably be the only boy at the dance with three dates!"

George blushed slightly, but his smile broadened. "I hope I can handle that!"

All that day, Elizabeth remembered George's smile, and she felt much better. Maybe there wasn't anything she could do about bringing George and his father back together, but at least she could help George feel better about himself.

When she got home from school that afternoon, her mother was going through the mail. "Oh, dear," Mrs. Wakefield remarked. "Here's something for Mr. Henkel that the mailman left in our box by mistake."

"I'll take it to him," Elizabeth offered. She took the letter from her mother and walked over to Mr. Henkel's house. Through a window, she could see him sitting in his chair, staring expressionlessly at a television. She rapped on the window and caught his attention.

Mr. Henkel looked up, and actually seemed pleased to see her. He beckoned for her to come in.

"Hi," Elizabeth greeted him. "What are you watching?"

"I don't know," Mr. Henkel said. "I'm not really watching it." He pointed to a book on his lap.

Elizabeth switched off the TV so she could hear herself talk. "I brought you a letter that was left in our mailbox."

"A letter?" Mr. Henkel asked in surprise. He took the envelope from Elizabeth. "Oh, it's just a bill."

He doesn't even get any personal letters, Elizabeth thought sympathetically. Then she thought about the boy described in the newspaper article, tearing across the football field. How could they be the same person?

Thinking of the newspaper article reminded her of something. "I got you some mystery books from the library," she told him. "But I left them at home. I can go back and get them now."

"Don't bother," Mr. Henkel said. "I'm in the middle of a mystery now."

"I'll bring them over on Saturday," Elizabeth promised.

"Thank you," Mr. Henkel said politely.

There didn't seem to be anything left to say. And yet, Elizabeth got the feeling he didn't really want her to leave. He must be so lonely, she thought. She should at least try to make some conversation with him.

"Speaking of the library," she said, "I saw your name there."

His brow wrinkled. "My name in the library?"

"I was looking at some newspapers from the sixties. You see, we're having a twenty-fifth anniversary celebration at school, and there's a contest to see who can bring in the best things from twenty-five years ago, when the school first opened. So I was going through these newspapers to get some ideas and I saw a story about you!"

A slow smile grew across Mr. Henkel's face. "The championship game," he murmured.

"That's right! The article said that you caught the winning touchdown pass."

His eyes misted over. "Yes, I did."

"Tell me about it," Elizabeth urged.

"Oh, I remember it well. We were a brand-new school, and we felt like we had something to prove. We didn't have a school song, or a mascot, or anything like that. But we knew how to play football, and we had a lot of spirit."

The book slid off his lap, but Mr. Henkel didn't even notice. He was completely caught up in his memories.

"The other team came from a school north of here. They'd been state champions for two years, and they were pretty sure of themselves. They thought they could just roll all over us." He laughed—not his usual bitter laugh, but a real laugh, a joyful one. "For a while, we thought they could, too! They had some really big guys on that team. But the coach gave us a great pep talk at halftime. He made us believe we could do anything. I remember thinking, I'm going to be a coach like that someday!"

Mr. Henkel began describing the play that won the game. Elizabeth didn't know too much about football, so she couldn't completely understand everything he was saying, but his description was so vivid, she almost felt like she was there. She could actually hear the roar of the crowd.

"A couple of guys hoisted me up and carried me on their shoulders back to the locker room. And boy, did we celebrate!"

Elizabeth laughed. "I'll bet you guys went crazy."

"We did," Mr. Henkel agreed, grinning. "Then the coach made a speech, telling us how proud he was. And he gave me something. Wait here. I'll show you."

He wheeled himself out of the room. Elizabeth held her breath. She had a pretty good idea what he was going to bring back.

Sure enough, he returned with a football in his lap. "This is the actual ball I caught in that game. Look, you can see where all the guys signed it."

Elizabeth carefully took the ball from him. The writing was faded, but the signatures were still visible.

"What a wonderful souvenir," she sighed. She debated asking the question that was on her mind. What harm would it do?

"This would be perfect for the contest," she began, but Mr. Henkel stopped her.

"I'm sorry, Elizabeth," he said, taking the ball back. "But I can't give you this. It's all I've got."

His voice had changed. His tone was cheerless and his usual melancholy expression had returned.

"I understand," Elizabeth said quickly. She got up. "I guess I'd better get home."

Mr. Henkel nodded. But his eyes remained glued to the ball he was clutching tightly.

"I'll be back soon with the library books," she called from the door.

How sad, she thought as she crossed the yard. His most precious possession is an old football. And he said it was all he had! What about his son? Wasn't a living person more important than a souvenir from twenty-five years ago?

At home, Jessica was sprawled in front of the television watching music videos. "Where have you been?" she asked Elizabeth.

"At Mr. Henkel's," Elizabeth told her.

Jessica made a face. "I don't see how you can stand that weird man."

Elizabeth was tempted to tell her that Mr. Henkel was once a football star, but she decided not to. If Jessica knew about the football he had, she just might go over there and pester him for it. "Have you collected all your things for the contest yet?"

"Maybe," Jessica said, grinning. "How about you?"

"We still need one more thing," Elizabeth said. "We're going crazy trying to think of something."

"Well, don't go too crazy," Jessica warned her. "I mean, it's not as if you could actually win."

"Why not?"

"Because if you could see what we've got already, you'd know your team doesn't stand a chance!"

Elizabeth laughed. "We'll see about that!" And she went upstairs to use the phone.

"Amy? Hi, it's Elizabeth. Guess what? Mr. Henkel *does* have the football."

"Oh, wow!" Amy squealed.

"Don't get excited," Elizabeth said. "I asked him, and he won't let us have it."

"Darn," Amy groaned. "Did you tell him George was on our team?"

"No. Why?"

"I was just thinking," Amy said slowly. "Maybe if he knew George wanted it, he'd give it to him."

"I don't think we could get George to ask him," Elizabeth said. "I told you how he acted when I mentioned his father."

"I know," Amy sighed. "It was just an idea."

"But I did talk George into going to the dance with us Friday night," Elizabeth added.

"You did? That's great! He's really a nice guy, Elizabeth. Maybe going to the dance will cheer him up."

"Maybe," Elizabeth agreed. "But I think it's going to take a lot more than a dance to make George really happy."

"Yeah," Amy said. " I know what you mean."

After she hung up, Elizabeth went to her room to start on her homework. But she found it hard to concentrate. She just kept thinking about George and the football.

Maybe Amy was right. Maybe they *should* try to talk George into asking his father for the ball.

Elizabeth had a feeling that ball could be more than just a winning item. It could be the one thing that might bring a father and son back together.

Six

On Friday afternoon, Jessica went into the kitchen clutching a battered magazine. "Mom, where's the ironing board?"

Her mother looked at her in astonishment, and Jessica couldn't blame her. Ironing was not known to be one of Jessica's favorite activities.

"Why, it's where it always is, honey, downstairs, in the laundry room," Mrs. Wakefield told her. "Are you ironing your things for tonight's dance?"

"Uh, yes," Jessica replied. *That wasn't really a lie,* she thought. She *was* planning to iron something for tonight. But it wasn't her clothes.

She ran downstairs to the laundry room and closed the door. Then she plugged in the iron and set it at its lowest setting. She waited a moment for the iron to heat up and then she bent down and spread her hair over the ironing board.

Behind her, the door opened.

"Jessica! What are you doing?"

Jessica raised her head and grinned at her sister. "I'm ironing my hair."

Elizabeth's mouth fell open. "What are you doing *that* for? Your hair's already straight!"

"It's not straight *enough*. Wait, I'll show you." Jessica opened her magazine and pointed to a picture. "Look at that girl." The model in the picture had long, completely straight hair, without even the slightest hint of a wave.

"I found this fashion magazine from the sixties," Jessica went on. "*All* the girls in it have their hair like this. That's how I want to look tonight. Tamara's mother told us she used to iron her hair to get it like this. So I want to try it."

Elizabeth shuddered. "If you ask me, it sounds kind of dangerous. Does Mom know you're doing this?"

"No! And you'd better not tell her, either."

Elizabeth didn't need to. At that very minute, Mrs. Wakefield appeared at the door, holding a can.

"Do you need some spray starch?" she asked Jessica.

Jessica pictured what her hair would look like if she starched it—sticking straight out like a petticoat. "No, thanks, Mom."

Mrs. Wakefield glanced around curiously. "Where are your clothes?"

Jessica tugged on a lock of her hair. "Uh, I was just going to get them."

Her mother eyed her suspiciously. "Jessica, what are you up to?"

Elizabeth started to giggle, and Jessica shot a furious look at her. Then she gave up, knowing that her mother would find out anyway. "I'm going to iron my hair so it's perfectly straight. You know, the way everyone had their hair in the sixties."

Mrs. Wakefield strode over to the iron and unplugged it. "Oh, no, you're not. Do you have any idea how dangerous this could be?"

"Mom!" Jessica wailed, but Mrs. Wakefield just shook her head.

"You know, I had a friend who used to do that when we were in high school. One day she lifted the iron, and half her hair came off."

"But I want to look like that," Jessica whined, pointing to the photo in the magazine. Her mother studied the picture.

"There are other ways to get your hair straight like that," Mrs. Wakefield said. "If you'd like, I'll show you how."

"I thought girls snarled their hair into big puffy styles in the sixties," Elizabeth said.

"That was in the early sixties," her mother told her. "Would you like to wear your hair like that?"

"You really should try that," Jessica said eagerly. "It sounds wonderful." In all honesty, she thought it sounded awful, but she didn't want Elizabeth looking the same way she did at the dance.

Elizabeth looked doubtful, but she nodded bravely. "Well, OK, I'll try it."

"Both of you, go wash your hair, and let me know when you're ready." Mrs. Wakefield left the room, and Elizabeth began flipping through the pages of Jessica's magazine.

"Where did you find this?" she asked. "Are you going to submit it for the time capsule?"

Jessica snatched it back. "Maybe." Actually, her team was only holding on to the magazine as a last resort. But she gave Elizabeth her haughtiest look. "Now I guess *you're* going to start running around looking for an old magazine."

Elizabeth smiled in a way that made Jessica uncomfortable. "No, we're working on getting something much more exciting than an old magazine." With that, she sailed out of the laundry room.

Jessica stared after her glumly. She was probably bluffing, but what if she really did have something wonderful? She'd find out one way or another, but right now she had other things on her mind. Like her hair.

A half hour later, she was sitting on a chair in her room while her mother brushed out her long blond locks. "This is how I did it when I was your age," Mrs. Wakefield said. "To get my hair really straight, I used to wrap it. I'd wind a lock around my head, and secure it tightly with clips."

"Ouch!" Jessica cried out as a clip dug into her scalp.

"Sorry," her mother said with a grin, "but it sometimes takes pain to be beautiful."

Jessica gritted her teeth as her mother wound the locks of hair tighter and tighter. "Boy, I'm glad I wasn't a teenager in your day," she complained. "I wouldn't want to go through this every day."

Mrs. Wakefield smiled. "Wait till you see what I do to Elizabeth."

"I hope she has to suffer as much as I'm suffering," Jessica muttered.

"All done," her mother declared. "Now you've got to let it dry, and I'll go start on Elizabeth."

Jessica followed her to Elizabeth's room. Elizabeth sat at her desk, looking apprehensively at a pile of big curlers stuffed with bristles.

Deftly, Mrs. Wakefield went to work, winding Elizabeth's hair on curlers and sticking in bobby pins. Elizabeth winced as the bristles hit her scalp.

"Would you believe I used to sleep on these things almost every night?" her mother asked.

"That must have been painful," Elizabeth sympathized.

"It was," Mrs. Wakefield agreed. "You girls are very lucky that the natural look is in style now."

Jessica started laughing. "You look like a creature from outer space."

Elizabeth looked at her reflection in the mirror, and she had to agree. The curlers made her head look twice its size.

Then Jessica looked at her reflection glumly. At least Elizabeth looked worse than she did.

The minute the twins walked into the dining room, Steven took one look at them and ducked under the table. "Help! We're being invaded by creatures from another planet!"

Mr. Wakefield glanced at the twins and practically jumped. "Oh no! Not again. I thought those days were gone," he declared.

"It's for the sixties dance tonight," Jessica informed him.

"Oh, that's right," her father said. "And how are your time capsule projects coming along?"

"My team's got two terrific things already," Elizabeth announced. "All we need is one more. And if we can get what we think we might get, we'll be a shoo-in."

Jessica glared at her. Then she beamed at her father. "My team's got great things, too."

"That's good," Mr. Wakefield said. "I'm glad to see this isn't turning into a battle between the two of you."

"Oh, no," Elizabeth said. "Nothing like that."

"There's no battle," Jessica echoed, looking at her sister. *Not yet*, she thought.

"Wow!" Elizabeth exclaimed as she entered the gym with Julie, Amy, and George. "This is cool!"

The gym was decorated with streamers and balloons. All over the walls were posters of rock groups and movie stars who were popular in the 1960s. At one end of the room, a disc jockey was playing records Elizabeth had heard on the local radio's oldies station. At the other end was a long table covered with refreshments.

And the kids looked wild. "Look at Bruce Patman," Amy squealed. Bruce was wearing a white guru shirt, blue bell-bottom pants, and a peace medallion around his neck. Another boy was wearing a long-haired wig.

Elizabeth adjusted her pale yellow shirtwaist dress. She'd found it at the junk shop, and her mother had assured her she had one almost exactly like it when she was Elizabeth's age. Then she touched her hair. It felt totally unfamiliar, all teased up in a big bouffant hairdo and stiff with hairspray.

Across the room she spotted Jessica with Lila and the other Unicorns. They were all wearing purple miniskirts but Jessica looked the best. She had added a pair of white patent leather go-go boots to her outfit. And her hair was absolutely straight, just like her mother had promised it would be.

"I'm going to get something to eat," Julie announced.

George looked around uneasily, and played with his wide, flowered tie. "I'll come with you," he said, and the two of them headed toward the refreshments.

"Are you going to ask George about the football?" Amy asked Elizabeth.

"Maybe later," Elizabeth said. "Let's get something to drink." They went over to the refreshment table to join Julie and George, who were watching the other kids dance. Then Ms. Luster, the librarian from school, joined them.

"Why aren't you kids dancing?" Ms. Luster asked, her bright eyes twinkling.

"I've never danced to this kind of music," Elizabeth confessed. She had a feeling most of the others hadn't either. The few who were actually on the dance floor were looking pretty awkward.

The disc jockey put on a new record. "That's a twist record!" Ms. Luster exclaimed. "Now, I know you can do that. It's very easy. Watch me!"

She pulled them out to the dance floor and gave a little demonstration. All four of them stared at each other in amazement. The librarian was twisting from the waist, back and forth, to the beat of the music.

"Awesome!" George declared.

Ms. Luster laughed. "We would have said 'far out'! Here, I'll show you how to do it. Bend your knees a little, put your arms out like this, and just go!"

By now, a small crowd had gathered around the librarian, and everyone was trying it. "Very good!" Ms. Luster declared. "Excellent, George! You're better than Chubby Checker!"

"Who's Chubby Checker?" Amy whispered to Elizabeth.

"I don't know," Elizabeth replied. "I guess he was a famous twister."

"This is a good dance to do when you're shy," Ms. Luster told them. "Because you don't even have to hold hands with your partner."

George turned a little red. "No wonder I'm so good at it," he told Elizabeth.

Elizabeth laughed. She had never heard George make a joke before!

"Look, Nora Mercandy just came in," Julie said.

Elizabeth waved to her. Nora looked great. She was dressed like a hippie, with a short, embroidered dress and strands of beads around her neck.

Then she noticed George was looking at Nora, too, and he was getting redder. He likes her, Elizabeth thought.

"George, why don't you ask Nora to dance?" Elizabeth suggested.

George was blushing furiously. "She might not know how to do this twist thing."

"Then you can show her!" Julie said. George bit his lip.

"Oh, go on and do it," Elizabeth urged.

"OK," George said. And with his face set determinedly, he started toward Nora. A few seconds later, they were on the dance floor.

She watched George and Nora for a few moments and then went back to dancing with her friends.

Every time Elizabeth saw George for the rest of the night, she could tell he was having a great time. He was dancing a lot, and talking to kids he had never spoken to before.

Since he was in such a good mood, Elizabeth decided she would ask him about the football. But it had to be at exactly the right moment.

It came when they were getting ready to leave. She and George were waiting for Julie and Amy outside the gym door, where Julie's father was going to pick them up.

"George," she said slowly, "remember when I told you about your father winning the football championship?"

She watched his expression carefully. He didn't freeze up like he had the last time she mentioned his father. He just nodded.

"Well, I was over at your father's a few days ago, and he showed me the football. I asked him if we could have it for our contest, but he said no."

"That's too bad," George said. "It would have been perfect."

"We were thinking," Elizabeth continued, "that maybe you could ask him for it. I mean, since you're his son, he just might let you have it."

She held her breath. Would George even consider doing this? It would mean he'd have to see his father, talk to him. But maybe, just maybe, this could start off a whole new relationship for them.

George was silent for a few minutes. He seemed to be thinking very hard. Then he smiled. "OK. I'll ask him."

Elizabeth wanted to jump for joy!

Seven

◇

The next morning, Elizabeth hummed a Beatles song as she fixed herself some breakfast. When her father walked in, she greeted him cheerfully.

"Good morning," she sang out. "Isn't it a beautiful day?"

She giggled at her father's expression as he looked out the window and saw all the clouds.

"I guess I just feel so good that it seems like a beautiful day," Elizabeth explained.

"I suppose this means you had a good time at the dance last night," her father remarked as he poured himself a cup of coffee.

"I did," Elizabeth said, sitting down at the kitchen table with her grapefruit. "But it was even better watching George Henkel have such a good time."

Mr. Wakefield joined her at the table. "And I'm

guessing from that pleased expression on your face that you had something to do with that."

In all modesty, Elizabeth had to admit she deserved a little credit. "You know, Dad, he's always been so quiet, no one ever knew who he was!" She bit into a section of her grapefruit and chewed thoughtfully.

"He wasn't even planning to go to the dance," she went on. "But I knew if he just relaxed and opened up to people, he'd have a good time. And I was right!"

"Good for you," her father declared. "That's a nice feeling, to know you've helped someone."

"And there's more," Elizabeth continued. "I think I've come up with a way to get George and his father together."

Mr. Wakefield's smile faded a little. "Now, Elizabeth, remember what I told you about getting involved in a family's problems. That's a very private business. And sometimes an outsider can do more harm than good." His expression was serious.

But Elizabeth wasn't discouraged. "It'll be OK," she assured him. "I just have a feeling everything's going to work out perfectly." She just hoped George wouldn't change his mind about going to see his father.

A little while later, Elizabeth was up in her room doing her homework. When she gazed out the window, she noticed George Henkel walking up the street past her house. *Where is he going?* She asked herself.

She squinted as his figure grew smaller. And then she almost bit the eraser off the pencil that she had pressed to her mouth. He turned onto the block where his father lived.

Elizabeth hugged herself in glee. It was actually happening! Everything was going to be OK. She couldn't concentrate on her math problems as she tried to imagine exactly what was going on in Mr. Henkel's house. She pictured George and his father hugging, making up over whatever it was that had kept them apart for so long. Maybe they'd start doing things together, like going to football games . . . Maybe right this minute Mr. Henkel was handing George the famous football for the time capsule project. They'd win the contest and get their pictures placed in the capsule. And twenty-five years from now, people would know who they were.

She was so caught up in her fantasies that she was only vaguely aware of the doorbell ringing downstairs.

"I'll get it," she heard her brother call out. A moment later Steven was standing in her doorway. "You'd better fix your hair. It's a *boy*."

Who could it be, Elizabeth wondered. She took a quick look in the mirror, and groaned. Her hair was still matted from the night before. She grabbed a brush and yanked it through her hair. It wasn't much improvement. Quickly, she pulled it back in a ponytail, and ran downstairs.

George Henkel stood awkwardly in the middle of the living room. Elizabeth took one look at his face, and her heart sank.

"George! What's the matter?"

"I went to see my father," he said woodenly. "Big mistake."

Elizabeth motioned for him to come sit on the couch with her.

"Oh, George," was all she could think to say.

"I asked him about the football." He looked up, and Elizabeth could see the pain in his eyes. "He said there was no way he'd give me the most important thing in his life."

Elizabeth gasped. How could Mr. Henkel talk like that to his own son?

"What's the matter with him?" she cried out.

George jumped to his feet. "He doesn't care about me," he said passionately. "He's a hateful person who just wants to sit around and feel sorry for himself!" For a moment George looked like he was going to explode. His face was red and his fists were clenched.

"Look, Elizabeth," he said flatly. "I'm sorry about the football. I guess we'll just have to come up with something else. I'll see you at school." With that, he walked out.

Elizabeth sat there, staring into space. Ten minutes earlier she had felt wonderful. Now she was miserable. And it wasn't because of the football. George was even sadder than he'd been before. And it was all her fault.

Jessica lay on her bed and stared up at the ceiling. Her team still hadn't found a third great item for the contest, and there was only a week left. Of course, they had that fashion magazine, but she knew that wouldn't impress the judges. They needed something big, something as important as the poster and the record album.

She went out into the hallway and dialed Lila's number. "Have you thought of anything?" she asked when Lila answered.

"No," Lila replied. "What about you?"

"Nothing," Jessica said mournfully. "I found out what Elizabeth's team has, though. I overheard her and Amy talking at the dance."

"Oh, really?" Lila's voice perked up. "What have they got?"

Jessica sneered. "Really dumb stuff. Some book and a picture of President Kennedy."

"Oh, well," Lila said in relief, "at least we've got better stuff than that."

"But I know they're working on getting something big," Jessica went on. "I just don't know what it is."

"Well, find out," Lila insisted. "And then

maybe we can get it before they do. Whatever it is."

"I will," Jessica promised. She hung up the phone, and went to Elizabeth's room. The door was slightly ajar, and she pushed it open.

Elizabeth was in the same position Jessica had been in moments before—lying on her bed, staring at the ceiling. But she looked even more depressed.

Her expression gave Jessica hope. Elizabeth obviously hadn't gotten her hands on whatever it was she was after for the time capsule contest.

"Don't you have a riding class today?" Jessica asked.

Elizabeth glanced at the clock on her nightstand, and leaped off the bed. "Oh my gosh, I'm late!" She dashed to her dresser, pulled out her riding clothes, and got her boots from the closet. Just as she was changing her clothes, something caught her eye.

"Oh no," she moaned. "I forgot to drop those library books at Mr. Henkel's and I promised I'd bring them today. Jessica, could you take them over to him for me?"

"Are you kidding?" Jessica yelped. "That man gives me the creeps. Take them over yourself."

"I don't have time," Elizabeth wailed. "*Please,* Jessica?"

Jessica was about to refuse again when Elizabeth grabbed a bracelet from her dresser. "I'll let you wear this," she said.

Jessica hesitated. She had been admiring Elizabeth's new bracelet. It would look absolutely perfect with the outfit she was planning to wear to school on Monday.

"OK," she relented. "I'll take the books."

Elizabeth flashed her a grateful smile. "Thanks, Jess." And she ran out of the room.

Jessica eyed the books distastefully. Well, she might as well get this over with. She grabbed the books and headed over to Mr. Henkel's.

When he opened the door, Jessica was surprised to see that he was smiling. Every time she'd seen him before, he looked mean.

"Hi," he said, "come on in."

Hesitantly, Jessica entered the house. "I brought these books," she began, but Mr. Henkel wasn't listening.

"I'm glad you're here, Elizabeth," Mr. Henkel said. "I wanted to talk to you."

Jessica was about to tell him she wasn't Elizabeth, but Mr. Henkel wouldn't let her get a word in. "I've changed my mind," he said. "I want to give you the football."

Jessica stared at him in bewilderment. What was he talking about? What football?

"I'm ashamed about the way I treated George this morning," he went on. "And I want to make it up to him. I don't know how I could have believed a football meant more to me than my own son."

Jessica shifted the library books to her other arm and gazed at the man uneasily. "Uh, Mr. Henkel, I think you made a mistake. I'm— "

"I know I made a mistake," Mr. Henkel interrupted her. "I just hope it's not too late to correct it. Wait here."

He wheeled himself out of the room. Jessica put the books on a table and debated running out of the house. But before she could decide, Mr. Henkel reappeared, clutching a football.

He held it out toward Jessica. Gingerly, she took it from him. It didn't look very clean.

"You know," Mr. Henkel mused, "I look back on that moment twenty-five years ago when I caught the pass and won the championship for Sweet Valley Junior High, and it seems like the happiest moment in my life. I wonder if I can ever be that happy again. That's why the football means so much to me."

He paused and sighed deeply. "But my own son means more to me, even if I can't show him my real feelings. So I want you to give him the football."

Slowly, the meaning of what he was saying came to her. It was all starting to make sense. George Henkel was on Elizabeth's team. This football came from a championship game twenty-five years ago. This was what Elizabeth's team had been desperately trying to get.

"I do love my son," Mr. Henkel was saying. "I

just can't seem to tell him that. Maybe this football can say it for me."

But Jessica wasn't listening. All she could think about was the football. With this old piece of leather, there was no doubt about it. Her team would win!

Eight

◇

Jessica was in a great mood when she jumped out of bed Monday morning. She dressed quickly and then began rummaging through her closet. She knew that somewhere there was an old tote bag big enough to hold—and hide—a football.

All she had to do was get the football to school, where she could hide it in her locker. After throwing a number of items out of her closet, she finally found the old tote bag. She tossed the ball in, hoisted the bag over her shoulder, and started to leave the room. Then she caught a glimpse of herself in the mirror and she groaned.

The bag was made of thin nylon and the outline of the ball was very clear. Anyone would be able to see that she was carrying a football—including Elizabeth.

She *could* try to get out of the house before Elizabeth saw her, but that was too much of a risk. And then came a rap on her bedroom door.

"Jess? Are you ready for breakfast?" Elizabeth called.

"Just a minute," Jessica called out. Frantically, her eyes swept the room. How could she hide the football?

In desperation, she opened a dresser drawer and began pulling out her heaviest sweaters. She stuffed them in the bag, around the football. Then she lifted it over her shoulder, and checked her reflection in the mirror.

It was big and heavy and bulky, and it would be a real drag carrying it to school. But at least no one would be able to tell what was inside.

With the tote bag over one arm and her schoolbooks cradled in the other, she went downstairs. She debated leaving the bag by the front door, but she didn't want to let it out of her sight. Keeping her arm clenched around it tightly, she went into the kitchen.

"What would you like for breakfast?" her mother asked.

"Nothing, thanks," Jessica replied. "I have to get to school early."

Elizabeth eyed her curiously as she buttered a slice of toast. Jessica wasn't surprised by her expression. Rushing off to school was not something she did regularly.

"If you wait one minute, I'll walk with you,"

Elizabeth offered, biting her toast. "You look like you could use some help carrying all that stuff."

"I can't wait," Jessica said. "I'm in a rush." Even though the sweaters hid the shape of the ball, she felt nervous having Elizabeth looking at the bag. And she certainly didn't want her carrying it.

"What are you carrying in that bag?" Mrs. Wakefield asked.

Jessica tried to sound casual. "Just some stuff for a school project."

Elizabeth smiled a little wistfully. "I'll bet you have something for the contest in there." Then she sighed. "I was hoping my team was going to have something really terrific, but it didn't work out."

Somehow, Jessica managed to keep a straight face. "Gee, that's too bad. Well, I'll see you later. Bye, Mom." And she dashed out.

When she got to school, she spotted Lila and Tamara in the hallway outside their homeroom, and ran up to them. "Wait till you see what I've got," Jessica crowed. She couldn't wait to see their faces when she opened the bag. "Right here, in this tote bag, is something from the sixties that's going to win this contest for us."

"Did you find out what Elizabeth's team was after?" Lila asked.

Jessica nodded proudly. "And I got it first."

Tamara peered into the bag. "What is it—a sweater?"

"No, dummy, it's under the sweater." Jessica motioned for them to move in closer. "I don't want anyone else to know about this." She pulled out the top sweater, revealing what lay underneath.

Lila gazed at it doubtfully. "A football? What's so great about an old football?"

"It's not just any old football," Jessica announced. "This is the football that was used in the first championship game at Sweet Valley Junior High."

She was pleased to see how impressed the others looked. In fact, they were more than impressed. They were ecstatic.

"Jessica, that's fantastic!" Lila exclaimed. "Where did you find it?"

Jessica giggled. "It belongs to this man who lives near me. He thought he was giving it to Elizabeth and I just let him believe I was her!"

"Wow," Lila said in awe, "that was brilliant." Tamara agreed enthusiastically.

Jessica basked in their admiration. "We better go put it in my locker with the other things." The girls hurried down the hall, meeting Ellen Riteman and Betsy Gordon along the way. They showed them the football and they were suitably impressed.

"Jessica, the Unicorns are going to love you," Ellen pronounced. And Jessica beamed.

They gathered around her locker while Jessica dialed the combination and opened it. Then she held the bag open while Tamara pulled the football out.

"Hey, what are you girls doing with that football?"

Jessica turned to see Bruce Patman standing there, watching them. She smiled pertly.

"None of your business," she said while the other girls giggled. She wasn't worried. Bruce would never figure out where the ball came from.

What worried Jessica was that Caroline Pearce had overheard their conversation about the football. She was the school gossip and she could never keep her mouth shut when she had interesting news.

But surely Caroline must realize how important it was to keep this quiet, she thought to herself. And she shut the locker.

Elizabeth left her social studies class feeling like a cloud of gloom was hanging over her head. No one else on her team had come up with anything for the time capsule. And George had looked even more dejected than ever.

As she walked down the hall toward her next class, Nora Mercandy came running up to her. Nora didn't look particularly happy, either. Her usually lively eyes were dark with concern.

"What's the matter?" Elizabeth asked.

"It's George Henkel," Nora said, frowning. "I tried to talk to him this morning, and he was really unfriendly. Honestly, Elizabeth, I don't understand him. I thought he liked me at the dance Friday night. Today he won't even look at me."

"I think he's got something on his mind," Elizabeth said vaguely. "Don't take it too personally." She didn't want to tell Nora the whole story.

"Well, I wish he had *me* on his mind," Nora murmured. "He's on your time capsule team, isn't he?"

Elizabeth nodded. "Are you on a team, too?"

"No," Nora said. "I didn't have time to start running around looking for things. Did you guys come up with some good stuff?"

"We've got two things," Elizabeth told her. "We haven't been able to find a third item, though."

"Your sister's team is doing great," Nora remarked. "I don't know what else she's got, but I heard about the football. That's really neat."

Elizabeth stopped suddenly. "What football?"

Nora's eyes widened. "Haven't you heard? Caroline Pearce told me, and I figured everyone must know by now."

"Know *what*?"

"Jessica has the football that was used in Sweet Valley Junior High's first championship game. The man who caught the winning pass gave it to her."

It took a moment for the words to sink in. And when they did, Elizabeth was stunned. She couldn't believe what she was hearing. "Nora, are you sure?"

Nora shrugged. "That's what Caroline told me."

For a second, Elizabeth felt dizzy from the shock. Then she told Nora she had to get to class and ran off. She needed some time alone to absorb this news and think it through.

It just doesn't make sense, Elizabeth thought. *Mr. Henkel told George the ball was the most important thing in the world to him. Why did he suddenly decide to give it away like that? And why would he give the ball to Jessica, whom he hardly knew, instead of his very own son?*

No, nothing was making sense. Something very strange was going on. And Elizabeth was pretty sure she knew exactly what it was.

Sitting at a table in the cafeteria, Jessica felt like a queen at a banquet. Word of the famous football had spread rapidly among the Unicorns, and everyone came by the table to congratulate her. Even Janet Howell, Lila's cousin and president of the Unicorns, left her table of eighth-graders and made a special trip to Jessica's table.

"The Unicorns are very happy about this," she told Jessica. "This is a great accomplishment and we won't forget it."

Jessica smiled at Janet's praise as Lila watched her through narrowed eyes.

"Don't forget," she noted, "*I* was the one who got us the poster. And *that's* an important item, too."

"Of course it is," Janet assured her. "But the football is even better."

Lila scowled. Jessica could tell she felt jealous. And that made her feel great. She loved being envied—particularly by someone like Lila. She was on top of the world.

"Uh, oh, here comes Elizabeth," Tamara muttered.

Sure enough, there was her sister, striding across the cafeteria toward them. And she looked *mad*.

She found out about the ball, Jessica thought, and a knot suddenly formed in her stomach.

But what could Elizabeth do about it, anyway? The ball was in Jessica's locker. And that's where it would stay. Jessica geared herself for the confrontation.

Elizabeth came up beside her and blurted out. "How did you get that football?"

Jessica was aware of the other Unicorns watching and listening. She stood up so she and Elizabeth would be eye to eye.

"I didn't steal it, if that's what you're thinking. Mr. Henkel gave it to me."

"That doesn't make sense," Elizabeth snapped. "He barely knows you. Why would he give you that football?"

Jessica shrugged innocently. "I have no idea. But when I went over there Saturday to drop off the library books, he gave it to me."

Elizabeth glared at her suspiciously. "He didn't by any chance call you Elizabeth, did he?"

Jessica faltered. "Why would he do that?"

"Because he thought you were me. And that's why he gave you the ball."

"He wasn't planning to give it to *you*," Jessica snapped. "It was George—" she stopped herself, but it was too late. Elizabeth's eyes were gleaming.

"That's just what I thought," Elizabeth declared in triumph. "He wanted George to have the ball. And he gave it to you because he thought you were me. And he wanted me to give it to George. Right?"

Jessica wasn't about to admit to anything. "You're just jealous because we've got the ball," she said.

"Oh, really?" Elizabeth smiled grimly. "I guess I'll just have to go call Mr. Henkel and ask him who he thinks he gave the ball to."

"That's blackmail!" Tamara declared.

Elizabeth didn't respond. She just stood there, looking at Jessica evenly.

Jessica knew it was all over. If Elizabeth called Mr. Henkel, she'd find out the truth. And Mr. Henkel might call her parents about it, and tell them Jessica took the ball under false pretenses. She could be in serious trouble. There was no way out.

"Where's the ball?" Elizabeth asked quietly.

"In my locker," Jessica muttered.

"Then let's go get it. Right now."

Jessica could barely bring herself to look at the Unicorns. Just a minute ago, she'd been the most popular member. Now they would all be furious with her. She gave them a helpless look and an apologetic shrug. Then she followed Elizabeth out of the cafeteria.

Clutching the ball tightly, Elizabeth waited outside the door at school. She knew George had to come out this way. She couldn't wait to show him the ball and tell him his father wanted him to have it. He would be thrilled!

Finally, she spotted him walking slowly toward the exit doors. She edged through the crowd of departing students to reach him. "George! Look!"

George stared at the football. "Where did you get that?"

Quickly, Elizabeth explained what happened. "I finally got Jessica to confess that your father told her to give it to you. He's changed his mind, George! He wants you to have it!"

She waited for a big smile to break out on his face. But it didn't appear. George just kept staring at the ball. And his eyes were cold.

"So he wants me to have it. Well, maybe I don't want it anymore."

Elizabeth was startled. "George, what are you talking about? Think of the time capsule! And think about your father! If he wants you to have this, it's because he loves you."

George snorted. "If he loves me so much, he can see me face to face and give it to me himself. Otherwise, I don't want it. And you can tell him that." Without another word, he walked away.

For the second time that day, Elizabeth was in a state of shock. She shook her head in disbelief. She realized she had to go right over to Mr. Henkel's to relay George's message. All Mr. Henkel had to do was ask George to come over and present the ball to him. Surely he could do that. It would solve everything. George would know his father loved him and their team would win the contest. There was still hope!

Elizabeth ran all the way home. She knew she looked pretty silly running with the ball tucked under her arm. And sure enough, when she passed Bruce Patman and some of his buddies, Bruce yelled out, "Hey, somebody tackle her!"

Luckily, nobody did. Elizabeth ignored them and kept on running. By the time she reached her block, she was out of breath. She didn't even bother to stop at her own house, but headed directly to Mr. Henkel's.

"Elizabeth! It's good to see you!" Mr. Henkel said with a smile when he opened the door. But he looked puzzled when he noticed the football. "Didn't you give it to George like I asked you to?"

Elizabeth didn't tell him about Jessica's scheme. "I tried to," she told Mr. Henkel. "But George said he won't accept it unless you give it to him personally. I thought maybe you could call him now, and—" Her voice trailed off as she saw the man's expression change. He looked cold, angry, and bitter.

"I see," he said harshly. "He wants me to apologize and ask his forgiveness, is that it?"

"Oh, no!" Elizabeth cried out. "That's not it at all! He only wants—"

"I know what he wants," Mr. Henkel barked. "I can see he wants me to beg him to accept this. And I guess he doesn't realize that I'm unable to get down on my hands and knees."

"Mr. Henkel, please listen to me," Elizabeth pleaded, but it was no use.

"You tell my son that if he doesn't want my football, that's fine with me. Goodbye, Elizabeth."

And he closed the door.

Nine

◇

Jessica was in disgrace. She had let the Unicorns down. She kept telling them that there was nothing she could do about it. If her parents found out how she had gotten that football, she could have been grounded for life!

But her teammates weren't very sympathetic. Both Tamara and Ellen believed she should have risked getting into trouble and kept the ball.

"A Unicorn stops at nothing to win," Ellen kept reminding her.

"You were only looking out for yourself," Tamara said. "A Unicorn should think about what's good for the group."

"It wouldn't be good for the Unicorns if *I* got into trouble," Jessica shot back. "Can you imagine what people would say about us if they knew I had fooled Mr. Henkel into giving me that football?"

That shut them up a little. And Janet Howell, who had witnessed the scene between Jessica and Elizabeth, stood up for Jessica.

"Jessica's right," she told the others. "She did the only thing she could do under the circumstances. It may not matter to us how she got the football, but other people might not understand. And if they found out, it could hurt our reputation."

Jessica was relieved to have the Unicorn president on her side. She knew that eventually the rest of the members would forget about it.

The team gathered in Jessica's bedroom after school that day. Ellen, Tamara, and Betsy were still a little angry at her. And, as Jessica suspected, Lila used the situation to her advantage. Even though she wouldn't show it, Jessica knew Lila was actually pleased that she had lost the football. It put her in a superior position again.

"Thank goodness we still have the poster *I* bought," Lila told them. "And the record album we found in *my* house. Otherwise we wouldn't have a chance."

"But what are we going to do for a third item?" Tamara whined. "We need three to win."

"We'll use the fashion magazine," Lila stated. "It's not great, but the other two things are so fantastic they'll make up for it."

"It's certainly a better collection than my sister's

team has," Jessica piped up. "I mean, who cares about an old book and a dumb photograph?"

"But now she's got the football," Ellen reminded her, as if Jessica needed reminding. "That's going to make a big difference."

Jessica tried to sound more confident than she felt when she said, "Not big enough. Not when her other two things are so stupid." She looked at Lila hopefully.

Lila raised her eyebrows and scowled for a second, but then she nodded. "That's probably true. And I've heard about some of the stuff the other teams have, and they're no better. I think we've still got a good chance at winning."

The others all agreed.

"Of course," Lila added, giving Jessica a disapproving look, "we would have had a better chance with the football."

Jessica wanted to change the subject. "I'll go get us some sodas," she declared, jumping up. She knew the minute she left the room, they'd all start criticizing her, but she didn't care. If she had to sit there for another one of Lila's looks, she was going to scream.

To her surprise, Elizabeth was in the kitchen, sitting at the table. "Why aren't you out celebrating with your team?" Jessica snapped as she opened the refrigerator and started pulling out sodas.

"Celebrating what?" Elizabeth sounded tired and depressed.

"Your precious football," Jessica said. "I suppose you think you're going to win now."

"We don't have the football," Elizabeth said quietly. "Mr. Henkel took it back."

Jessica stared at her twin. Her first impulse was to ask why. But she could tell from Elizabeth's expression that she was in no mood to talk.

Besides, it didn't matter why. They didn't have the football either, and that was all that mattered. Jessica raced back up to her room with the sodas.

"Guess what?" she announced quietly. "Elizabeth doesn't have the football! She gave it back to Mr. Henkel!"

Three sets of eyebrows shot up. "You're kidding!" Ellen exclaimed. "Then they don't have a chance!"

Even Lila looked satisfied. "That's good news. At least there's no way they'll win now."

Jessica happily agreed, and handed out the sodas. She couldn't honestly say she was back on top of the world. But at least she'd crawled up from the bottom.

Elizabeth's group spent the next couple of days following up leads.

"My aunt's got an attic filled with stuff she's

saved for years," Amy told them. "Maybe we can find something there."

So they spent an entire evening searching through Amy's aunt's attic. But they didn't find anything related to the sixties.

Then Julie remembered seeing something at the junk shop—a collection of souvenir plates from a World's Fair that had taken place in the sixties. The next day after school, they went tearing back to the shop. The plates were still there—but they cost two hundred dollars.

"I can't sell you just one," the lady told them apologetically. "It's part of a set, and it's very valuable."

George wasn't much help in their search. He didn't even seem interested anymore. Elizabeth had one faint hope—that Mr. Henkel would change his mind and call his son. But she knew that wasn't likely. Mr. Henkel was a very proud man. And if he believed that his son had rejected the football, he wasn't going to offer it again.

On Thursday, they gave up. "We have to turn everything in today," Elizabeth told her teammates. "The judges have to examine everything before the ceremony on Saturday, when they dedicate the dugouts. That's when they'll announce the winner."

Nobody said, ". . . and it won't be us," but that's what they were all thinking.

"Well, we tried," Julie said.

"I didn't," George said glumly. "I think I blew it for all of us."

"That's not true," Elizabeth told him firmly. "You did what you had to do."

"That's right," Julie said, and Amy agreed, too. George gave them a small smile.

"Thanks," he whispered.

"And we're all going to the ceremony together," Elizabeth announced. "Who knows? Maybe the judges will be so impressed with the two things we submitted that they won't care if we don't have three."

"Absolutely!" Amy declared.

"That's a definite possibility," Julie echoed.

Elizabeth could tell that they didn't really believe that. They were all mainly interested in cheering up George.

But from the sadness in George's eyes, Elizabeth knew they weren't having much success.

Saturday morning was bright and warm, a perfect day for an outdoor ceremony.

"They're going to have all the items we collected for the contest on display," Elizabeth told her parents as they prepared to leave the house.

"That ought to bring back memories for some of the parents," Mrs. Wakefield said. "What did your team contribute?"

"An old textbook from Sweet Valley Junior High, and an autographed picture of President Kennedy. There was a third thing we were hoping to get, but it didn't work out."

"Well, you made a fine contribution anyway," her father assured her. "Now, where's your sister? We want to have some time to look at all those things you kids collected before the ceremony starts."

"I'll get her," Elizabeth said, and went upstairs to Jessica's room. As she expected, her sister was still fixing herself up in front of the mirror.

"C'mon, Jess, we're ready to go."

Jessica gave her hair one last brush. "I want to look absolutely perfect," she declared. "They're going to take pictures of the winners, remember?"

Elizabeth remembered all too well. "You already look perfect," she said. She caught a glimpse of herself in the mirror, and pushed a stray lock of hair out of her eyes. Not that it mattered how she looked. No one was going to be taking her picture.

When Jessica was finally ready, the whole family piled into their maroon van and drove over to the school. Elizabeth had arranged to meet her team by the exhibit, and they were all there, including George. The items were set up on several tables in the center of the softball field, and the air was filled with conversation and laughter as students and families looked over the collection.

"Good grief, what's that?" Elizabeth asked. "It looks like a mound of hair."

Amy read the card that was attached to it. "'Beatles wig, 1964.' I guess people wore them so they'd look like the Beatles."

Farther down the table, they saw a photograph of the Beatles and ticket stubs from a Beatles concert.

"There's Jessica's team's stuff," Julie announced from farther down the table. "They have some interesting things," she commented.

Amy sniffed. "They have a Beatles album. Big deal. Everybody's got Beatles stuff."

"It's still a good collection," Elizabeth said loyally. No matter what nasty schemes Jessica pulled, she was still her sister, and she had to stand up for her.

"Ours is better," Julie insisted. "Our things are more important. The textbook stands for education, and the photograph stands for government."

"That's true," Elizabeth admitted. But two great items wouldn't win the contest for them.

"Attention!" a voice boomed out over the field. Elizabeth saw Mr. Clark, the principal, standing at a microphone. "Will everyone please take a seat in the stands so we may begin our program."

Elizabeth, Amy, George, and Julie took seats. Down the row from them, she saw Jessica and her team. They were all examining themselves in mirrors.

As the crowd settled down in the bleachers, Mr.

Clark began. "In celebration of Sweet Valley Middle School's twenty-fifth anniversary, we are burying a time capsule containing items from the sixties. Our students have been holding a competition to see which team could bring in the three most distinctive items representing that time. As you saw from the display, we have a very fine collection, and the judges have had a difficult time making a decision."

Behind him, Elizabeth could see three teachers examining the items on the table. Mr. Clark beckoned them to the microphone to announce their decision.

Just as he was about to step aside and hand the microphone to one of the judges, something seemed to catch his eye. He was looking at the entrance to the field. Following his gaze, Elizabeth turned to look in that direction and saw a figure in a wheelchair heading onto the field toward Mr. Clark.

"It's my father!" George exclaimed.

"And he's got the football," Elizabeth said, gasping.

A murmur went through the crowd as Mr. Clark covered the microphone with his hand and spoke with Mr. Henkel. Then the judges joined them. Then Mr. Clark spoke into the microphone.

"Would George Henkel please come down here?"

Elizabeth turned to George. He got up and made his way down to the field, his face pale.

"What's going on?" Amy asked in bewilderment.

Elizabeth felt a thrill shoot through her. "I don't know, " she said. "But I have a feeling it's something good!"

Ten

◇

No one spoke as Mr. Clark handed the microphone to Mr. Henkel and Mr. Henkel moved closer to speak into it.

"I hope you all will excuse this interruption. But I have something important to say, and I want everyone to hear it."

He held up the football so they could see it. "Some of you may remember me from twenty-five years ago, when I caught this ball during Sweet Valley Junior High's first championship game. That was a big moment for me."

He paused, and even from a distance Elizabeth could tell that this was difficult for him. He turned and looked for a moment at George, who was standing by his side. Then he continued speaking.

"A lot has happened since then. I'm not the man I used to be. And I've had a hard time dealing with that. I've wasted a lot of time feeling sorry for myself."

He paused again, and lowered his head. When he looked up, he was smiling. "You know, this football was very special to me. And when my son asked if his team could have it for their project, I said no. I didn't want to part with it, because it was the only thing I had to remind me of better days. I said it was the most important thing in my life. Well, I was wrong. There's a person who is much more important to me. My son, George."

Elizabeth clutched Amy's hand. She felt an enormous lump forming in her throat.

Now Mr. Henkel's voice was trembling. "This football is only a memory. It's time for me to stop looking back, and start looking ahead. That's why I'm giving it to my son, with the hope that we can start making a future together."

He held the football out to George. George took it, held it for a moment, and then handed it to a judge, who placed it on the table with the other things. And then, despite the fact that a whole audience was watching, George threw his arms around his father.

For a moment, there was total silence. Then, suddenly, everyone was applauding. Elizabeth, Amy, and Julie all hugged each other. "That's the most beautiful thing I ever saw," Amy cried.

Elizabeth tried to wipe away her own tears. See-

ing George and Mr. Henkel embracing was exactly
what she had hoped for.

George wheeled his father away from the microphone to the edge of the stands and sat down beside
him. Then Mr. Clark returned to the microphone.

"Thank you, Mr. Henkel, not only for giving us
the football, but for reminding us what's really important in life. Now, I believe the judges have
reached a decision. Mrs. Arnette?"

He stepped aside so the social studies teacher
could speak into the microphone.

"First of all, I want to congratulate all the teams
who participated in the time capsule project. Because of your efforts, students in twenty-five years
will know what the 1960s were like in Sweet Valley.

"We judges did not have an easy time picking
the winners. In deciding which collection of items
was the finest, we did not look for the most unusual,
or the most expensive. We wanted to see items
which best represent what we at Sweet Valley Middle School believe in—yesterday, today, and tomorrow."

"The winning team members are Elizabeth
Wakefield, Amy Sutton, Julie Porter, and George
Henkel."

The applause was so deafening that Elizabeth
could barely hear her own squeal of joy. The three
girls leaped up, hugged each other, and then ran
down the bleachers to where George was sitting

with his father. Elizabeth spoke first. "We wouldn't have won without you, Mr. Henkel. Thank you."

"Thank *you*, Elizabeth," Mr. Henkel said. "Because of you, I've got my son back."

It was all Elizabeth could do to keep from crying. Hearing those words meant more to her than all the time capsules in the world.

As the applause died down, Mrs. Arnette began speaking again. "I'd like to ask the members of the winning team to step forward and tell us about each item, and what they mean to them."

"Oh my gosh!" Amy whispered. "I didn't know we'd have to give a speech!" But they all joined Mrs. Arnette at the microphone, and Julie went first. She picked up the photograph and held it high.

"This is a signed photograph of President Kennedy, the first president elected in the 1960s. To us, this photo represents leadership."

With a little push from Elizabeth, Amy went next. She held up the book. "This is a textbook that was used by one of the first classes at Sweet Valley Junior High. It's a symbol of education, and it stands for our belief in our school."

As Amy stepped aside, Elizabeth took George's hand and the two of them went to the microphone together. Elizabeth spoke first. "This football is a symbol of teamwork. It stands for working together to accomplish a goal."

Then George took a deep breath and spoke. "And it's a symbol of something passed on from one generation to the next. It stands for our belief in our parents."

Once again, applause swept over the bleachers. Only this time, the crowd stood up.

"It's a standing ovation!" Elizabeth exclaimed. And it seemed to go on forever.

Then a photographer came forward to take their pictures. "Does anyone have a mirror?" Julie asked anxiously. Elizabeth produced one, and they all spent a few moments frantically fixing their hair. Then the photographer took a photo of each of them, and another of the whole group.

Elizabeth felt like she was walking on air. What a day! She was so dazed, she was barely aware of the dugout dedication going on. As soon as it was over, she looked for her parents.

She found them shaking hands with Mr. Henkel.

There were more hugs, more congratulations. And then Elizabeth saw her sister coming toward them. She eyed Jessica a little nervously. Jessica didn't look upset at all, though. She congratulated Elizabeth, and then stepped back, looking at her critically.

"I'm glad you brushed your hair."

"Why?" Elizabeth asked.

"I wanted your picture to come out nicely, because in twenty-five years, people will be looking at it. And who knows?" Jessica grinned mischievously. "They just might think it's me!"

Eleven

◆

It was a week after the contest and Elizabeth was still basking in the glow of the time capsule victory. She hurried home after school, clutching a red folder tightly in her hand. It was an essay she had written for her English class, and it was one of the most difficult papers she had ever written. She had revised it three times

But all her hard work paid off. The essay had been returned that day, and she had received an A plus! She couldn't wait to tell her family.

"Mom!" she called as she ran in the door. "Mom, guess what?"

But there was no answer. Elizabeth sighed in disappointment. Her mother was probably still at work. She checked the refrigerator door for a note, but there was no message.

Elizabeth helped herself to some cookies and milk, and sat down at the kitchen table. It seemed to her that her mother had been working more than usual lately. She was hardly ever home when the twins got home from school.

The house was so silent that when the phone rang, Elizabeth jumped. *That's probably Mom*, she thought as she got up to answer it. "Hello," she called into the phone.

"Hi, honey. Let me talk to your mother." It was Mr. Wakefield.

"She's not here."

There was a brief silence on the other end. "Do you know where she is?"

Elizabeth glanced around the kitchen to make sure she hadn't overlooked a note. "No, she didn't leave any message."

She could hear her father sigh over the phone.

"I have to take a client out to dinner, and I wanted her to join us."

"I'll tell her to call you as soon as she gets home," Elizabeth offered.

"It doesn't matter," Mr. Wakefield said. "I'll just take him out by myself. I'll see you later, honey."

That's odd, Elizabeth thought as she hung up the phone. *Dad almost always knows where Mom is.* And she'd never heard of her father going out to dinner without her mother.

Just then, Jessica came in through the back door. "Where's Mom?" she asked Elizabeth breathlessly. "We're supposed to go shopping."

"She's not here," Elizabeth told her. "I don't know where she is."

Jessica frowned. "This isn't like her to break a promise."

"Maybe she's just late getting back from work," Elizabeth suggested.

Jessica sat down and drummed her fingernails on the table. "She's *always* working late these days. What's going on? Did everyone in Sweet Valley decide to redecorate their houses at the same time?"

"It seems like it," Elizabeth agreed. "I feel like I hardly see Mom at all anymore."

"I saw her at the mall yesterday," Jessica said. "But she didn't see me."

Elizabeth was surprised. "What was she doing there?"

"She was on her way into a restaurant with some man."

"Maybe it was someone who's having his house decorated," Elizabeth said.

"Then why weren't they at his house?" Jessica demanded.

Elizabeth was puzzled, too. "I don't know, Jess. Maybe they were taking a break. Are you sure you don't know who she was with?"

"I'm positive," Jessica said. "It wasn't one of Mom and Dad's friends. I've never seen him before." Then she grinned. "Maybe Mom has a secret boyfriend."

Elizabeth was shocked. "Jess! That's not funny!"

"I was just kidding," Jessica said quickly. She took a cookie and bit into it. The two girls sat eating in silence for a minute. Then Jessica looked at Elizabeth thoughtfully. "Have you noticed that Mom and Dad haven't been spending much time together lately?"

Elizabeth *had* noticed that, but she didn't want to think about it. "I guess they've both been very busy with work," she murmured lamely.

"*Maybe*," Jessica said darkly. "But it's weird."

Elizabeth gazed at her in alarm. "What do you mean, weird?"

"Well, Mom's hardly ever around these days. And who was that man she was with? Just between us, I think something strange is going on."

And Elizabeth, feeling troubled, could only agree.

SWEET VALLEY TWINS

Jumping to Conclusions

Written by
Jamie Suzanne

Created by
FRANCINE PASCAL

A BANTAM BOOK®
TORONTO · NEW YORK · LONDON · SYDNEY · AUCKLAND

To Jake Michael Nardi

One

◇

"The decorations look beautiful!" Elizabeth Wakefield said, clapping her hands in delight as she surveyed the family's living room. Pink-and-white streamers were looped from wall to wall above her head. Through the picture window she could see the sun just beginning to set over Sweet Valley, California. "What a perfect night for a party!" she exclaimed.

Elizabeth and her twin sister, Jessica, had spent the entire afternoon decorating and cooking. Today was their parents' sixteenth wedding anniversary and it had been Jessica's idea to have a special party to celebrate. For two weeks the twins had thought of nothing but their big secret.

"I hope they're surprised," Jessica called from

the kitchen. "I'm sure they will be," Elizabeth called back as she straightened the "Happy Anniversary, Mom and Dad!" banner stretched across the entryway. "I haven't breathed a word to anyone."

"This is going to be great," Jessica declared as she entered the dining room. She carried a large bouquet in her hands. The sisters had picked sixteen yellow roses from their mother's rose garden, then carefully mixed them with wildflowers.

As they set the flowers on the sideboard, they both noticed their reflection in the mirror on the wall. They were identical in almost every way. Their blue-green eyes were the color of the Pacific Ocean and their shiny blond hair fell in waves over their shoulders. Even the dimples in their left cheeks matched when they smiled.

Only their family and closest friends could tell the girls apart, and those who knew them best knew that their similarities were only skin-deep. When it came to their personalities, they couldn't have been more different.

Elizabeth loved nothing more than to indulge in a good mystery, preferably one by Amanda Howard, her favorite writer. In addition, Elizabeth worked hard in school and was proud to be a member of the staff of *The Sweet Valley Sixers*, the sixth-grade paper.

Jessica, on the other hand, loved clothes and boys and her after-school activities, especially being a member of the Unicorns, an exclusive all-girls club at Sweet Valley Middle School. And it was just like Jessica to think that no party ever really got started until she entered the room. But, in spite of all their differences, the twins were still the best of friends.

"You know," Jessica said, "it feels like ages since our family has been together. Sometimes I feel like we should schedule family meetings, just to remind us all what we look like."

Elizabeth laughed. "It hasn't been that bad, Jess."

"Well, ever since Dad started that big case, we hardly see him," Jessica pointed out. Their father was a successful lawyer in Sweet Valley, and his hours could be very demanding.

"That's true," Elizabeth said.

"And what about Steven?" Jessica put her hands on her hips. "He's never home."

"I know," Elizabeth agreed. "He's always at basketball practice."

"Which is fine with me," Jessica added with a smile.

Since he had begun his freshman year at Sweet Valley High, their brother had been harder to live with than ever. Even Elizabeth found his constant bragging about being older and wiser a little irritating.

"But it's Mom who's been gone the most," Jessica said, her voice suddenly turning serious.

Elizabeth nodded. "She's been spending a lot of time working with her clients." Mrs. Wakefield worked part-time as an interior decorator but lately it seemed as if it was full-time.

"She's also been dining with strange men," Jessica added.

"Now, Jessica," Elizabeth scolded. "Be fair. You saw her in a restaurant with a man *once*—and you never even asked her about it."

Jessica had seen their mother having lunch with a man whom she didn't recognize a few days earlier and had been brooding about it ever since. Elizabeth guessed that, similar to the time when Mrs. Wakefield had been ill, Jessica's overactive imagination was hard at work again.

"Well, she *has* been gone a lot," Jessica insisted, "and if it weren't for you and me running things, this house would be a mess."

Elizabeth grinned. It was just like Jessica to take credit for the extra chores they had been asked to do—chores which Elizabeth usually wound up doing.

"Well, what do you think?" Jessica pointed to a platter full of sandwiches on the sideboard.

"They served these at our last Unicorn party and they were a big hit."

Elizabeth picked up one of the sandwiches and took a bite. "Hey! These are delicious."

"Don't eat them all!" Jessica said, swatting playfully at her sister's hand. "Save some for Mom and Dad."

"Did you call about the cake?" Elizabeth asked.

"Steven was supposed to pick it up from the bakery but he's late—as usual."

"Don't panic. Mom and Dad aren't supposed to be back for another half an hour."

"Half an hour!" Jessica raced toward the kitchen. "We'll never make it in time."

The front door slammed and Steven called from the hallway, "You can start the party now. I'm here."

"Very funny!" Jessica shouted, walking back into the kitchen. "Bring that cake in here, quickly."

Elizabeth carefully placed four long-stemmed roses around two tiny figures that stood in the center of the dining room table. They were the figures that had been on Mr. and Mrs. Wakefield's wedding cake sixteen years ago.

Steven strolled into the dining room, and looked over Elizabeth's shoulder. "Wow, where did you find those?" he asked.

"In Mom's trunk."

Steven stared at the tiny man in his formal tuxedo and the tiny woman in her frilly wedding dress and shook his head. "Boy, why would anyone want to dress up like that!"

"Because it's romantic," Jessica said, coming up behind them. "I can just see them on their wedding day."

Elizabeth sighed. "I'll bet Mom looked beautiful!"

"Cut it out, you two," Steven said, making a face and groaning. Then he caught sight of the tray on the sideboard. "Hey, sandwiches!"

"Don't you dare, Steven Wakefield!" Jessica leapt in front of him. "Those are for the party."

"But I'm dying of hunger," he pleaded.

"You'll have some later." Elizabeth cut in.

Steven reluctantly backed off.

"We'd better do a last minute check to make sure everything is ready," Elizabeth told her sister.

"The hors d'oeuvres are done. I have the casserole ready to pop in the oven," Jessica said, counting the items on her fingers. "The cake is here and—"

"Did you hear that?" Steven rushed to the window. "It sounded like a car," Elizabeth whispered.

Jessica raced to the living room and peered through the drapes. "It's them!" she shouted. "Hurry, turn off the lights."

Elizabeth flicked the switch and the three of them scrambled behind the couch to hide.

"Ouch!" Jessica cried as Steven stepped on her foot. "Steven, watch where you're going."

"*You* watch where—"

"Shhhh!" Elizabeth hissed.

The three held their breath and listened for the sound of the key in the lock. The front door creaked open.

"Hello?" It was their mother's voice. "Anybody here?" When there was no response, she said, "That's strange, the children should all be home by now."

Then their father's voice rumbled in the darkened room. "I thought I saw a light on when we pulled into the driveway."

Jessica started giggling. Steven jabbed her to make her stop, but within seconds Elizabeth was laughing as hard as her sister.

"Ready?" Steven whispered hoarsely. "One, two, three—"

"SURPRISE!" they all shouted.

"What's all this about?" their father asked as the light flicked on. He looked over at his wife, who was equally confused.

"I don't know," she replied. "Kids, is this a joke?"

"A joke? How can you ask that, Mom? It's for your anniversary," Jessica explained. "Don't you remember?"

"Anniversary?" Their parents clapped their hands to their foreheads. "Oh, no!" they echoed in unison.

"Did you both forget?" Elizabeth asked in amazement.

"How *could* you?" Jessica couldn't hide the disappointment in her voice.

"I guess we've been kind of busy," Mr. Wakefield replied, lifting his hands in a helpless gesture.

Mrs. Wakefield sighed dramatically. "We knew the romance couldn't last forever."

"Don't say that!" Jessica cried out. "It's not funny."

Mr. Wakefield looked at Jessica sharply. "It's just a joke, Jessica."

"Does this mean we can't eat the cake and sandwiches?" Steven asked.

Jessica turned to him, her eyes blazing. "Is your stomach all you can ever think of?"

"Well . . . sometimes."

Elizabeth decided this was a good moment to

interject. "How do you like the decorations? It was Jessica's idea to give you a party."

Jessica nodded but said nothing. Her stomach was starting to feel queasy. *They haven't kissed, or hugged, or anything,* she thought. *Don't they care anymore?* Suddenly, she remembered seeing her mother with that other man.

"Jessica?"

Jessica looked up to see Elizabeth waving at her. "What?"

Elizabeth made eating motions with her hand and pointed toward the kitchen.

"Oh. Right." Jessica decided just to concentrate on the anniversary party for now.

That night as Elizabeth was getting ready for bed, she heard a soft knock at her door.

"Lizzie, it's me," Jessica whispered. "I need to talk to you."

"What's the matter, Jess?" Elizabeth asked as her sister entered her room.

"It's Mom and Dad," Jessica whispered. "I'm really worried."

"Just because they forgot their anniversary?"

Jessica sat on the edge of the bed. "People don't forget an important event like that unless there's something really wrong."

"They've both been awfully busy recently." Elizabeth sat down next to her sister.

"I know. And that's another thing." Jessica whispered, "Have you noticed they hardly go out together anymore?"

"Look," Elizabeth said patiently. "Dad has that big case right now and Mom's had to spend more time on the job than usual. It's not going to be this way forever."

"Well, I'm not so sure," Jessica said.

"What's that supposed to mean?"

"Maybe it's like Mom said, the romance is all gone. Lizzie, what if they're just pretending for our sakes?"

"Now you're being silly." Elizabeth stood up. "I'm really tired. Let's get some sleep. I'm sure everything will look better in the morning."

"I hope you're right." Jessica hugged her sister and trudged back to her room.

As she drifted off to sleep she couldn't help thinking, *People who love each other just don't forget their anniversary.*

Two

◇

At lunchtime on Monday Amy Sutton looked up from her tray and declared, "Why did the Hairnet do this to us!" Everyone at Sweet Valley Middle School called Mrs. Arnette, the social studies teacher, "the Hairnet" because she always wore a brown net over her tight bun. Amy picked up a handful of potato chips and stuffed a few into her mouth. "Can you believe it? A big report due in two weeks."

Elizabeth smiled at her best friend. They had decided to meet at lunch to think up ideas for their new social studies project. So far they had gotten nowhere.

"Amy, it's not that bad," Elizabeth said. "With three of us working on it, it should be easy."

"A report for Mrs. Arnette is never easy," Pamela Jacobson announced as she slid her lunch tray onto the table and sat down next to Elizabeth.

Pamela had only started attending Sweet Valley Middle School a few months earlier, but she had quickly become good friends with Elizabeth and Amy. She had eagerly volunteered to be in their group working on the report.

"I'm glad you're here, Pamela." Elizabeth smiled at the pale brunette. "Tell Amy that our Living History report will be fun."

Pamela turned toward Amy and with a serious expression repeated Elizabeth's words. "Our Living History report will be fun."

Elizabeth laughed and gave Pamela a playful punch. "You're just as bad as Amy!"

Amy sighed. "I can't help thinking that history's just a lot of boring dates. Every time Mrs. Arnette starts to write one on the blackboard . . ." She stopped talking and dropped her head onto the table, letting out a loud snore. Elizabeth and Pamela couldn't resist a giggle.

Pamela opened her carton of milk and put her straw in it. "Why don't we go over the assignment again to see how much work we have to do?"

"Good idea." Elizabeth flipped open her notebook. "First we have to find someone in Sweet Valley to interview."

"Right." Amy took a huge bite of her grilled cheese sandwich and mumbled, "Then we ask them questions."

"Then we go to the library and do a little research on the era or subject they discuss," Elizabeth said.

"And finally, we put it all together and present the report to the class," Pamela finished.

Elizabeth smiled at her friends. "It could be a lot of fun."

Amy groaned. "Or it could be a lot of work. Besides, who do we know who's interesting? I can't think of anyone."

Elizabeth sighed. "I wish we could do a report about romance—maybe something about love and adventure." Elizabeth turned to Pamela. "How did your parents meet?"

Pamela began to answer, then paused, a surprised look on her face. "Gee, I don't know."

"Do you know how your mom and dad fell in love?" Elizabeth asked Amy.

She shook her head slowly. "I never asked."

"Me, neither," Elizabeth said.

"I guess I never really thought about it," Amy added. "I think of my parents as always having been married. It's hard to imagine them apart."

Amy lowered her voice dramatically. "I've got it," she declared. ". . . Mom and Dad are in a crowded airport. They bump into each other accidentally and Mom's suitcase falls on the ground. Dad reaches down to pick it up, their eyes meet—it's *fate!*"

"Oooh!" Elizabeth let out a squeal of delight. "This is just like a romance novel. Let's do our project on our own parents."

"What a great idea!" Pamela clapped her hands together.

"We could call it 'Sweet Valley Sweethearts,'" Elizabeth added. Amy nodded enthusiastically. "This could be a really interesting report."

"Don't forget, we still have to find other stories to go along with the interviews," Pamela reminded them.

"We could go to the library and each do a report on romance. You know, famous romantic couples in history," Elizabeth said excitedly.

"And literature," Amy added.

"And we could end our report with a love poem," Pamela concluded.

"Then it's settled." Elizabeth shut her notebook. "We'll each interview our parents and find out how they met."

"This is going to be great," Amy declared. "I never thought I'd get excited about a project for the Hairnet."

Amy and Pamela chattered on about their

project while Elizabeth sat quietly, thinking about her parents.

This project will be just the thing to put the romance back in their lives. Elizabeth couldn't wait to get home and tell Jessica about her plan.

Jessica checked her watch for the fifteenth time. School had been out for over an hour and there was still no sign of Elizabeth. Finally she spotted her sister coming down their street and she ran to meet her.

"Lizzie, I have to talk to you!"

"What's the matter?" Elizabeth asked.

Jessica motioned for Elizabeth to follow her around the side of the house to the old pine tree. The twins used to go there to share secrets when they were younger and they had called it their "thinking seat."

Elizabeth frowned. Whatever Jessica wanted to talk about must be pretty serious because only Elizabeth still went there when she had a problem to think through.

"Jessica," she pleaded. "Please tell me what's wrong."

"It's Mom," Jessica whispered. "I heard her on the phone, talking to someone."

"So? It's probably just a client calling about a

job." Mrs. Wakefield's clients were always calling her at home.

"I couldn't really hear what they were saying because Mom finished the call in the bedroom and shut the door." Jessica crossed her arms. "But I'll tell you this—she was sure doing a lot of laughing for a business call."

"Jessica, you're being silly."

"And that's not all." Jessica lowered her voice. "The phone rang again five minutes later and it was the same man."

"How do you know it was a man?"

"I listened on the extension."

"Jessica!" Elizabeth was shocked. "That's spying. How could you?"

"I had to!" Jessica's blue-green eyes glistened with tears. "Oh, Lizzie, don't you see? First Mom is away half the time. Then she forgets her wedding anniversary. And now she's flirting with a strange man on the phone—"

"What do you mean, flirting? Mom wouldn't—"

"Right after Mom hung up she rushed out of the house." Jessica paced back and forth on the grass in front of the tree. "She's going to leave us, I just know it. She'll run off with some rich Arab. He'll promise her all the things Dad can't afford, and then we'll never see her again!"

"You're being ridiculous," Elizabeth cut in. "Where in the world did you come up with a story like that?"

"I saw it on a late-night movie once," Jessica replied matter-of-factly. "It was called *The Desert Siren* and it was based on a true story. Things like this happen *all* the time, Lizzie."

"Look, Jessica," Elizabeth interrupted, "there's a simple way to find out if you're right. Let's just ask Mom about the call when she gets home."

"She won't admit she's fallen in love just like that!"

"Mom has *not* fallen in love," Elizabeth declared. "With a rich Arab or anyone else!"

Jessica opened her mouth to protest but Elizabeth was already marching toward their back door. "I just hope you're right," Jessica whispered under her breath.

When they came through the door, Mrs. Wakefield was standing at the kitchen counter, removing a cardboard box from a brown paper bag. Her face was flushed with excitement and she turned to greet her daughters with a smile.

"There you both are! Sorry I'm late but I had to go back to the office."

Jessica pinched Elizabeth's arm.

"Since we're stuck with eating TV dinners tonight," Mrs. Wakefield said, "I thought a special surprise was in order."

"What sort of surprise?" Elizabeth asked, rubbing her bruised arm.

"Blueberry cheesecake!" Mrs. Wakefield flipped open the lid of the box to reveal the luscious dessert inside.

Elizabeth and Jessica stared solemnly at their mother.

"Oh, I know you're disappointed that I haven't been able to cook a proper dinner lately," their mother said. "But you'll have to bear with me for a while. I started working on a new account for a man from L.A."

Elizabeth felt a nudge from Jessica but tried to ignore it.

"He's opening a new office here in Sweet Valley and he wants me to decorate it! It's one of the biggest accounts we've ever had and I'm in charge of the whole thing." She grinned proudly. "Not bad, huh?"

"What's this guy like?" Jessica demanded. Elizabeth winced at the suspicious tone in her sister's voice. Their mother didn't seem to notice but rattled on gaily.

"Well, for one thing, he's very wealthy."

This time the nudge in her side was so sharp, Elizabeth gasped with pain. She spun around to face Jessica, who glared back at her as if to say, "I told you so!"

"He's got a huge home in Beverly Hills," their mother continued, as she popped some frozen dinners into the oven. "But he's hardly ever there. Most of the time he calls in from his private jet."

Mrs. Wakefield reached into her briefcase and pulled out a magazine. "Here's a picture of his house. It was the featured home in this month's issue of *Designer's Monthly*."

The twins stared at the photograph in awe. The mansion was three stories high and looked like a castle. Off in the distance they could see a pool and tennis courts. A big silver limousine sat in the driveway with a chauffeur standing at attention beside it.

"Wow." Jessica's stomach did flip-flops.

"What's his name?" Elizabeth asked.

"Francis Howard," Mrs. Wakefield replied. "Everyone calls him Frank, though. He's a very nice man."

"What's he look like, Mom?" Jessica asked in a shaky voice.

Their mother paused for a moment, then shrugged. "He's pretty normal-looking, I guess. He has a nice smile."

The phone rang suddenly and both girls jumped at the sound. Elizabeth answered it.

"Hello." A deep voice rumbled in her ear. "May I speak with Alice—I mean, Mrs. Wakefield?"

"Just a minute, please," Elizabeth said. She covered the mouthpiece with her palm and said, "Mom, it's for you."

"Thanks, honey." Mrs. Wakefield took the receiver from her and said, "Hello? Oh, hi, Frank. Just a minute. Let me go into the other room." She handed the phone back to Elizabeth. "Hang that up for me, OK?"

She walked briskly out of the kitchen and into their father's study. "I've got it!" she called out. Then they heard her voice fade away as the door to the study shut behind her.

Elizabeth stared at her sister. Jessica's lower lip was trembling. "*Now* do you believe me?" Jessica said sadly.

Three

◇

"I made up a list of sample questions for us to use in our interviews," Elizabeth announced, handing Pamela and Amy each a neatly printed copy from her binder. "What do you think?"

The three girls had gone to Pamela's house after school on Wednesday to plan the next step for the Living History project. They had made themselves comfortable in the den, and were now discussing the finer points.

"Oh, this is great, Liz!" Pamela said as she passed around sodas and chips. "I thought maybe we could interview my mom this afternoon."

"Good idea." Elizabeth took a sip of her

drink. "That will give us a chance to practice some interview techniques."

"I hope you guys don't mind," Amy said sheepishly, "but I talked to my parents last night. I just couldn't wait to find out how they met and fell in love."

"That's OK." Elizabeth smiled at her friend. "Did you take a lot of notes?"

"No, but I have every detail memorized." Amy, who was sitting on the floor, raised herself up on her knees. Her voice became hushed and excited as she began to tell her story.

"When my parents were both seniors in high school, they got summer jobs working at an amusement park. Dad ran the loop-the-loop ride and Mom took tickets at the gate."

"Did they know each other from school?" Pamela interrupted.

Amy shook her head. "No, Dad went to Crestview High. They'd never even seen each other before the Fourth of July. Anyway, that night, after the park was closed to the public, the owners kept the rides running for the employees."

"Sounds like fun," Elizabeth said, settling back on the couch.

"So Mom decided she'd ride the Ferris wheel and—"

"And that's where they met?" Pamela asked eagerly.

"Yes, but first—"

"I thought you said your dad ran the loop-the-loop," Elizabeth cut in.

"He did but he decided to go for a ride on the Ferris wheel, too." Amy sighed with exasperation. "But wait, I haven't even gotten to the good part yet.

"So there they were, all standing in line, waiting to get on the Ferris wheel. Then the man who ran the ride put Mom and Dad together in the same chair."

Elizabeth's eyes grew bigger with anticipation.

"Now here's the best part." Amy took a long sip of her soda and then whispered, "The Ferris wheel got stuck when the two of them were at the very top."

"Oooh, how scary!" Pamela blurted out.

"They were up there for almost an hour!" Amy continued.

"I'd have died of fright," Elizabeth said.

"Mom told me she was absolutely petrified and started to get hysterical. Dad had to calm her down by explaining how the ride worked and what the problem might be. He talked her right out of being scared. Then Mom noticed the full moon above them." Amy beamed happily. "By the time they got back down to the bottom, they were in love."

Both Pamela and Elizabeth sighed. "How romantic!" Elizabeth said.

Amy leaned back on her elbows. "Yes, isn't it a great story?"

All three girls sat silently, dreamily imagining the couple in the moonlight, perched high up on the top of the Ferris wheel.

"Elizabeth, have you asked your parents how they met?" Amy asked.

Elizabeth felt her cheeks turn pink, thinking of how little time her parents spent together these days. "Uh, n-no. I haven't asked, yet. They've both been really busy with their work, you know."

Elizabeth was relieved that neither of her friends seemed to notice how uncomfortable she was.

"Well, I can't wait to hear about it next time," Pamela said enthusiastically.

"Hello, girls." Mrs. Jacobson stood at the door to the den, holding a tray in her hands. "I thought you might need some healthy snacks to get you through your research."

"Thanks, Mom," Pamela said, as her mother

placed a tray of celery sticks, carrots, and dip on the coffee table.

"Have you girls been working hard?" Mrs. Jacobson asked as she passed around napkins. "Pamela told me all about your Living History project. I think it's a wonderful idea."

Elizabeth couldn't help feeling a pang of jealousy. It just didn't seem like there was any time, lately, when she could sit down and talk to her mother.

"Mom," Pamela said, "we thought we'd try out our interview techniques on you. Is that all right?"

"Sure." Mrs. Jacobson laughed and took a seat on the couch. "Fire away."

Pamela opened her notebook and reached for a pencil. "How did you and Dad meet?"

"And when did you fall in love?" Amy chimed in.

"Unless, of course, they happened at the same time," Elizabeth added, getting back into the spirit of things.

"Well, not exactly," Mrs. Jacobson replied slowly.

"You mean, it wasn't love at first sight?" Pamela sounded disappointed.

"No," Mrs. Jacobson replied with a laugh. "It was more like third sight."

"Oh," Pamela made a note on her pad, "what does that mean, Mom?"

"You see, the first time I met Dr. Jacobson," Pamela's mother explained, "I was in such pain from my sprained ankle that I hardly noticed how handsome he was."

"How'd you sprain your ankle?" Elizabeth asked.

"Playing volleyball with my sorority team. They rushed me to the emergency room and he was the doctor who wrapped my ankle. That was the first time I saw him. When I had to go back to the hospital for a follow-up examination, I was in better spirits and I noticed his good looks. But I wasn't sure if he was interested in me until he scheduled a house call for my sprained ankle." Mrs. Jacobson smiled at the memory. "He paid me a visit at the sorority house and the next thing I knew, we were engaged."

Elizabeth sighed wistfully. "I hope the next time I sprain my ankle, a handsome doctor rescues me and we fall in love, just like that."

"Thanks, Mom," Pamela said, giving her mother a big hug. "That was terrific!"

"Well, I'll leave you girls alone," Mrs. Jacobson said. "I'm sure you've got lots more to do."

After she had left the room, Elizabeth sat quietly, nibbling a carrot stick. "I hope my parents' story is half as romantic as yours both are."

"It will be," Amy said. "Your parents are the perfect couple. They're so much in love."

Elizabeth didn't respond. *Maybe they're just pretending to be in love, for our sake,* she thought. She shook her head to chase the thought away.

"You're right," she said, smiling bravely. "They *are* the perfect couple."

That afternoon Jessica walked home after school with Lila Fowler, a fellow Unicorn and one of her best friends. Lila was one of the prettiest girls in the sixth grade and she knew it. She dressed only in the best and latest fashions. Sometimes Jessica felt envious of her friend, whose father was very wealthy and gave her anything she wanted.

As they strolled along, the two Unicorns chatted about clothes, boys, and the latest gossip. Lila did most of the talking, but Jessica was having a hard time keeping her mind on the conversation.

"So I said to her, 'Caroline, do you really think I care?'" Lila laughed with satisfaction as they rounded the corner to the Wakefield home. "Oh, Jessica, you should have seen her face! She looked like a prune."

Jessica froze suddenly and stared straight ahead.

"Jessica? Are you listening to me?" Lila demanded, tossing her perfectly combed hair over one shoulder.

Jessica didn't reply. She was too busy staring at the silver limousine that was parked in front of her house. The windows were made of dark glass so you couldn't see inside. The door opened and a man stepped out onto the sidewalk.

"Who's that?" Lila whispered. Jessica shook her head in awe. He was without a doubt the most distinguished-looking man she had ever seen. Tall and ruggedly built, he was dressed in an elegant suit. He walked briskly up to the front entrance and slipped a skinny cardboard tube between the screen and the door. As he turned around to walk back to the car, the girls got a closer look at his tanned face.

"He looks like a movie star," Jessica exclaimed.

"I know who that is!" Lila hissed.

"Who?"

"Frank Howard, the millionaire."

Jessica felt like she'd been hit in the stomach. "No!"

"Yes," Lila continued, her voice trembling with excitement. "I read about him in *Faces* magazine. Women go crazy over him but he's never gotten married."

The man got back into the limousine and the car pulled away from the curb. The girls watched in silence as the sleek car disappeared around the corner.

A sudden breeze rustled the leaves and Jessica shivered. She thought to herself miserably, *Mom will never be able to resist a man like Frank Howard.*

Four

◇

That evening, Jessica and Elizabeth entered the kitchen with a chorus of questions.

"What's for dinner?" Elizabeth asked.

"Where's Mom?" Jessica demanded.

Mr. Wakefield was standing by the counter, leafing through the phone book. "You're just the pair I need to see," he said. "Your mom just called to say she won't be home for dinner."

"Not again!" Jessica exclaimed.

"Where is she?" Elizabeth asked.

"She had to work late," her father replied. "So dinner is up to me. What do you say we send out for pizza and watch a little TV?"

"Sounds great to me," Steven announced from the refrigerator. He had poured himself a huge glass of milk and was balancing a plate piled high with cookies. "I'm starved."

"Steven!" Jessica snapped. "How can you think of eating at a time like this?"

He stared at her blankly. "What are you talking about? It's dinnertime. What else should I be thinking about?"

Jessica didn't answer but stormed past him into the hall.

"What's with her?" Steven asked.

Elizabeth shook her head and shrugged. Steven turned his attention back to Mr. Wakefield. "Hurry up and order, Dad. The basketball game is about to start."

"Orders, anyone?" Mr. Wakefield asked. "What would you like on the pizza?"

"Anything's fine with me, Dad," Elizabeth said quietly.

"Pepperoni. Or sausage," Steven declared as he walked into the family room to turn on the television. "Maybe both," he shouted back as an afterthought.

Elizabeth stepped into the hallway and leaned against the wall. Behind her she heard her dad's voice call out from the kitchen.

"Set your timers, everybody! They have exactly thirty minutes to get it to us piping hot, or else!"

He sounds awfully cheerful for a man whose wife has told him she's working late. Too cheerful as a matter of fact. Maybe even glad that Mom isn't with us, Elizabeth thought.

"Elizabeth." She looked up to see Jessica behind the banister, gesturing for her to come closer.

"What?"

"I think Mom is out with Mr. Howard."

"So what if she is?"

Jessica looked deeply into her sister's eyes. "I'm starting to get really worried."

"Jessica!" Elizabeth crossed her arms impatiently. "Mom told us all about Mr. Howard yesterday. He's just a rich client from Beverly Hills. That's all."

"Oh, yeah?" Jessica stuck out her lip stubbornly. "Mom left out one very important fact."

"What?"

"Mr. Howard is gorgeous!"

"How do you know?"

"I happened to be coming home this afternoon just as he stopped by to drop off some stuff for Mom." Jessica clutched her twin's arm. "Lizzie, he looks just like a movie star!"

"So?" Elizabeth blinked at her sister.

Jessica threw her hands in the air. "So why did she tell us Mr. Howard was just a normal-looking guy? Maybe she was trying to hide the fact that she was in love with him."

Elizabeth folded her arms in front of her and stared at her sister. "That's an awful thing to say!"

"Are you just going to stand there while some millionaire breaks up our parents' marriage and takes Mom off to his mansion?"

"No," Elizabeth said, marching past her sister on the stairs. "I'm going to talk to Mom tonight."

"*If* she comes home," Jessica called after her. "She could be at some restaurant with Mr. Howard right now, eating dinner by candlelight and planning how they're going to run off together."

"Jessica," Elizabeth cried out. "Those things only happen in the movies."

Her sister looked unconvinced.

"Besides," Elizabeth added, "you're forgetting Dad."

"What about him?"

"He'd never let something like that happen."

"That's just it, Elizabeth," Jessica said. "What if he doesn't know what's going on until it's too late? Mom will be gone, and his life will be ruined."

Elizabeth shook her head. "Jessica, I'm not going to listen to you anymore." With that she turned and headed for the den.

Just then, the pizza arrived. Mr. Wakefield

paid the delivery boy and carried the hot carton into the den.

"Clear the decks, gang," he declared. "The food's here."

"Just in time, Dad," Steven said. He grabbed a slice and pointed at the television. "The game's starting."

"Tell Jessica to come down and eat, would you, Elizabeth?" her father asked.

Elizabeth nodded and went into the hallway. "Pizza's here," she called up the stairs. "Want any?"

"I'm not hungry," Jessica yelled back. Elizabeth shrugged and went back into the den.

"She'll be down in a little while," she said, placing a piece of pizza on a plate and cutting it with a fork. "Dad?"

"Umm?"

"How did you and Mom—"

She was interrupted by an explosion of cheering from her brother and father.

"What an unbelievable shot!" Mr. Wakefield exclaimed.

"Way to go!" Steven crowed, waving his fists over his head.

Mr. Wakefield glanced at Elizabeth. "I'm sorry, honey. What did you say?"

"Well, I was just curious," she began again. "How did you and Mom meet?"

He tilted his head up to look at her. "What's this all about, anyway?"

She described the Living History project, and told him how she, Amy, and Pamela had come up with the Sweet Valley Sweethearts idea.

"Was it love at first sight?" she asked.

"Love at what, Elizabeth?" her father murmured absentmindedly. He had obviously not heard a word she'd said.

"At first sight," she repeated loudly. "Did you know Mom was the girl for you the moment you saw her?"

"Hmm . . . Well, I guess so."

There was suddenly a lot of cheering on the television again. "Looks like another championship year," Mr. Wakefield pronounced grandly.

"Number one!" Steven yelled hoarsely, "Number one!"

Elizabeth looked at her brother in disgust. The interview was getting nowhere. She was about to give up when she heard the front door slam and Mrs. Wakefield call out, "Hi, everybody. I'm home."

"Boy, am I glad to see you!" Elizabeth sang out happily, as she ran to meet her.

"Me, too!" Jessica chimed in from the top of the stairs.

"What a day." Mrs. Wakefield sighed loudly as she put her briefcase down on the floor by the front door. She collapsed onto the living room couch and sighed. "I am simply exhausted. And I'm not even done. Elizabeth, will you bring me a glass of water?"

"Sure, Mom." Elizabeth ran toward the kitchen.

"Did you eat yet?" Jessica said. "We sent out for pizza."

"Oh. Thanks, but I already ate. I grabbed a bite on the way home."

"Mom, I'm doing a Living History report for social studies class," Elizabeth said, after she handed the glass of water to her mother.

"That's interesting, dear," her mother replied, flipping through an envelope filled with papers.

"And she chose you and Dad for her subject," Jessica added pointedly.

"Mmm. That's nice."

"So can I interview you now?" Elizabeth finished. "It's kind of important."

Mrs. Wakefield didn't raise her head from her work. "I guess so. Sure."

Elizabeth took a deep breath and dove in. "Did you and Dad fall in love at first sight?"

"How did you meet?" Jessica asked. "Was it incredibly romantic?"

"Or a complete surprise, like a chance encounter in an airport?" Elizabeth added.

"One at a time," Mrs. Wakefield protested, holding up her hands. She sat up as if to answer, but then she said, "I'm sorry, Elizabeth, I am so tired, and it's a long story. Could you ask me again tomorrow?" She heaved herself up and headed for the stairs. "I'll be in better shape to tell you about it then. Good night, girls."

"Mom! Aren't you even going to say good night to Dad?" Jessica cried out after her.

"Oh, I almost forgot he was here," Mrs. Wakefield murmured. "Silly me." She stuck her head into the den and called, "Good night, you two. I'm going right up to bed."

Mr. Wakefield and Steven were still glued to the basketball game. Mr. Wakefield glanced up and blew his wife a kiss.

"Steven, did you do your homework?" Mrs. Wakefield asked. Steven nodded without looking up. "OK, then. See you tomorrow, everybody."

Jessica and Elizabeth watched her leave them with a growing sense of dread.

"Did you hear that? She almost forgot Dad was here," Jessica repeated.

"And she wasn't excited about telling us how they fell in love, either," Elizabeth whispered.

"That's because she's in love with somebody else," Jessica whispered back. "We've got to do something before it's too late!"

"But what?"

"Meet me in my room. I'll get Steven. It's time he knew what's been going on around here."

Elizabeth nodded and hurried up the stairs. Jessica squared her shoulders and marched into the den. "Steven," she announced. "Elizabeth and I have to talk to you, *now*!"

Steven looked up at her, an angry reply on his lips, but the intense look on her face stopped him. He seemed to know immediately that something serious was up. Without another word he followed Jessica out of the room.

"What's all the secrecy for?" Steven asked, once they had gathered in Jessica's room. "Are we planning another surprise party?"

"No!" Jessica hissed. "We're really concerned about Mom."

"What's wrong with Mom?" Steven asked.

Elizabeth took a deep breath and began. "Steven, we think Mom has been spending too much time with a man named Frank Howard."

"Is he the guy she was with yesterday?" Steven asked.

"What do you mean, 'yesterday'?" Jessica pounced on her brother's words.

"Well, I was downtown and I passed the Ritz Cafe and Mom was having lunch with some guy."

"Was he really, really handsome?" Jessica asked.

Steven shrugged. "I guess so."

"What did Mom say to you?" Elizabeth asked.

"Nothing. I waved to her but she was so busy talking, she didn't see me."

Jessica and Elizabeth looked at each other, eyes wide. Jessica's words were barely a whisper. "That proves it."

Elizabeth swallowed hard and nodded at her sister.

"What does it prove?" Steven looked from one twin to the other.

"Steven," Elizabeth said gently, "we think Mom has fallen in love with Mr. Howard."

"That super-handsome, rich man you saw her with yesterday," Jessica added.

"What? You two are nuts!" Steven said in disbelief.

Jessica shook her head. "We are not! We know all about *that* man. He lives in Beverly Hills in this fabulous mansion. It's got a huge pool, tennis courts, and lots and lots of bedrooms!"

"Whoa!" Steven held up one hand. "How do you know all this?"

"Mom showed us an article that was written about him in *Designer's Monthly*. It had a lot of pictures of his mansion," Elizabeth explained.

"Oh, Lizzie!" Jessica suddenly covered her mouth in horror. "Do you think Mom showed us those pictures for a reason?"

"What reason?" Steven was completely confused.

"Maybe she wanted us to see the mansion that we'd be living in."

"Wait a minute," Steven cut in. "She didn't show me the pictures."

Jessica paced around the room. "I wonder what it will be like living in a forty room mansion. I mean, it's practically a castle."

Elizabeth hopped up off the bed. "Jessica, stop talking like that. I don't want to leave Dad."

Jessica spun to face her twin. "Well, I don't either."

"Then don't even think about it."

"You're right. I'd probably hate it in Beverly Hills. I mean, they have so many stars and beautiful people, nobody would notice me."

Steven's voice cracked as he said, "I don't want Mom and Dad to split up. That'd really be awful!"

Elizabeth folded her arms in front of her and put on her most adult voice. "Then we had better take action."

Jessica nodded enthusiastically. "We need a foolproof plan."

Jessica sat on the edge of her bed and bit her lip thoughtfully. "I think we should devise a way to drive Mom and Mr. Howard apart."

"You mean, scare him off?" Steven asked.

"That's it!" Jessica jumped up off the bed. "We'll make Mr. Howard think we're the worst kids on earth."

"Great!" Steven slammed his fist in his hand. "We'll be loud and rude—"

"And insulting," Jessica added. "We'll wear ugly, dirty clothes. Mr. Howard won't know what hit him."

Elizabeth, who hated being mean, hesitated. "I don't know about this. That seems a little too extreme."

"Extreme?" Jessica protested. "We're trying to save our parents' marriage! Now we just have to find a way to see Mr. Howard."

"I say we go with Jessica's plan." Steven held his hand out and Jessica placed hers on top of it.

Elizabeth looked first at her brother and then at her sister and choked back a sob. She realized how much she loved them both and how awful it would be if the family ever split up.

She very solemnly placed her hand on top of theirs. "Count me in."

Five

On Saturday they had a chance to put their plan into action. Mrs. Wakefield had some designs she needed to deliver to Mr. Howard.

"I'll take them, Mom," Jessica said. "I can ride them over on my bike."

Before Mrs. Wakefield had a chance to say no, Jessica had grabbed the designs and raced upstairs to change her clothes and tell Elizabeth.

"This is it, Lizzie," Jessica called. "Operation Shock Mr. Howard."

Five minutes later she tiptoed into her sister's room. Elizabeth was shocked. "You look terrible!"

Jessica had put on an old striped blouse she had outgrown two years before. The sleeves were too short and she had deliberately buttoned it up wrong. She was wearing a pair of plaid shorts that clashed with the blouse.

Jessica smiled. "Thanks. So do you."

Elizabeth was wearing a faded orange sweatshirt with holes in the elbows. She also had on a purple-and-green patchwork skirt that she'd worn in a play at school.

They had both combed gel through their hair to make it look stringy.

"Do you think this stuff will ever wash out?" Elizabeth asked, patting her head with distaste.

"Of course it will," Jessica replied, feeling her own hair gingerly. "It's just styling gel. But it makes us look like we haven't washed our hair in three weeks."

They tiptoed down the stairs and, just as they were leaving, Jessica called, "We're on our way to Mr. Howard's, Mom."

"Do you have his address?" their mother called back. "It's on the right-hand corner of the plans."

"I see it," Elizabeth shouted. "'Bye."

"Hurry back," Mrs. Wakefield said. "I'm going to start lunch soon."

They pedaled fast to reach Mr. Howard's office building. As they turned the corner, Jessica yelled, "There he is. That's him!"

Elizabeth almost fell off her bike when she saw who Jessica was pointing at. "Wow," she whispered. "He really does look like a movie star."

Mr. Howard was standing in front of the building's glass doors, talking to another man. He was even more handsome than Elizabeth could have imagined—tall, tanned, with blue eyes that sparkled.

"Now's our chance," Jessica said, hopping off her bike and propping it up on its kickstand. "Let's go!" Grabbing the folder of designs out of her basket, Jessica dashed toward the man. Elizabeth climbed off her bike, gulped nervously, and hurried after her twin.

"Mr. Howard! Mr. Howard!" Jessica waved and ran straight up to him. He turned at the sound of his name, a pleasant smile on his face. The smile faded to a look of shock when he saw the strangely dressed duo in front of him.

"Hi, Mr. Howard. I'm Jessica Wakefield and this is my sister, Elizabeth."

"You're Alice Wakefield's daughters?" he asked, an uncertain look on his face.

"She asked us to bring these plans to your office," Jessica continued. "I'm glad we caught up with you."

"Thanks," Mr. Howard said, looking them up

and down curiously. "Looks like you two have been doing some yard work today, hmm?"

"Oh, no," Jessica answered. "This is how we always dress. Right, Elizabeth?" Elizabeth nodded.

"Always?" Mr. Howard was staring at their clothes in amazement.

"You see, Mom designs all of our outfits," Jessica explained. "Don't you think she has wonderful taste?" Jessica took a full spin for him.

Mr. Howard looked too shocked to reply.

"I bet she'd love to design a suit for you," Jessica said.

"Oh, that's all right," he replied hastily. "I've got tailors of my own."

"Are you sure?" Jessica persisted.

He nodded quickly.

"Oh, well. It's your loss." She grabbed Elizabeth by the hand and dragged her down the sidewalk. "See you around."

As soon as they were out of sight, the twins fell back against the side of the building, laughing like crazy.

"He must think Mom is the strangest designer who ever lived!" Elizabeth motioned to her twin to peek around the corner back at Mr. Howard.

He hadn't moved. He shook his head slowly, a dazed look on his face. Then he waved goodbye to his friend and went into the building.

As they got on their bikes and headed home, Elizabeth said, "I just hope we don't get into trouble."

"Don't worry," Jessica reassured her sister. "I bet we never see him again!"

An hour later, Jessica and Elizabeth had washed their hair and changed their clothes and were setting the table for lunch when the doorbell rang.

"I'll get it!" Jessica called to her mother in the kitchen. She waltzed to the front window and peeked out through the curtain. When she saw who it was, her knees almost buckled.

"It's Mr. Howard!" she whispered to her sister. "He's here!"

"What should we do?" Elizabeth asked. "I never thought he'd come to the house."

At that moment Steven appeared at the top of the stairs. Jessica, thinking fast, hissed, "Steven, it's *him*. Turn up the stereo and be obnoxious!"

"Sure thing!" Steven grinned and raced into the living room. Then the twins casually opened the front door.

"Well!" Mr. Howard's eyes widened at their

very different appearance. He quickly recovered and flashed them a dazzling smile. "Hello. I barely recognized you two. Is your mother in?"

Jessica cupped one hand over her ear. "You'll have to speak up. I can't hear you!"

Mr. Howard leaned forward and said, more loudly, "Maybe if you turned the music down, it would be a little easier to converse."

"Good idea." Jessica turned and screeched, "Ste-ven! Turn that down!"

The music stopped immediately and Elizabeth smiled at Mr. Howard. "That's our brother, Steven."

"He always plays his music that loud!" Jessica added.

Elizabeth was afraid they were pushing things a little too far so she said cheerfully, "Come on in, Mr. Howard. Mom's in the kitchen."

Mr. Howard relaxed a little at her politeness. "Why, thank you."

Then Steven danced into the room, wearing headphones and moving in jerks and fits.

"It's useless trying to talk to him," Jessica explained. "He hardly ever takes those off."

"Mom, Mr. Howard is here," Elizabeth called toward the kitchen.

"Frank?" Mrs. Wakefield sailed into the room, removing her apron. "What a nice surprise!" The twins watched closely as Mr. Howard and their mother shook hands.

"I initialed the changes you made on the plans," Mr. Howard said. "So I thought I'd just drop them by." He handed Mrs. Wakefield the thick manila envelope and smiled. "I'm very impressed with your work, Alice."

Mrs. Wakefield smiled back and a deep red blush colored her cheeks. "Why, thank you, Frank."

Jessica made a move to usher Mr. Howard back to the front door when Mrs. Wakefield said, "Why don't you join us for lunch? Unfortunately, my husband had to go to the office today, but I was just about to sit down with the kids."

Jessica held her breath, waiting for his answer. Her heart sank as he said, "I'd love to."

The twins exchanged worried looks behind his back.

"You kids go and wash your hands," Mrs. Wakefield instructed, "while I pour Mr. Howard a glass of iced tea."

"Sure, Mom." Jessica and Elizabeth raced to the upstairs bathroom.

Steven appeared in the doorway. "Now that we've got him here, what do we do?"

"It's time for Plan Two!"

"I don't remember a Plan Two," Elizabeth said

as she joined her sister at the bathroom sink. "When did we come up with that?"

"Just now, and it's perfect!" Jessica dried her hands on the towel. "We're going to kill him with kindness! And then we'll spice up his food."

Jessica ran down to the kitchen, followed by Elizabeth. "Mom, why don't you join Mr. Howard in the dining room. Elizabeth and I can handle everything."

When their mother was out of the kitchen, Jessica whispered to Elizabeth, "Wait till he gets a taste of my special salad dressing."

"What?"

Jessica threw open the refrigerator door and began tossing different-size jars and spices onto the counter. "Lizzie, you prepare individual salad plates while I whip up my special spicy dressing."

"Right!" Elizabeth dished large portions of chef salad onto five plates. Then she poured Italian dressing on four of them.

"If this doesn't get him," Jessica giggled as she ladled her special dressing onto Mr. Howard's salad, "I don't know what will."

"What's in it?" Elizabeth asked, setting the plates on a bright yellow tray.

"Molasses, garlic, catsup, soy sauce, and my secret ingredient—hot chili peppers!"

Before Elizabeth could say another word, Jessica swung open the door to the dining room and announced, "Ladies and gentlemen, lunch is served."

Once everyone had their plates, Mrs. Wakefield raised her glass of iced tea. "I would just like to say welcome to our guest. *Bon appétit.*"

Jessica raised her eyebrows at Elizabeth. They both knew that Mrs. Wakefield only used French when she was trying to impress people.

The twins each picked up their salad forks and paused to watch Mr. Howard take his first bite of Jessica's special concoction.

He chewed carefully for a second. Then his eyes widened and he started coughing.

"Frank, are you OK?" Mrs. Wakefield asked, scooting her chair back.

"Water!" he wailed. He was barely able to choke out the word.

"I'll get it!" Jessica leaped to her feet and raced into the kitchen, happy for an excuse to hide her laughter.

Elizabeth bit her lip and stared hard at her plate, trying not to laugh. Steven, knowing his sisters must have done something to Mr. Howard's salad, was smiling.

Jessica returned with a tall glass of water which she handed to Mr. Howard. Tears were streaming down his cheeks. "Thank you," he said gratefully. "I think the salad dressing went down the wrong way."

"That dressing is Mom's specialty," Jessica said, with a twinkle in her eye. "We have it practically every day. Isn't it good?"

Mr. Howard took a long sip of water and then nodded. "It certainly is different. So, uh . . . spicy and different."

"Spicy?" Mrs. Wakefield looked at Jessica in confusion.

Before Mr. Howard could say another word, Jessica reached for his plate. "I'm glad you like it, Mr. Howard. I'll bring you some more."

"No!" Mr. Howard nearly knocked over his chair trying to stand up. "No, thank you. I'm really pretty full. I had a big breakfast."

"Oh." Jessica set the salad back in front of him. "Well, I hope you have room for Mom's special casserole. It really goes well with the salad."

Mrs. Wakefield blushed. "Jessica, you certainly are full of compliments today."

Jessica smiled her sweetest smile at her mother. "I just want Mr. Howard to know what a good cook you are."

"I-I'm sure she is," Mr. Howard said, placing his napkin on the table. "Unfortunately, I'm afraid I can't stay for the rest of this, uh, delicious lunch.

Please forgive me, but I just remembered a special meeting that was scheduled for this afternoon."

Mrs. Wakefield looked completely bewildered. "I'm sorry you have to leave so soon, Frank. Maybe we can have lunch another time."

Mr. Howard nodded vigorously. "Let's plan on it."

Mrs. Wakefield started to stand up, but he stopped her. "No, Alice, please don't get up. I know my way out."

"We'll walk you to the door," Jessica announced. She grabbed her sister's hand. "Come on, Elizabeth."

"I hope you do come back, Mr. Howard," Jessica said. "Mom is famous for her unusual dishes."

Mr. Howard tried to smile. "I'll bet she is."

Jessica's voice squeaked as she said, "It's too bad you didn't get a chance to meet the rest of our brothers and sisters."

"The rest?" Mr. Howard looked very confused. "I thought there was only three of you."

"Living in Sweet Valley," Jessica explained quickly. "But we've got lots of half-sisters and -brothers around California. They're from Mom's first two marriages." Jessica lowered her voice and added, "We're hoping this one will last."

"Well, I think your mother is a wonderful designer and a fine woman," Mr. Howard said, stepping out the front door. "She really seems to have come a long way."

He backed away slowly, almost tripping over the stone planter at the end of the walk. As he was getting into his car Jessica called out, "Be sure and come back soon. We'll have Mom make her special tuna casserole. It's really unusual."

The last the twins saw of Mr. Howard was his startled face disappearing into the car. The sight made them burst out laughing. "Jess, you're terrible!" Elizabeth managed to say.

"I know," Jessica whispered between giggles. "But remember, it's for the family."

As they watched him speed off down the road, Elizabeth wondered out loud, "Do you think that'll stop him from liking Mom?"

Jessica's tears of laughter suddenly stopped. "Oh, Lizzie, I hope so," she said softly. "I really do!"

Six

◇

Elizabeth met Amy at the park on Monday afternoon. The two of them walked over to Pamela's house where they were supposed to do more work on their Living History project. Lately, though, Elizabeth hadn't been able to concentrate on anything. Her stomach was always in a knot from worrying about her parents. Neither of them had ever gotten around to telling her how they first met. And that made her worry even more.

"Elizabeth," Amy asked, after they had walked an entire block in silence. "Is something wrong?"

"No!" Elizabeth replied, a little too quickly. "Why?"

"Well, for the last few days you've been so

quiet. I thought you might be sick or something."

Elizabeth shook her head miserably. "I'm not sick."

"Well, are you mad at me?" Amy stared down at her feet.

"Of course not, Amy!" Elizabeth couldn't hold her secret in any longer. Before she knew it, the entire story had tumbled out of her mouth, starting with the forgotten anniversary and ending with the lunch with Mr. Howard.

"I'm really afraid my parents are going to break up." Elizabeth fought hard to hold back her tears.

Amy patted Elizabeth's shoulder. "You know, a lot of parents get busy with their work, but that doesn't mean they don't love each other. Are you sure you're not imagining things?"

"But it's not just me," Elizabeth protested. "Jessica feels the same way."

"Well, you know what a wild imagination Jessica has. She always exaggerates."

That was true. With Jessica things were either really awful or really wonderful. There was never any in-between.

Elizabeth tucked a strand of hair behind one ear. "I guess you're right. It's just that my parents have been apart so much lately—"

"But you said your father was all tied up, working on that important case."

"I know—"

"And your mother has a big new account."

Elizabeth nodded. "With a *really* handsome, *really* rich man."

"So?" Amy shrugged. "I think your father is really handsome."

Elizabeth smiled gratefully at her friend.

"Look," Amy said, "my parents are always working late. They end up leaving messages for each other on the refrigerator door."

Elizabeth couldn't help laughing at that. "Really?"

Amy put her hand on her chest. "Cross my heart."

Elizabeth suddenly felt relieved. She was lucky to have such a good friend. As they strolled along, she thought, *Amy's right. Lots of families get busy and don't fall apart. Why should mine?*

At the Jacobsons' house, Amy reached up to ring the doorbell, but before her finger touched the buzzer, the door flew open. Pamela stood just inside, a big grin on her face.

"Hi! Come on in! I've got a surprise for you."

Mrs. Jacobson was standing in the living room behind Pamela. "Hello, girls," she said, "I'm taking everyone to Casey's Place for a Sooper-Dooper Banana Scooper."

Elizabeth pointed to her notebook. "But what about the project?"

"I've finished my interview with my parents and so has Amy," Pamela said. "I've completed my report on romantic couples in literature, like Romeo and Juliet. And Amy collected love sonnets by Shakespeare."

Elizabeth stared down at the notebook she was holding. She had made a list of a few romantic couples in history, but she hadn't even begun her library research. Elizabeth's cheeks burned. She was holding up the entire project.

Amy noticed her blush and said quickly, "We've still got a whole week till the report is due. That's lots of time. We should take an ice cream break."

Elizabeth smiled shyly at Mrs. Jacobson. "Well, OK. Let's go! It's too hard to turn down a Casey's Special."

At Casey's Place, the most popular ice cream parlor in Sweet Valley, Mrs. Jacobson ordered four banana splits at the counter.

"Let's sit over here!" Pamela skipped over to the round table by the window. Elizabeth smiled. She knew why Pamela wanted to sit by the window. A lot of the kids from Sweet Valley Middle

School came to the mall and this was the perfect place to watch them go by.

"Oh, look, there's Bruce Patman." Pamela pointed to the dark-haired boy leaning against one of the pillars by the escalators. Bruce was one of the cutest, and most conceited, boys in the seventh grade.

"And Jerry McAllister and Charlie Cashman are with him," Elizabeth said, dipping her spoon into her banana split.

"So what else is new?" Amy cracked. "Those boys stick together like glue." All three girls giggled as they dug into their ice cream.

Suddenly, her mouth full, Amy said, "Hey, Elizabeth! Isn't that your mom?"

Amy pointed toward a woman looking at the display window of Brass and Glass, a fancy furniture store at the mall. Her mother's back was turned but Elizabeth recognized her immediately. She also recognized the man standing next to her.

"Oh, no," Elizabeth cried. Their plan to scare Mr. Howard away had obviously not worked at all. Her mother was still seeing him and she looked happier than ever.

"Is anything wrong, Elizabeth?" Mrs. Jacobson asked.

"No!" Elizabeth fumbled for her napkin and

pretended to wipe her lap. "I spilled some ice cream on myself. That's all."

As Elizabeth dabbed at her skirt, she raised her eyes to meet Amy's. Amy mouthed the words, "Is that him?"

Elizabeth nodded.

"Are those your parents?" Mrs. Jacobson asked, as Mr. Howard and Mrs. Wakefield stepped into the store.

"That's my mother and a client of hers." Elizabeth tried to sound as calm as possible. "My mom's a decorator. She often takes her clients shopping."

"That's strange," Mrs. Jacobson said, staring at the store across from them.

"What is?" Pamela asked, following her mother's gaze.

"This may sound silly, but I think someone is following them." Mrs. Jacobson pointed with her spoon toward a pillar. "Look."

A figure in a long trench coat and large felt hat peeked out from behind the marble pillar, then scurried in little steps to the door of Brass and Glass. From the pocket of the tan coat, the person took out a newspaper and pretended to read.

Elizabeth nearly choked on her banana split. She recognized the coat and hat as her mother's, but the tennis shoes definitely belonged to her sister!

"Jessica!"

"Where?" Pamela looked back to where Bruce and the boys were still gathered. "Is she here, too?"

Elizabeth was relieved to find no one had recognized her sister as the person in the trench coat.

"Wh-what I mean is," Elizabeth stammered, "Jessica and I were supposed to meet here. I almost forgot. She's probably waiting for me in front of Sweet Valley Fashions right now."

Elizabeth sprang to her feet and thanked Mrs. Jacobson for the ice cream. "I'll talk to you guys later," she said to Pamela and Amy.

"Call me tonight!" Amy called out after her.

Elizabeth nodded and raced out of the restaurant.

She had to figure out how to communicate with Jessica without letting Amy, Pamela, and Mrs. Jacobson see her. She marched straight to the door of the furniture store and pretended to wave at her mother. At the same time she whispered out of the corner of her mouth, "Count to thirty, then follow me." Then she added, "And Jessica, we're being watched, so act natural!"

As soon as they were safely out of view, Elizabeth put her hands on her hips and shook her head at her sister. "What do you think you're doing?"

"I'm following Mom." Jessica took off her hat and shook out her long blond hair. "We were at home having a snack when the phone rang. It was Mr. Howard calling to tell Mom to meet him at the mall. I thought I'd better follow them so I hopped on a bus and came down here."

"Well, did you find out anything?"

Jessica nodded sadly. "Oh, Lizzie, it doesn't look good. They've been shopping for china and silverware together."

Elizabeth took a deep breath to calm herself. "Remember, Mom is a decorator. She's always running off with clients to shop for furniture and stuff."

A familiar laugh interrupted their conversation. Both girls held their breath as their mother and Mr. Howard passed right by them. Jessica peeked out from their alcove to watch them.

"What are they doing now?" Elizabeth asked.

"They're going into Sweet Valley Jewelry Store," Jessica answered.

"What are they going in *there* for?"

Jessica's voice was barely a whisper. "Oh, Lizzie, they're looking at engagement rings!"

"Jess, no!" Elizabeth covered her mouth in horror.

Jessica nodded and her voice shook. "How many decorators do you know who choose their client's engagement rings?"

Seven

◇

Dear Elizabeth,

I've got a plan. Meet me in front
of Dad's office at 3:30. I'll be
waiting.

Love, Jess

Jessica read the note she had written and her eyes
started to fill with tears. Seeing their mother looking at rings with Mr. Howard had been very
upsetting. Once their mother had left, she and
Elizabeth had gone into Sweet Valley Jewelry
Store to see the ring for themselves. It was
beautiful—a huge diamond surrounded by tiny
sapphires. This just *had* to be a bad dream, and
Jessica was going to end it once and for all.

Jessica folded the note, tucked it into Elizabeth's locker, and turned to run to her next class. She was in such a hurry that she almost crashed into Janet Howell, one of the most popular girls in the eighth grade and president of the Unicorn Club.

"Hi, Jessica. Don't forget about the big meeting this afternoon."

"Meeting?" Jessica's mind was a blur.

"Of course," Janet said. "Today's the day we talk about the service award. You remember, don't you? The one that's to be awarded to the organization that does the most good in the community." She smiled knowingly. "I'm sure you'll have some great ideas."

"Is that today?" Jessica fell back against one of the lockers. Ever since Mr. Howard had come on the scene, she'd forgotten everything else.

"Of course it's today!" Janet exclaimed. "And *all* members should be there."

For a half-second Jessica debated whether to run back and remove the note from Elizabeth's locker, or to go ahead with her plan. Then the bell rang, and she knew she wouldn't have time to retrieve the note.

"I'm sorry, Janet," Jessica said. "But I can't be there today."

The older girl raised her eyebrows in disapproval, but before she could say anything else, Jessica broke away and ran down the hall. "'Bye, Janet," she called over her shoulder.

For a moment Jessica felt awful. Janet Howell would think she didn't care about being a Unicorn. But that didn't really matter now.

I've got more important things to worry about, she thought. *Like saving Mom and Dad's marriage.*

"So what's your plan?" Elizabeth asked, as she joined Jessica on the sidewalk. They were standing in front of the plate glass doors leading into the offices of Mr. Wakefield's law firm.

"Elizabeth," her twin declared, "it's time to tell Dad what's going on between Mom and Mr. Howard."

"Do you really think that's a good idea, Jess? Isn't there anything else we can do?"

"Like what?" Jessica shot back. "We can't stand by and just let Mr. Howard take Mom away from us."

"But what will Dad do?"

"I don't know." Jessica pursed her lips in thought. "I hope he doesn't try to shoot Mr. Howard or anything."

"Daddy would never hurt anybody," Elizabeth said quickly.

"Well, he *is* a lawyer. Maybe he'll just sue Mr. Howard for millions and millions of dollars." A small smile crept across Jessica's face. "You know, that wouldn't be such a bad idea."

"How are we going to tell him?" Elizabeth asked.

"Elizabeth," Jessica said sternly. "We can't be cowards about this. We have to stick together and tell Dad so he can bring Mom to her senses. Then things can be just the way they used to be."

Elizabeth wiped her nose with a tissue and nodded. "You're right. Let's go."

Within minutes they were ushered into their father's office by his secretary. He looked up from his desk in surprise. "Well, to what do I owe this delightful interruption?"

Jessica opened her mouth to speak, then shut it. Her father sat in front of them, grinning widely. He seemed so pleased to see them, she didn't have the heart to tell him her bad news.

"How's your big case going, Dad?" she finally blurted out.

"I'm very glad you asked." He folded his hands in front of him. "It should be all wrapped up by tomorrow and . . ." He paused dramatically. "It looks like we're going to win!"

"Oh, Dad, that's great!" Elizabeth rushed forward and wrapped her arms around his neck. She fought hard to hold back her tears. Just thinking about her mother leaving her wonderful father made her want to cry.

"That's terrific, Dad." Jessica ran to hug him, too.

"Hey, what's all this?" he asked, looking pleased at his daughters' attention.

"We just want you to know we love you and—" Elizabeth's eyes misted up again and she couldn't go on. "And we've missed you lately," Jessica finished for her. "An awful lot."

"Well, I've missed you, too," Mr. Wakefield replied. "Which is why I'm going to take us all out to a big dinner tomorrow night to celebrate."

Jessica and Elizabeth exchanged quick looks over their father's head. Being a twin was a big advantage at times like this because they each knew what the other was thinking.

"Dad, I've got an idea," Jessica said. "Why don't you take Mom out instead?"

Elizabeth nodded eagerly. "To a special restaurant."

"Then you could have a romantic dinner for two by candlelight," Jessica added. She was sure it was their only hope.

"Oh, and find one with a violin player that

comes to your table and serenades you," Elizabeth said dreamily.

Mr. Wakefield chuckled. "Listen to you two. You sound like a pair of matchmakers."

"Well, you forgot your own anniversary," Jessica reminded him, putting her hands on her hips. "I think you owe it to Mom to treat her to a special dinner."

"I do, too," Elizabeth said.

Mr. Wakefield looked from one daughter to the other. "Is this an order?" he asked.

"Yes!" they said in unison.

"OK, then." He put his arms behind his head and relaxed back in his chair. "You know, that's not a bad idea," he said thoughtfully. "There was this little Italian restaurant over on Seaview Drive that your mother and I used to go to a lot, before we were married. Haven't been back in years."

"Oh, Dad!" Jessica hugged him again. "You have to go there. You just *have* to!"

"OK, OK!" He held his hands up in front of him. "Listen, you two, I've still got work to do this afternoon. If I'm going to win this case, you'd better scoot."

"Yes, sir!" They saluted as they marched out the door.

* * *

That night, before she went to bed, Elizabeth tiptoed to Jessica's room and knocked softly on the door.

"Come in."

Jessica was already under the covers. The lamp on the nightstand glowed in the darkened room. "Jess, do you think the dinner will make everything OK between Mom and Dad?" Elizabeth whispered.

"I'm not sure, Lizzie. It's a good start, but just to be on the safe side . . ." Her voice trailed off.

"Jessica, you have that funny look in your eyes."

"What look?" Jessica blinked innocently.

"The one you get when you're planning to do something that will get us into lots of trouble."

"Elizabeth!" Jessica looked offended. "I am not going to get anyone in trouble."

"Promise?"

Jessica drew her face into a pout. "I can't believe you don't believe me."

"Promise?" Elizabeth insisted stubbornly.

Jessica looked at her sister for a moment, then flicked off her bedside lamp.

"Trust me." Jessica's voice came out of the darkness. "Good night, Elizabeth."

Eight

◆

After school on Friday, Jessica hopped on her bike and pedaled straight downtown to Mr. Howard's office. *I'm going to go right up to Mr. Howard and tell him to leave Mom alone.*

She hadn't told Elizabeth about her plan because she knew her sister would have tried to talk her out of it.

"I'll tell him that our family was perfectly fine until he came to Sweet Valley," she said out loud as she rode along. "I'll tell him that Mom and Dad love each other, and if Mom leaves, we'll be orphans. Then I'll politely ask him to go back to Beverly Hills—*alone.*"

Jessica swallowed hard. The gleaming steel-

and-glass exterior of Mr. Howard's new office building loomed in front of her. She locked her bike in the stand at the entrance and marched to the elevators, where she headed directly for the penthouse floor.

The elevator stopped and opened to show a large reception area. A pleasant-looking woman with white hair and glasses greeted her. "May I help you?"

"I'm Jessica Wakefield," Jessica announced, "and I would like to talk to Mr. Frank Howard, please."

"Oh, Alice Wakefield's daughter?" the receptionist asked. Jessica nodded and the woman smiled. "Have a seat, Jessica. I'll tell Mr. Howard you're here." The woman gestured toward a gray leather couch set against the wall.

Looking around, Jessica realized that her mother had done a wonderful job decorating the office. The thick carpet was a deep shade of maroon. Chrome-and-glass tables holding beautiful lamps were placed at both ends of the couch. The wall hangings made the whole room look rich and elegant.

Just as she was starting to change her mind about being there, Mr. Howard stepped out from his office. "Why, Jessica, what a nice surprise!" He flashed a dazzling smile and once again Jessica noticed how handsome he was.

"Hello, Mr. Howard," Jessica said in her most businesslike voice. She didn't want him to charm her out of her speech. "I was wondering if I could talk to you."

"Certainly." He gestured for her to follow him but the secretary interrupted. "Excuse me, Mr. Howard, but there's a call for you on line one."

"Pardon me, Jessica," he said, moving back to his office. "I'll only be a minute."

She watched him pick up the phone on his desk and then, with one hand, give the door a push. The heavy oak door didn't close all the way.

Jessica had no intention of eavesdropping but his words carried clearly to the reception area. They made her stomach fill with butterflies.

"Darling, how are you?" Mr. Howard said. "I've missed you."

Jessica pursed her lips. *This is worse than I thought. They just saw each other Monday night and they already miss each other.*

"I've got the ring, dear," he went on. "I can't wait until Saturday night. Then we'll be together, once and for all."

"Saturday night!" Jessica sprang up and ran for the elevator. "That's tomorrow!"

"Wait a minute, Jessica," the secretary called after her. "Don't you want to talk to Mr. Howard?"

"It's too late to talk," Jessica said as she flew into the elevator.

Nine

◆

Elizabeth stared down at the blank page in her notebook. It was the final meeting of her Living History group, and once again she wasn't prepared. The three girls were just settling down in the den of the Suttons' house.

"I'll go get us some sodas," Amy announced, jumping up and disappearing into the kitchen.

Pamela got up to call her mother and Elizabeth ran into the kitchen to talk to Amy.

"Amy," Elizabeth whispered. "I don't have my interview."

"Weren't you able to talk to your parents?"

Elizabeth shook her head miserably. "Too many things are going on at home." She looked her best friend in the eye. "I think I'm going to have to drop out of this project."

"Elizabeth, you can't!"

"It's not fair to you and Pamela. If I don't get this done, Mrs. Arnette will give all of us a bad grade."

"Don't worry, Elizabeth. You still have the whole weekend to do it."

"But, Amy, I don't know when I'll be able to talk to my parents." She picked up a glass of soda and followed her friend back into the den.

When they were all seated again, Elizabeth closed her notebook and said, "I'm going to quit. It's better this way, you'll see."

"You can't quit!" Pamela exclaimed. "No matter what's going on with your family, we're all in this together."

Elizabeth looked over at Amy in surprise. "Pamela knows, Elizabeth," Amy explained. "I had to tell her."

Before Elizabeth could respond the doorbell rang and within seconds Jessica burst into the room. She looked as if she had seen a ghost.

She hurriedly recounted the conversation she'd overheard at Mr. Howard's office. Then she sobbed, "Oh, Lizzie, I never believed Mom would go away so soon."

"We've got to stop her!" Elizabeth said with determination.

"We'll help!" Amy and Pamela chimed in.

For the next ten minutes no one said a word. Jessica paced anxiously in the corner. Amy chewed thoughtfully on a piece of apple. Elizabeth concentrated all her energy on thinking up a plan to stop Mr. Howard.

"I've got an idea," Jessica suddenly announced. "It's a long shot, but it just might work!"

"What is it?" Elizabeth demanded, as all three girls leaped to their feet.

"First we need to get Steven out of basketball practice," Jessica said. "Then I'll tell you everything."

The girls hopped off the bus in front of Sweet Valley High, and Jessica led her sister, Pamela, and Amy up the sidewalk to the entrance of the high school gymnasium.

"Good," Jessica said. "The team's still practicing."

They stepped through the doors and were met with the noisy sound of basketballs pounding against the wooden floor, mingled with shouts and the squeak of sneakers. Steven, who played on the junior varsity team, was one of the players on the court.

"I hope we can get him away to talk," Elizabeth said to Amy, a worried frown on her face. "We don't have much time."

Just then the coach blew his whistle and all the boys jogged toward the sidelines.

"Good workout, guys," the coach said. "Hit the showers." As they obediently filed by, he tossed a fresh towel at each one. "See you tomorrow."

Steven was just about to disappear into the locker room when Jessica caught his attention.

"Steven Wakefield!" she called out loudly. "Get over here!"

Steven turned around and jogged toward them, a huge grin on his face. "So you came to see the star in action, did you?"

Elizabeth could tell that Jessica was going to snap back at him and quickly said, "Steven, we need your help. It's really important."

He looked closely from one twin to the other, then nodded. "What is it?"

"Mom is going to elope with Mr. Howard tomorrow night," Jessica exclaimed.

"What!" Steven looked aghast at the news.

"That's right," Elizabeth chimed in. "Jessica

heard him planning it with her on the phone at his office."

"It's true, Steven," Jessica said solemnly. "We have to do something fast to stop them."

"But what can we do?" he sputtered.

Jessica crossed her arms. "We're going to convince Mr. Howard, once and for all, that getting involved with our mother would be the worst disaster in the world."

"How are we going to do that?"

"Mr. Howard is coming to our house for dinner tonight—that is, after I invite him."

"But Mom and Dad are going out."

"That's right!" Jessica's eyes gleamed. "After they leave, Mr. Howard will arrive and meet the *real* Wakefield children—all *ten* of them."

"Ten?" Steven cocked his head in confusion.

"That's right. From all of Mom's marriages."

"Oh." Steven chuckled. "I get it."

Jessica smiled with satisfaction. "He'll wish he'd never heard of any of the Wakefields after tonight."

"We're going to need lots of people to help," Elizabeth said hurriedly.

Steven turned and raced for the locker room. "Meet me outside in five minutes," he shouted over his shoulder.

The four girls hurried outside the gym and anxiously paced back and forth in front of the exit. True to his word, Steven emerged from the locker room minutes later. Behind him trooped six lanky members of the basketball team.

"Will these volunteers do?" he asked, a huge grin on his face.

"Oh, Steven, they're perfect!" Elizabeth said, grinning widely.

"Come on, everyone," Jessica ordered happily, clapping her hands. "Follow me. I'll explain what you have to do on the way home."

"Jessica!" Elizabeth grabbed her sister by the sleeve and pulled her to a stop. "We haven't called and invited Mr. Howard yet. What if he's made other plans?"

"Oh, that's right." Jessica slapped her forehead. "We'd better find a phone."

"There's one by the grocery two blocks from school," one of the basketball players said.

They ran down the street. Jessica stepped into the phone booth and pulled the door shut. Elizabeth watched anxiously as her sister dialed the number. After a brief conversation, Jessica hung up the phone, stepped out of the booth, and smiled slyly. "I talked to his secretary. She actually believed I was Mom. Mr. Howard is coming over at seven-fifteen."

"Seven-fifteen?" Elizabeth repeated. "But Mom and Dad aren't leaving for dinner until seven o'clock. What if they're late and they run into Mr. Howard?"

"We'll just have to make sure they leave on time, that's all."

"What's the plan, Jessica?" Steven asked impatiently.

"OK, everybody, listen carefully." Jessica raised her voice a little so the whole group could hear. "I want you all to go home and put on the oldest, dirtiest clothes you have. Then I want you to come over to our house at exactly five after seven."

"What'll we do when we get there?" the tallest basketball player asked.

Jessica smiled and answered sweetly. "You'll see."

Ten

◇

At two minutes to seven, Mrs. Wakefield was still upstairs, putting on her earrings. Mr. Wakefield stood waiting for her in front of the television, catching the end of the sports report.

"Mom!" Jessica called up the stairs. She was almost frantic. "You're going to be late!"

"Don't worry, Jessica," her father called. "This restaurant is pretty casual. They'll hold a table for us."

"When was the last time you were there?" Jessica demanded.

Mr. Wakefield scratched his head. "Gosh, I don't know. Years ago?"

"Well, things could have changed," Jessica practically shrieked. Her father looked up in surprise.

"She's right, Dad," Steven joined in. "If De-Salvio's takes reservations, they probably want you to stick to them. In fact, I hear it's become one of the hot spots in town."

"Really? Maybe you're right." Mr. Wakefield turned off the television set. "I'd better hurry your mother along."

"She's on her way," Elizabeth announced from upstairs. She was guiding her mother down the hall toward the stairs.

"Wait a minute, Elizabeth," her mother protested, trying to turn around. "I don't have my purse."

Elizabeth waved her bag in the air. "It's right here. Your lipstick and brush are inside."

"Boy, the way you kids are scurrying around tonight," Mrs. Wakefield said with a smile, "you'd think you were trying to get rid of us." She tucked the bag under her arm.

"That's because we've got a wild party planned right after you leave," Steven joked.

Jessica shot him an angry look. "That's not funny, Steven," she snapped.

"He's just kidding, Jess," Elizabeth said hurriedly. "We all want you both to have a terrific time."

"Mom, you look beautiful!" Jessica called from the foot of the stairs. "Doesn't she, Daddy?"

Mr. Wakefield smiled approvingly at his wife.

"She certainly does. Just like the girl I first dated."

Mrs. Wakefield giggled as she came down the steps. "Oh, Ned, don't be silly."

When Mrs. Wakefield reached the bottom of the stairs, Mr. Wakefield kissed her lightly on the cheek. Jessica grabbed her sister's hand and squeezed it with all her strength. "It's working," she whispered.

Elizabeth nodded excitedly.

Steven checked his watch and announced loudly, "It's seven o'clock!"

"You don't want to miss your reservations!" Jessica grabbed her parents' elbows and ushered them out the door. Steven raced down the sidewalk to the car. "Curfew is midnight!" he cracked, holding the door for his mother.

"'Bye! Have a wonderful time," Elizabeth called out. She and Jessica waved gaily as Mr. and Mrs. Wakefield drove off.

As soon as the car rounded the corner, Jessica declared, "Time to get to work."

Elizabeth looked up and down the empty street. There wasn't a sign of the volunteers. "Where is everyone?" she wondered out loud. "Do you think they deserted us?"

There was a violent stirring in the bushes beside the house. The twins turned to see the most outlandish spectacle emerge from behind them.

Amy Sutton led the pack, dressed in a tattered pair of overalls. Mud was streaked over her face and she had arranged her hair into a messy pile on her head.

Pamela Jacobson was right behind her, followed by the boys from Steven's team. They had all gotten into the spirit, wearing baggy, worn jeans and T-shirts smeared with axle grease. No one looked as if he or she had taken a shower in weeks.

Jessica quickly set the group to work. "We've got to pull all the nice furniture from the living room out on the back porch. We can throw a dirty cover over the couch."

"Then we'll bring up the old tattered stuff from the basement," Elizabeth said. "The house will look like a tornado hit it."

They set to work and within minutes the house was a wreck. Elizabeth and Jessica took a second to make sure their own outfits were suitably awful. They had on Steven's old workout clothes which were way too big. Jessica looked her sister over critically, then reached out and enlarged the small hole in her sweatshirt.

"Jessica! What are you doing?"

"Come on, Elizabeth," Jessica chided. "This is no time to get prissy."

Just then the doorbell rang.

"It's him!" Steven whispered from the hall.

"OK, everybody hide!" As the gang ducked out of sight, Elizabeth and Jessica walked to the front door and threw it open.

Mr. Howard was standing on the step, elegantly dressed in a crisp pinstripe suit, a small rose tucked in his lapel. He took a look at the twins and almost lost his balance.

"Why, Mr. Howard," Jessica said, "what a surprise!"

"Please come in." Elizabeth took him by the elbow and ushered him into the hall.

"Surprise?" The man looked confused. "I thought your mother called my secretary and invited me to dinner tonight."

"Oh, you mustn't fall for everything Mom does, you know," Jessica said lightly. "Sometimes, she gets . . . well, a little confused."

"She does?" Mr. Howard looked nervously back toward the front door. Steven shut it firmly behind them.

"Oh, yes," Jessica rattled on. "Sometimes she'll call us down to dinner, when there isn't even any food ready."

"I don't understand."

"Oh, yes," Elizabeth chimed in. She lowered her voice and added, "We're a little worried about

Mother. Lately she's taken to talking to herself again."

"Again?" Mr. Howard blinked his eyes. "Why would she do that?"

The twins looked at him solemnly and mimed someone drinking from a bottle. Jessica added a little hiccup for extra effect.

Elizabeth led him into the ramshackle living room. "Just make yourself comfortable."

Mr. Howard's eyes widened as he surveyed the soiled chair Elizabeth pointed him toward. He positioned himself gingerly on the edge and tried to look comfortable.

"But where's your father?" he asked.

Just then a huge crash came from the hall. The entire gang of basketball players burst into the room, dragging Amy by the arms and legs.

"Wh-what are you doing to that child?" Mr. Howard demanded, leaping to his feet. The two tallest guys looked down at him dumbly, then dropped Amy onto the carpet.

"Nuthin'!" one of them said. "We was jus' horsin' around, like usual."

"Yeah," the other boy said. "We're playin' our favorite game."

"Drop The Sister," another one explained. He made a move to grab Jessica.

"Sister!" Mr. Howard said. "Now, wait a minute. Are all of these children your brothers and sisters?"

"As far as we know," Steven replied. "Of course, it's hard to tell."

"Let's climb up on the roof," one of the boys said as he grabbed Amy again, "and play up there."

"Just a minute!" Mr. Howard ordered. "Hold it right there. You put her down this instant." The boy did as he was told. Then Mr. Howard looked over at Amy and said, "Are you all right?"

She nodded, then grinned at him. It looked as if her front teeth were missing. Elizabeth noticed the shocked look on Mr. Howard's face and tried not to giggle. Steven, however, could not hold back anymore. He burst out laughing and Jessica tried to nudge him back to silence. But the damage was done. The rest of the team began to chuckle, and soon Elizabeth, Amy, and Pamela were laughing, too.

Mr. Howard watched without a word. Finally, when everyone had calmed down a little, he said, "I see what's going on. This is some kind of practical joke." He turned around and glared at Jessica and Elizabeth. "And I am not amused."

Elizabeth watched Mr. Howard march to the front door and she suddenly felt a little ashamed.

"Maybe we've gone too far," she whispered to Jessica.

Her sister shook her head vehemently. "This is exactly what we wanted," she hissed. "Now he'll go back to Los Angeles and leave Mom alone."

Mr. Howard swung open the front door and stopped in his tracks. Elizabeth looked up and nearly fainted with shock. There, framed in the doorway, were Mr. and Mrs. Wakefield.

"Frank? What are you doing here?" Mrs. Wakefield exclaimed.

"*What* has happened to this house?" Mr. Wakefield demanded, gaping at the wreck of a living room. "And who are all of these people?"

"I'm completely confused," Mr. Howard said. "First I receive a call telling me I'm invited to dinner. I cancel a previous engagement to come here. Then, when I arrive, I find out it's all some kind of silly prank."

The room, which had been packed with people, suddenly emptied as Steven's basketball team, Amy, and Pamela hurried out the back door. The Wakefield children were left standing in the middle of the living room, alone.

"I'm sure there must be a good explanation for all of this," Mrs. Wakefield stammered to Mr. Howard.

"There had better be." Mr. Wakefield narrowed his eyes at his children. "I want to hear some talking. And I want to hear it now!"

"Excuse me," a soft voice interrupted. "Is this the Wakefield home?"

Everyone spun around to see a beautiful, dark-haired woman standing in the doorway. She smiled shyly. "I'm looking for Mr. Frank Howard. His secretary told me I might find him here."

"Karen? Is—is that you?" Mr. Howard asked as the beautiful woman peered into the room over Mr. and Mrs. Wakefield's shoulders. "I wasn't expecting you until tomorrow."

Jessica and Elizabeth stared at each other in horror. Mr. Howard was supposed to meet her tomorrow?

Mr. Howard quickly introduced Karen Barclay to the Wakefields as his fiancée.

Out of the corner of her mouth Jessica whispered, "I guess I made a mistake."

Elizabeth slowly turned to face her sister. "You *guess*?"

Steven muttered behind them, "Boy, are we in trouble now!"

Eleven

◇

For the next half hour, the Wakefield children tried to explain their antics to their parents and Mr. Howard. Jessica had to do most of the talking.

She could feel her cheeks getting redder by the minute. Only hours before, there had been no question in her mind that a terrible crisis had hit the family. With each word, however, the whole thing sounded more and more ridiculous.

Mr. Howard and his fiancée Karen sat side by side on the old sofa, holding hands. With each description of how Jessica had discovered a new "clue," his face relaxed more and more. Soon he was grinning. When she told how she had followed them to the jewelry store, Mr. Howard threw back his head and laughed uproariously. Even Mr. and Mrs. Wakefield were smiling.

Finally Jessica shrugged and stared down at her hands. "So, you see, we thought Mr. Howard and Mom were going to elope, tomorrow night."

"And we had to stop it," Steven added. "For your sake, Dad," Elizabeth said. "And for the whole family."

"I can't say that I approve of your methods," Mr. Howard interrupted with a chuckle. "But I admire your determination. Not too many children would go to such lengths to keep their family together."

"Not too many children have the wild imagination our Jessica has," Mr. Wakefield commented, raising an eyebrow at his daughter.

"I don't think it's wild," Jessica protested. "What would you think if your parents forgot their anniversary?"

"We told you, honey," Mrs. Wakefield replied. "We've both been working very hard."

"But you didn't even give each other a present, or flowers, or go out to din—" Jessica stopped in midsentence. "Hey, what are you two doing home, anyway?" she demanded. "This was supposed to be your romantic night out."

Their parents glanced at each other, then Mrs. Wakefield said, "Well, your father and I got to the restaurant and suddenly realized we were missing something."

"What?" the twins and Steven asked.

Their mother smiled at them. "You."

"We wanted to celebrate our wedding anniversary," Mr. Wakefield explained, "but the best part of our marriage has been having you children."

"So we decided to come back and get you," Mrs. Wakefield added. "Of course, we didn't expect to find this." She gestured to the shambles of a living room.

Jessica winced at the reminder. "We'll clean it all up, I promise." Elizabeth and Steven nodded in agreement.

"I know you will," their father said with a smile. "Tonight your mom and I realize we haven't been spending enough time at home. Sometimes it takes a little crisis to remind us all of—"

"Ahem." Mr. Howard cleared his throat. "This sounds like private family talk. I think Karen and I should leave you alone now." The couple stood up to leave.

"No, no," Mrs. Wakefield said, motioning for them to sit back down. "Frank, this concerns you, too." She leaned against the arm of the wingback chair their father sat in. "You see, kids, Mr. Howard has made me a very generous offer. He wants me to redecorate his main offices in Los Angeles."

"Are you going to?" Elizabeth asked, holding her breath.

"I've decided to say no." She smiled at Mr. Howard. "You see, I started decorating as a part-time profession. Lately, it's been taking up more and more of my time." Mrs. Wakefield put her arms around her daughters. "Now I know it's going to have to stay part-time. Because, Frank, I think you'll agree that raising three children is definitely a full-time job."

Mr. Howard grinned and nodded. "I'm going to miss your artistic touch, but I understand."

"So it looks like we're just one big happy family again," Mr. Wakefield concluded. "And I'd just like to say one more thing."

"What's that?" Steven asked. The twins looked up expectantly.

"I'm starved." Mr. Wakefield clapped his hands together. "If we hurry, I'm sure we'll be able to find a table at DeSalvio's. Of course, you kids will have to get cleaned up a bit first." He turned to Mr. Howard and his fiancée. "We'd love it if you two would join us."

"Yes, please do," Elizabeth said happily. "It'll be our way of making it up to you."

"I promise not to add any of my special dressing to your salad," Jessica promised, holding up her hand solemnly.

"My eyes water just thinking about it," Mr. Howard joked.

The twins and Steven quickly ran upstairs to change their clothes and wash up. When they came back down, they all put on their coats and moved to the front door.

"I think you and Frank will like this little restaurant," Mrs. Wakefield said to Karen. "It's so romantic. Ned and I went there on our first date."

Elizabeth's ears perked up. "Your very first date?"

"Yes," Mrs. Wakefield replied. "I've been meaning to tell you."

Elizabeth could hardly contain her excitement. Finally she'd be able to finish her interview. "Let me get my notepad and pen."

"It's really pretty silly," Mr. Wakefield said, chuckling. "Let's get in the van and we'll tell you all about it on the way over."

"Why don't we take the limousine?" Mr. Howard cut in. "There's plenty of room."

"Could we drive by the Dairi Burger?" Jessica asked excitedly. She was sure some of the Unicorns would be there and this would really impress them.

Mr. Howard nodded and the children raced for the front door.

"A silver limo. This is all right!" Steven shouted as the sleek car pulled away and headed toward the heart of Sweet Valley.

When they got home that evening, Elizabeth could hardly wait to call Amy. She raced to the telephone in the hall, and quickly dialed Amy's number, then carried the phone with its long cord into her bedroom.

"Elizabeth!" Amy shrieked into the receiver the minute she picked up the phone. "I've been sitting here all night, waiting for you to call. Boy, your dad sure looked angry."

"Sorry," Elizabeth apologized, "but I never got a chance to call. After we explained the whole mess to everyone, my dad took us all out to dinner. But here's the *best* news! I found out how Mom and Dad first met."

"Oooh, great! Tell me everything."

"Well, it was seventeen years ago," Elizabeth began. "Dad was in law school and Mom had just finished college and was working as a waitress while she was looking for a job in the design field."

"Where?"

"At DeSalvio's, the restaurant we went to tonight. She only worked there a short time because she found a job decorating windows at Morgan's. But anyway, it was close to graduation and Dad and his three roommates had reserved a table to celebrate. Each one of them had a date."

"Was your mom your dad's date?"

"No, she was his waitress."

"What! Your dad was out with someone else?"

"Amy, if you'll just listen, I'll tell you how they met. You see, this was Mom's first night as a waitress. She was really nervous to have a table of eight to serve."

"Especially if one of them is a handsome man like your dad."

Elizabeth giggled. "That's exactly what Mom said. So, anyway, she put all of the food on one of those big silver trays and—"

"Oh, no!" Amy broke in. "Did she spill it?"

"Yes, all over Dad! Spaghetti, lasagna, and eggplant, with tons of tomato sauce."

"Oooh, how awful!"

"Mom said she was never so embarrassed in her life," Elizabeth continued. "She ran back into the kitchen and cried and cried."

"What did your dad do?" Amy asked. "Was he mad?"

"No, he said it was so awful that it was funny. There he was with his clothes all ruined, the entire table's dinner on the floor, and his date mad at him for laughing about it."

"And then what happened?"

"Chef DeSalvio had Dad go into the kitchen and put on a pair of white pants and a shirt while he cleaned his clothes."

"That's where he found your mom?"

"Yes, and Mom said he looked really cute in the chef's outfit. He sat down and the two of them started talking—"

"And he forgot all about his other date," Amy jumped in. "He only had eyes for your mom."

"Right. Then Chef DeSalvio came in and told Dad that the restaurant owed him a full dinner. Dad's date and his friends had left so he invited Mom to join him. The chef set up a little table with candles on it in the kitchen, and they fell in love while the chef's brother, Tony, serenaded them with his mandolin."

"How romantic!"

"Isn't it?" Elizabeth said dreamily. "After they told us that story, Jessica made them promise to go back to DeSalvio's every year on their anniversary."

"Do you think they'll do it?" Amy asked.

"Well, if I know Jessica, next year she'll have arranged for their anniversary dinner to be served in the kitchen with Tony serenading them. She'll probably even find a way to have Dad wear a chef's outfit."

Jessica, who was just about to knock on her sister's door, overheard Elizabeth's comment and smiled to herself. *What a great idea!*

She went back to her room and as she hopped into bed, she thought, *I'll get started on it right away. Next year's anniversary will be the best one ever!*

Twelve

◇

"Jessica! Over here, quick!" Elizabeth called across the noisy lunchroom.

"We did it!" Amy Sutton shouted out. "We got an—"

"Amy!" Elizabeth gave her friend a gentle shove. "I think I should be the one to tell my sister the good news."

"Good news?" Jessica slid into an empty seat. "What is it?"

"Our Living History project," Pamela Jacobson explained.

"Mrs. Arnette gave us an A on it," Elizabeth said happily.

"Lizzie, that's great!" Jessica gave her sister a hug. "You deserved it."

Elizabeth smiled. "I think that was the hardest report I've ever done."

"You know something?" Amy broke in. "I think that is the first A I've ever gotten from the Hairnet. This really calls for a celebration. Like an extra piece of peach cobbler." She looked hungrily at Pamela's plate. "Who's not going to eat hers?"

"No, you don't!" Pamela snatched up her plate to keep it away from Amy. But it was too late.

"Amy!" Pamela squealed. "Give it back."

"It's mine, all mine!" Amy chortled.

Elizabeth and Jessica laughed as Pamela struggled to get back the cobbler. Suddenly the cobbler flew off the plate. The girls watched the sticky dessert sail through the air and land in a gloppy mess at the feet of a girl walking by.

It was Billie Layton, one of the best athletes in the sixth grade and an ace pitcher on the neighborhood Little League team. Her real name was Belinda but everyone called her Billie.

"Watch what you're doing!" Billie snapped. "I could've stepped in that."

"Sorry, Billie," Amy giggled. "We were just joking around."

"Great!" Billie checked her sneakers to see if any of the sticky dessert had gotten on them. "Next time keep your jokes to yourself."

Amy looked stunned. "I said I was sorry."

Billie didn't say any more but turned and marched out of the lunchroom.

"What's the matter with her?" Jessica asked after Amy had wiped the dessert off the floor with a napkin and tossed it in the trash.

"I don't know," Pamela said. "She's usually so nice."

Amy shook her head. "Something must be wrong. I heard Billie caused a scene in baseball practice yesterday."

"What?" Elizabeth exclaimed. "She's always so easygoing."

"She struck out," Amy continued. "She got so mad, she threw her bat over the fence."

"Who told you?" Pamela asked.

"Jim Sturbridge," Amy replied. "He's the catcher. Jim told me that the coach made her go straight home."

"She's sure acting weird," Elizabeth whispered. "She didn't even look like herself just now."

"Well, if I was the only girl on a team full of boys," Jessica said, "I guess I'd act funny, too."

"Maybe she's doing badly in school," Amy suggested.

"I don't think so," Elizabeth answered. "She got a hundred on that big math test last week."

"Did you know her mom works in the library?" Pamela said.

"You mean, that pregnant lady?" Jessica asked.

Pamela nodded. "Maybe that has something to do with it."

"Oh, I doubt it. It would be really neat to have a baby sister or brother," Elizabeth said.

"Unless the baby turned into another Steven," Jessica cracked. They all laughed and the subject soon changed to other school gossip.

As they left the cafeteria to go to class, Elizabeth noticed Billie leaning against a row of lockers, staring at the floor. She looked so sad, Elizabeth's heart went out to her.

Well, Elizabeth thought to herself. *If I can find out what's bothering her, maybe I can help her.*

SWEET VALLEY TWINS

Standing Out

Written by
Jamie Suzanne

Created by
FRANCINE PASCAL

A BANTAM BOOK®

TORONTO · NEW YORK · LONDON · SYDNEY · AUCKLAND

To Sara Anne Weiss

One

◇

"Hey, Billie, wait up!" Jessica Wakefield called as Belinda Layton turned to leave the locker room after gym class.

"What's up, Jess?" Billie asked, slinging her red duffle bag over her shoulder. As usual, Billie's slender figure was hidden by the loose sweatpants and sweatshirt she always wore. Her light brown hair was pulled back in a pony-tail.

"I just wanted to tell you what a great job you did for our side," Jessica said breathlessly. Thanks to Billie's great dribbling and long throws, their team, the Stars, had defeated the Condors by eight points.

Billie looked pleased at Jessica's praise, but she didn't smile. "Thanks," she said sadly. "It's nice to know that somebody appreciates me."

Jessica tossed her long blond hair behind her shoulders and stared at Billie in disbelief. Had she just heard Billie Layton—all-around athlete, high-scorer on the basketball team, *and* star pitcher of the neighborhood Little League team, the Rangers—feeling sorry for herself?

"Of *course* people appreciate you," Jessica exclaimed. "How could they not?"

"Easily," Billie said.

"What's *wrong*, Billie?" Jessica demanded, pushing up the sleeves of her purple cardigan. "You've been acting so strange lately." Jessica had heard from someone on the Little League team that Billie had been sent home from baseball practice the day before. She'd struck out and thrown her bat over the fence in anger.

Billie's mouth turned down at the corners and Jessica thought she might cry.

"You'd act strange, too, Jessica, if your mom was having a baby," she blurted out.

"But that's great news, Billie!" Jessica exclaimed. "When is the baby due?"

"*You* may think it's great," Billie grumbled, beginning to walk away, "but *I* think it's awful. And it's due in just a few weeks, right in the middle of Little League season."

"But what's wrong with that?" Jessica asked, trying to match her shorter strides to Billie's longer, more powerful ones. "Babies are so cute! Imagine having your very own little sister or brother!" she added.

"It's a boy," Billie growled.

Jessica's blue-green eyes widened. "You mean, you already *know*?"

Billie nodded. "My mom's older than most mothers. So the doctor sent her to have a test to make sure the baby's healthy. That's how they found out it's a boy."

"Just think how *simple* that makes everything!" Jessica said excitedly. "You don't even have to worry about whether to buy pink or blue stuff for the baby's room."

"Yeah," Billie interrupted. "My dad put up the curtains Saturday afternoon. They've got these stupid little blue football players all over them." She scowled. "It's the first time my dad ever put curtains up."

Jessica giggled to herself. She had once seen Billie and her father out jogging together. He was a distinguished-looking ex-Navy commander who looked like he was standing at attention even in a sweatsuit. She couldn't imagine Commander Layton hanging baby curtains. "I guess he was trying to help your mom, huh?"

"I guess." Billie sighed. She looked straight at Jessica for the first time since they'd started to talk. "Listen, if you really don't mind hearing about it, I feel like I need to talk to someone— confidentially, I mean."

"It must be hard for you," Jessica sympathized. "I'm so lucky to have Elizabeth to listen to my problems."

Elizabeth was Jessica's identical twin and although they were different in many ways, they were closer than any two girls could be. They looked exactly alike with their long, silky blond hair, sparkling blue-green eyes, and dimples in their left cheeks. In fact, the only way to tell them apart was by their very different personalities.

Jessica was fun loving and always eager to gossip about boys, movie stars, and the latest fashions. She loved to be the center of attention in a large gathering of friends. Most of all, Jessica liked intrigue and high adventure which usually got her in a great deal of trouble.

Lucky for Jessica, Elizabeth was there most

of the time to bail her out of her messes. Older by four minutes, it often seemed more like four years. Like her sister, Elizabeth was fun loving, but she also had a serious side. She loved the time she spent talking with her closest friends, Amy and Julie, and the time she had alone to read a good mystery or do some writing.

What a shame that Billie doesn't have someone as caring as Elizabeth to talk to, reflected Jessica.

"Of course, there *is* Jim Sturbridge," Billie said, interrupting Jessica's thoughts. "Jim's my best friend. I can always count on him, and I can talk to him about *anything*." She bit her lip. "Except this. He'd think I was being a crybaby."

The bell that signaled the beginning of the lunch period almost drowned out her words, and kids began to spill out of the classrooms into the hall.

"Oh no!" Jessica moaned. "I'm sorry, Billie, but I've got to run. The Unicorns are having an emergency meeting at lunch, and I've just *got* to be there."

The Unicorn Club was an exclusive group who thought they were as special as the animal for which their club was named. They had adopted purple, the color of royalty, as their group color, and each day they tried to wear something purple. Elizabeth thought the Unicorn meetings were nothing more than gossip about boys and clothes. She also thought the girls in the club were snobs. Jessica loved being a Unicorn and took it all very seriously—especially emergency meetings. She put her hand on Billie's arm and flashed a wide smile. "Let's get together later, OK?"

Billie looked hurt, and Jessica, feeling a pang of guilt, thought that maybe she should skip the Unicorn meeting just this once. Then Billie's glum look disappeared when she spotted Jim Sturbridge walking past them down the crowded hall. "Hey, Jim!" she called, waving to him. But Jim didn't turn around. He was deep in conversation with a girl. "He must not have heard me," Billie muttered. "Well, see you later, Jessica." She walked away, looking a little disappointed.

Jessica couldn't help wondering why Jim was walking around with Sally Holcomb, one of the biggest flirts in the whole sixth grade, if he was *Billie's* best friend.

"This emergency meeting will come to order," Janet Howell, president of the Unicorn Club, commanded crisply. All the members stopped chattering and looked at Janet.

"Why are we having an emergency meeting?" Ellen Riteman asked, sounding worried.

"Don't tell me we're out of money again," Lila Fowler said with a weary sigh. The Unicorns were always overspending their budget for parties and dances, so fund-raisers were a constant topic of conversation.

Jessica smiled. Lila Fowler was one of her closest friends. Mr. Fowler was one of the wealthier men in Sweet Valley, and in Lila's mind, it was impossible to run out of money. She was used to getting anything she wanted.

"The problem can't be money," Mary Wallace reported confidently. "We've got sixteen dollars and thirty-two cents in the treasury."

"The problem *isn't* money," Janet said sternly. She leaned forward and lowered her voice so only the Unicorns could hear her. "The problem is image."

"Image?" Jessica asked, surprised. "How can there be anything wrong with our image?"

"Jessica's right, Janet," Lila said. She looked at all the members around her. "There isn't anybody here who doesn't fit the Unicorn image perfectly. Everyone here is both pretty *and* special."

The other Unicorns looked flattered, but Janet looked impatient. "You're all missing the point," she said. "Our image *is* our problem. People think we're stuck-up—that we're snobs."

Lila laughed and shrugged. "Well, of course that's what they think! They're jealous because *they're* not special enough to be Unicorns!" There was a general nod of agreement around the table.

"Actually, I wouldn't care about our image," Janet persisted, "if it weren't for the service award."

"What service award?" Mary asked.

"The one that's to be given next month to the organization that contributes the most to the community," Janet went on. "There's a prize that goes with the award." She paused, making sure that she had everyone's undivided attention. "The prize is an all-expense-paid, one-day trip for the whole organization—to the place of their choice within a fifty-mile radius."

Conversation buzzed around the table. Jessica sighed happily as she imagined the whole club taking a trip to a TV studio to see their favorite soap operas live. Or maybe they could all go to one of Johnny Buck's concerts! Johnny Buck was her favorite rock star.

Janet held up her hand for silence. "As I was saying," she went on, "if we want to win the service award, we will have to come across as helpful, rather than stuck-up. I want everybody to start thinking about ways to change our image," Janet continued. "We'll meet again in a few days, and I'd like everybody to have at least one suggestion. In the meantime, just practice being helpful—little things, like helping your teacher hand out papers, volunteering to be hall monitor, giving people directions. It's not all that hard, you know. And it could go a long way toward changing our image." With that, Janet took a sip of milk and turned her attention to her lunch. Then she cleared her throat and said, "Oh, and one more thing. It wouldn't be very good if word got out that we're worried about our image. So keep this confidential."

That evening, Elizabeth sat at her bedroom desk, typing a story for *The Sweet Valley Sixers,* the sixth-grade newspaper. Elizabeth was the

editor and her hard work was largely responsible for its success.

"Hi, Lizzie!" Jessica bounced into the room
and plopped down on the bed. "Got a minute?"

"Sure, Jess." Elizabeth sat back and
stretched. She looked at the clock. "Fifty-nine,"
she said, counting seconds. "Fifty-eight, fifty-
seven . . ."

Jessica giggled and tossed a pillow at her
sister. "I mean, do you have a minute to *listen*,
Big Sister? I need some advice."

Laughing, Elizabeth tossed the pillow back
at Jessica. "Sure, I've got a minute," she said
cheerfully. "What's up?"

"Well, it's about Billie Layton. She's pretty
upset," Jessica said, leaning back against the pillows on the bed and tucking her feet under her.
"I'm not supposed to repeat this, but since
you're my twin, it's almost like telling myself."

Elizabeth wrinkled her brow. "Well, I'm not
sure I understand what you just said, but go
ahead."

"Did you know that Billie's mother is about
to have a baby?" Jessica announced untucking
one of her legs.

Elizabeth grinned. "Yes, I know. Don't you

remember when we were talking about Mrs. Layton at lunch the other day?" Billie's mother worked part-time in the school library. Then she frowned. "*That's* upsetting Billie? How come? It's so exciting! Being an only child must get kind of lonely sometimes."

For a second, Elizabeth tried to imagine how boring her life would be without Jessica or her older brother, Steven.

"She's getting a little brother," Jessica said, making figure eights with her foot. "They know that already."

"Well, maybe that's what's got her down," Elizabeth suggested. "I know she spends a lot of time with her father. And he comes to all of her ball games. Maybe she's afraid he won't have much time for her when the baby comes."

"But that's not the *problem*, Liz," Jessica said, sitting up. "The problem is Jim Sturbridge and Sally Holcomb," she added. "Billie says that Jim is her best friend, but I think maybe he means more than that to her. This morning we saw him walking with Sally Holcomb and Billie looked really upset." Jessica frowned. "Don't you think we should do something?"

"*We* should?" Elizabeth asked. Jessica had

an unsettling way of including her in her schemes. "Just what do you have in mind?" she asked suspiciously.

"Well, nothing, actually," Jessica said, waving her hand vaguely. "I just thought we could help somehow, that's all."

"It's nice that you want to help Billie," Elizabeth said, "but Jim has a right to be friendly with anybody he likes. It does sound as if Billie could use some cheering up."

Jessica stood up with a sigh. "I wish we could do something for her. Anyway, just remember not to tell anyone about this, OK?"

Elizabeth nodded, deep in thought. "The secret's safe with me," she said.

Two

◇

"Hey, Billie, are you ready to go?" Jim Sturbridge asked, as Billie opened the door of her house on Tuesday morning.

"Yeah, I'm ready." Billie grabbed her books and called goodbye to her mother. She was glad that she and Jim were going to walk to school together. She wanted to discuss strategy for the big baseball game coming up on Saturday. They were scheduled to play the Rebels, their long-time rivals.

"So," Jim said, as they walked along, "are you all set for the game or do you need an extra workout or two?"

"Are you kidding?" Billie scoffed. "Hey, don't forget that this is the arm that wiped out the Cardinals last week." She whirled and threw an imaginary ball.

Jim looked serious. "Maybe so. But the Cardinals aren't good hitters. The Rebels are great hitters! Their first baseman is the top hitter in the league, and they've got a couple of other guys who are pretty good, too."

Billie cocked her head, feeling confident. "So what? I'll hold them to a couple of hits and you guys can get in there and score some big ones off their pitching." She grinned. "Piece of cake."

Jim laughed. "Boy, you sure make it sound easy, Billie." He put a friendly arm around her shoulders. "But there's no doubt about it, it's got to go that way. We can't win this game unless you can keep them from scoring." He dropped his arm. "We're counting on you."

Billie squared her shoulders. It felt good to know that he was relying on her. She wouldn't disappoint him.

There was something else that made her feel especially happy this morning. She and her father had had a talk the night before and had made plans to go fishing the day after the big game. In the old days, they'd gone fishing almost every weekend—just the two of them. But now with her mom's pregnancy, everything had changed and not for the better. Her mom hadn't felt well in the early months, so instead of going fishing with Billie on weekends, her dad had stayed around the house, helping her mother with the housework and other chores. Yet now that her mom was feeling better, he *still* stayed around the house, just to make sure that she had everything she needed—so he said. Billie suspected that he was worried about her mom, but even so, she felt left out. That's why the fishing trip was so special. Once the baby was born, Billie knew it would be a long time before she'd get to spend time alone with her dad again.

But what made Billie happiest of all was that during their talk, her father had promised to come to the big game on Saturday. This would give her a chance to show him how far she'd come since the last game he'd attended, weeks ago. She would put just the right spin on that super fastball he'd taught her. And then, after the game, they would sit down together and go over every play. It was too bad that her mother couldn't come, too, but she was so busy getting things ready for the baby. She hardly had time to think about anything else these days.

As Billie ambled down the sidewalk beside Jim, she decided she felt too good to dwell on any troubling matters—least of all, having seen Jim, the day before, with boy-crazy Sally Holcomb.

"Hand me those raisins, Jessica," Lila ordered, pushing her light brown hair out of her eyes. The girls were baking oatmeal cookies in Mrs. Gerhart's Tuesday morning home-ec class.

"Here you are," Jessica said.

Lila stirred the raisins into the dough. "And now the nuts."

Jessica handed Lila the nuts she'd just finished chopping. She and Lila were good friends, even though Lila could be bossy. Lila frequently insisted on doing the easy jobs, like mixing the dough, while her friends did the harder jobs, like chopping nuts.

"Now," Lila remarked, adding the nuts, "what was it you were saying about Billie Layton?"

"I was saying that Billie said Jim Sturbridge is her best friend," Jessica told her.

Lila began to drop little mounds of cookie dough onto the cookie sheet. "Well, if Jim

Sturbridge is Billie Layton's best friend," she said, "how come he's hanging around with Sally Holcomb? I saw the two of them having ice cream at Casey's Place the other day."

Jessica sighed and began to wash out the empty bowl Lila handed her.

Lila put the cookie sheet into the oven. "Somebody should tell Billie what's going on behind her back." She took off her apron and folded it up. "After all, Jessica, wouldn't *you* want to know if your boyfriend was sneaking around with some other girl? And while we're on the topic of Sally Holcomb, did you *see* that sweater she had on this morning? What gives her the right to wear a purple sweater? She's not a Unicorn!"

"Hi, Jessica."

Jessica whirled around and saw Elizabeth leaning on the counter next to her. Her sister had obviously finished making her cookies.

"Oh, hello, Elizabeth," Lila said smoothly. She rinsed her hands off in the sink, dried them, and then glanced at her watch. "Listen, Jessica, would you mind doing the rest of the dishes? I promised Mrs. Gerhart I'd talk to her the minute we were through."

Without waiting for Jessica's response, she added: "And I really think you ought to tell Billie about Jim and Sally. After all, it's not fair to keep her in the dark about something so important. Remember what Janet said about Unicorns being helpful? Well, this is a perfect opportunity." She picked up her books and walked toward the teacher's desk.

Elizabeth laughed. "I thought *you* were a whiz at getting out of the dishes, Jess, but Lila takes the grand prize." She gave her twin a sympathetic look. "Want me to help?"

Furious, Jessica reached for the dish towel. It was just like Lila to leave her with the dirty work. "Sure, thanks," she said gratefully. "If you'll wash, I'll dry."

Elizabeth ran water into the sink. "I thought you promised Billie not to talk about her problem, Jess."

"But I didn't mention the family stuff Billie told me about," Jessica countered. "Just the part about Jim Sturbridge, and then Lila brought up Sally Holcomb. Everyone but Billie knows about *them*."

Elizabeth turned to face her twin, her

hands covered with soapsuds. "You're not going to tell Billie, are you?" she asked.

Jessica dried the dish Elizabeth handed her. "Don't you think I should?"

"No!" Elizabeth snapped. "Jim and Billie are just friends, and what happens between Billie and Jim or Jim and Sally is entirely their own business. It's wrong to meddle or be a tattletale."

Jessica sighed and hung up the dish towel. "I guess you're right," she conceded.

Billie, still preoccupied by how much better things were, arrived at gym class a little late. Every girl had changed into her gym suit already and had lined up out on the floor—everyone except Jessica, who was standing in front of the locker-room mirror pulling her hair back.

"Hi, Billie," Jessica said. "I've been waiting for you. Maybe we can talk while you're getting ready."

Billie quickly opened her locker and pulled out her gym suit. "Oh, that's OK, Jessica," she said with a sheepish grin. "Everything's back to normal again—at least for now."

She took off her shoes and padded into one of the lavatory stalls. A clutch of panic seized her when she sat down. She had started her period—her very *first* period!

Billie sank down on the toilet lid. She'd studied all about menstruation in Health class, and her mother had explained it to her when she was younger, so this wasn't exactly a surprise. But still, she didn't feel prepared, and she certainly didn't have any of the things you needed.

"Billie, are you all right?" Jessica asked urgently, rapping on the door. "You've been in there a while."

Billie mustered up all of her courage. "Uh, Jessica," she said, nearly in a whisper, "do you happen to have any . . ." She swallowed. "I mean, uh, there's a machine on the wall by the door that sells . . . Could you put a quarter in it for me?"

"You mean," Jessica asked unbelievingly, "the machine by the *door*?" That was a machine that mostly seventh- and eighth-graders used.

"Yes," Billie said miserably. "That's the one I mean."

Jessica flew to get her purse and then

dashed to the machine. A moment later, she was back outside the stall again. "It's empty," she reported.

"It *can't* be," Billie moaned.

"Listen, don't move a muscle," Jessica commanded. "Lila and I share a gym locker and she keeps that stuff in there. It hasn't happened for her yet, but she says you have to think ahead about these things. I'll be right back."

Inside the stall, Billie fought back tears. *Don't move a muscle?* Where could she go? Just when she was thinking everything was back to normal, this had to happen.

In a jiffy, Jessica was back with a small box. "Here you are," she said, thrusting it through the door. "Do you need any help?"

"Thanks," Billie said glumly. "I think I can manage." But truthfully, she wasn't sure at all.

Three

◇

A little while later, Billie was in the cafeteria having lunch with Jessica, Elizabeth, and Mary Wallace. She didn't have much of an appetite for the lasagna, though. Instead, she kept wondering which other girls in the cafeteria had gotten their periods. Her eye fell on Sally Holcomb, who was laughing and flirting with two boys. She didn't realize that she was staring until Jessica nudged her.

"Sally Holcomb is the boy-craziest girl in the whole sixth grade," Jessica said disgustedly. "Don't you think so?"

"Uh, I guess," Billie replied, flushing. She ducked her head, thinking about how shapely Sally was. Was *she* going to look like that in the next few months? What would happen when she tried to break her curveball over the plate?

Would her chest get in the way of her arm? And more horrible than that: Would she have to give up being a pitcher? The thought was so awful that Billie felt herself turning pale. Jessica patted her hand sympathetically, as if encouraging her to say what was on her mind.

But Billie didn't want to think about any of these disturbing matters any longer than she had to. She stood up and picked up her tray.

"I've got to go to music class," she said glumly. "I'll see you later."

Usually Billie enjoyed singing in music class, making her voice blend with the other voices, but today she had too much on her mind. She thought about Ms. McDonald, the new music teacher. Ms. McDonald had a well-developed figure, but she didn't seem to have any trouble using her arms, at least not that Billie could notice.

"Eyes up here, everybody," Ms. McDonald said, as she tapped on her music stand with her baton. "Now, let's try it once again, from the beginning."

Billie closed her eyes and tried to concentrate on her part, but all she could think about was class ending.

By the time her last class rolled around, Billie was tired of thinking about the changes in her body. She was ready to think about her schoolwork and nothing else, but when she walked into the classroom, she met Jessica and the rest of the class walking out, led by the vice principal, Mr. Edwards.

"Where's everybody going?" she asked, curious, falling into step with Jessica.

"To the library for a study hall," Jessica reported. "Ms. Wyler got called away and Mr. Edwards came in to tell us that they couldn't get a substitute on such short notice. And boy, am *I* glad!" she confided with a sigh of relief. "I didn't have my homework finished."

Billie nodded. She was happy, too. Now she'd get a chance to see her mom, who was working in the library this afternoon. What a lucky break!

Billie didn't spend as much time with her mother as she did with her dad, but today she could hardly wait to see her. She could tell her about getting her period and ask for some advice.

Mrs. Layton looked up from her desk in surprise when Mr. Edwards led the class into the library. He bent over and whispered something to her and then she stood up and came over to the tables where the class was sitting.

Billie blushed. Her mom looked awfully big, in spite of the loose top she was wearing. It was obvious that the baby was due very soon.

"Welcome, all of you, to your unscheduled library period," Mrs. Layton said with a warm smile. "If there are questions I can answer, or a book I can help you find, please let me know." She laughed. "Let's just hope it isn't on the bottom shelf," she added, and everybody giggled.

Billie stuck up her hand. Boy, did she have questions. "I'd like to talk to you," she said.

But Randy Mason, one of the smartest boys in the sixth grade, had beaten her to it. He was following her mother back to her desk with a long list of books in his hand. Billie watched as her mom spent almost fifteen minutes helping Randy.

Impatiently, Billie waited for her chance to approach her mother's desk and when it came she flew up front.

"Hello, Belinda," Mrs. Layton said cheerfully. "How's your day going?"

"Terrible," Billie groaned, pulling up a chair beside the desk. Her mother was the only one in the family who called her Belinda. "It's been just awful."

"Oh, I'm so sorry, honey," Mrs. Layton said sympathetically. "What happened?"

Billie looked around to make sure that nobody was within earshot, and then she leaned forward. "I was changing for gym this morning when I discovered—"

Julie Porter came around the bookshelf and stepped up to the desk. "Mrs. Layton, I have a question about a flute book." She looked at Billie. "Oh, hi, Billie," she said. "Listen, don't forget about my birthday party on Saturday. You *are* coming, aren't you?"

"Well, actually . . ." Billie began, a little embarrassed. She'd decided not to go to Julie's party, but she'd forgotten to tell her. The party was right after the big game, and since her father had promised to come, they'd probably stop off for ice cream afterward.

"A birthday party?" Mrs. Layton interrupted, smiling. "What fun! We'll have to see that you get a new party dress, Belinda! Something pretty and lacy, don't you think?"

A dress? Billie stared at her mother, alarmed. She didn't *need* a new party dress, especially one with lace on it. What she really needed—and before the game, too—was a new pair of sneakers.

"I know you've got a game on Saturday, Billie," Julie was saying, "but the party doesn't start until afterward, because most of the boys will be at the game. Just come whenever you get changed."

"Why, that sounds perfect, Belinda," Mrs. Layton said, getting slowly to her feet. "Now, let me help you find that book you're looking for, Julie."

Billie sighed dejectedly. "I guess we can't talk now, Mom," she said.

Mrs. Layton smiled down at her. "We can have the whole evening together if you want, honey. Right now I have to help Julie."

Billie trudged back to the table and put her head down on her arm. Didn't her mother even care about her? Everybody seemed more important than she did. First there was the baby, disrupting the family and taking everybody's attention, and now her mother didn't have time to talk to her because she had to answer all the other kids' questions. Nobody seemed to have time for Billie.

It just wasn't *fair*!

Four
◇

After school on Tuesday, Elizabeth and Billie waited for Jessica in front of the school.

"Hi, Jessica," Elizabeth called when she spotted Lila and Jessica coming down the front steps. "Over here." She and Jessica had made a date to go to Billie's house in the hope of cheering up their friend.

"Hi," Jessica said, as she and Lila joined Elizabeth and Billie.

"Are you ready to go to Billie's?" Elizabeth asked eagerly.

"Oh, no!" Jessica's hand flew to her mouth. "Gosh, Billie, I forgot all about . . . that is, the Unicorns are meeting this afternoon at Janet's house to talk about something really important. I mean, it's *crucial*. There's no way I can miss it."

"That's right," Lila chimed in. "It's crucial."

At that moment, Aaron Dallas, one of Billie's Ranger teammates, came along, and Billie started talking to him about the upcoming game. While she was occupied, Elizabeth leaned toward her twin. "But we *promised* we'd spend this afternoon with Billie," she whispered. "Don't forget, you're the one who wanted to do something to help cheer her up."

"And I still do," Jessica whispered back, with a stricken look. "I really want to help! It's just that—"

"Jessica," Lila interrupted abruptly, "if we're going to get to the meeting on time, we'd better go. You know how Janet feels about people being late."

Jessica gulped. "I'm coming," she said hastily, as Lila started to walk away. "Billie," she added, "I'm really sorry about today. I'll come over to your house one day soon, OK?" She turned and dashed off after Lila.

"I apologize for Jessica," Elizabeth said soberly, as they started walking home. "Sometimes she has a little trouble remembering all the plans she's made."

"That's OK, Elizabeth," Billie said with a sigh. "Sometimes it's hard to keep track of everything." She paused. "Especially when things happen so fast."

"Are things changing that quickly with you, too?" Elizabeth asked gently.

Billie gave a little laugh. "Boy, you can say that again. Changes, changes, and more changes. And none that I'd exactly wish for. I got my period today in gym class," she confided, staring at her feet.

"You did?" Elizabeth exclaimed. "Wow, that's great!"

"Yeah, I guess it is," Billie said. "It's just that there are so *many* changes in my life right now, I didn't quite feel ready for another one." She kicked at a stone on the sidewalk. "I've been trying to tell my mom, but these days she's either too busy or too tired."

Before the girls realized it, they were at Billie's house. On their way in, they stopped in the kitchen to grab some snacks and then headed directly up the stairs to Billie's room.

"Welcome," Billie said with mock formality, as she ushered Elizabeth into her bedroom.

Elizabeth looked around and grinned. The neat, sunny room was *exactly* like Billie. The yellow-and-white walls were decorated with baseball pennants and posters of sports heroes, and a fishing rod leaned against a wall in the corner. Piled up in the opposite corner were a pitcher's glove, a baseball, some bats and a red batting helmet. An autographed football sat on her desk.

"The football belonged to my dad when he was at the Naval Academy," Billie said proudly, picking it up for Elizabeth to get a closer look. "It's my most valued possession."

"So your dad is into sports, too," Elizabeth commented, as Billie opened one of the sodas they'd brought up.

"He's taught me everything I know," Billie said simply. "Sometimes I think he was disappointed I wasn't a boy. But it didn't stop him from teaching me everything he would have taught a boy to do. We used to do everything together. But—"

"But what?" Elizabeth prompted softly.

"But we don't do many things together anymore," she said sadly, burying her face in her arms.

"If you ask me," Lila commented tartly, as the Unicorns were settled into the den at Janet

Howell's house, "this whole thing is a lot of nonsense."

"I don't see how you can say that, Lila," Janet replied, raising her chin. "You can't deny that the Unicorns have an image problem."

"It all depends," she said, fingering the unicorn charm that hung on a gold chain around her neck, "on your definition of an image problem." She smiled at the others. "Personally, I like our image just the way it is."

"Me, too!" Ellen Riteman agreed.

"Well, I think Janet's right," Mary Wallace said quietly. "The Unicorns *are* special, and that's good—for us. But lots of kids feel left out because they can't belong. If we could include them in some of the things we do, it might change the way they look at us."

"Include other people in our club?" Ellen asked in horrified disbelief. "You mean, girls who *aren't* Unicorns? People like Lois Waller?" Lois was the chubbiest girl in the sixth-grade class.

At the mention of the girl's name, everybody giggled. When they all quieted down Jessica turned to Mary.

"Go on, Mary," she said encouragingly. "What kind of plan did you have in mind?"

"Well, it's not a plan, exactly. And I wasn't suggesting that we bring other people into the club. I was thinking that maybe the Unicorns could start a tutoring service." She looked around the table. "After all, a lot of us have pretty good grades. And there are lots of kids who need help after school. We could meet in the library and—"

Lila Fowler shrugged. "Well, I for one have *no interest* in tutoring students after school," she said firmly. "In the library or anywhere else."

"Well, then," Jessica volunteered, "how about running errands for sick people?" The idea had just popped into her head. For a moment she imagined herself with a basket, buying bread for a little old lady with a broken hip or a sore throat. Maybe she'd even bump into Tom McKay or Colin Harmon, the cutest boys at school, who'd offer to help her with the errands.

Kimberly Haver frowned. "But how would we find out who the sick people are?" she asked. "Would we just knock on doors and say, 'Pardon me, but are there any sick people here I can run an errand for?'"

Everybody laughed and Jessica sat back, wishing she hadn't volunteered her idea.

"It's clear that this matter requires more discussion," Janet said. "Mary's and Jessica's ideas are both good, but we ought to have some other suggestions to consider, too."

Lila pushed her chair back. "Well, my suggestion is that we table this idea for now and talk about more important things, like Julie Porter's birthday party." She looked around the table. "I've got a fabulous new dress, with purple velvet ribbons on it. What are the rest of you going to wear?"

"Gosh," Elizabeth exclaimed, looking at her watch. "It's after five o'clock. I've got to get home and help my mom with supper."

Billie got up from the floor and stretched. They'd talked for a while and then decided to play Scrabble. The game had been close, but Elizabeth had finally beaten her.

"Belinda?" Billie could hear her mother calling from downstairs. "Belinda, we're home."

"I'm up here, Mom," Billie called. "My dad took my mom to the doctor this afternoon for a checkup," she explained to Elizabeth.

Elizabeth finished putting away the tiles. "I hope everything's OK."

"Oh, it is," Billie said. She took the box Elizabeth handed her and put it on the closet shelf. "Thanks for coming over," she said. "Too bad Jessica couldn't make it."

Elizabeth didn't say anything. She was looking at the clothes in Billie's closet. Then she turned to Billie. "Listen," she said, "speaking of Jessica, the two of us are planning to go shopping on Thursday, over at the mall. Jessica wants to get something new for Julie's party. Would you like to come along?"

"Shopping?" Billie asked, screwing up her face. "I was going to go to the park after school on Thursday to practice for Saturday's game." Then she remembered her mother's idea about buying her a new dress for the party. Maybe she should go shopping with the twins in order to pick out her own dress, and maybe she could even get those sneakers she needed, too.

"On second thought," she added, "that's not such a bad idea."

"Terrific!" Elizabeth exclaimed happily. "Mom can pick us up and drive us to the mall right after school. I'll tell Jessica you're coming. She'll really be glad."

Billie walked Elizabeth downstairs and said

goodbye to her at the front door. Then she wandered down the hall in the direction of the kitchen, where she could hear the faint murmur of her parents' voices.

Billie didn't mean to eavesdrop, but when she got near the kitchen door, she heard her father say, "The doctor's report we got today was super, Margaret. It won't be long now."

"No, it won't," her mother said. "In fact, I think it's time to decide on a name." Billie heard her mother sigh. "I think you're right, David. We ought to name the baby William Arthur, after your father."

Outside the door, Billie leaned against the jamb and sucked in her breath sharply. *William?* They were going to name the baby *William?*

"Are you sure, Margaret?" her father asked. "It's bound to cause Belinda difficulties. After all, we've been calling her Billie—" He paused and corrected himself. "—*I've* been calling her Billie for almost twelve years now. She might feel like we're taking something away from her—something that *belongs* to her."

"I know," her mother said. "She may be a little upset when we tell her, but I think she's mature enough to understand why it's so important that we name her brother after her grandfather."

"Right," her father agreed. His voice dropped a little, and Billie could almost hear her heart pounding. "Now we've got a boy to carry it on. My father would be so proud."

Billie swallowed. Her name. They were taking her name away from her. And then, shoulders sagging, tears blurring her eyes, Billie turned and ran upstairs.

Five

◇

"Elizabeth!" Jessica poked her head out of her door and into the upstairs hall as Elizabeth walked by. "Could you come here for a minute?"

"What's up?" Elizabeth asked. "What do you want to borrow now?" The minute she entered her sister's room, she shrieked in mock horror. "Jess! What's happened to your *room*?"

Jessica looked around her neat, spotless room, and said proudly, "It does look rather nice, doesn't it?" She had picked up all her clothes and magazines and record albums, and she'd straightened her shelves. She'd even vacuumed the cookie crumbs off the rug and taken all the dirty dishes down to the kitchen.

"I don't believe it," Elizabeth said, stunned. She shook her head and took another look around the room. "I can *walk* without tripping over something! And look! There's your bed!"

"Very funny, Elizabeth," Jessica said. It was true she wasn't usually very neat but she thought Elizabeth was exaggerating just a bit.

Elizabeth gingerly approached the closet.

"I'll bet," she said, "that your closest is so full that . . ." She slid the door open and jumped back, as if to escape an avalanche. To her surprise, nothing happened. Cautiously she stuck her head inside and then moved back out. She came over to the bed and put her hand anxiously to Jessica's forehead.

"You're not sick or anything, are you Jess?" she asked. "Should we call a doctor? An ambulance? Where did you put everything? Your room hasn't looked like this since the day you moved into it."

Jessica tried to suppress her giggles but soon both girls roared with laughter.

"Well, Jess," Elizabeth said at last, looking around. "Congratulations. This is *certainly* a new you."

"It is?" Jessica asked, wide-eyed. "Do you really think so?" She was about to tell Elizabeth that cleaning her room actually was part of a campaign to change her image when she remembered the strict orders not to discuss the Unicorns' plan with *anybody*.

Instead she said, "Speaking of changes, how was Billie today?" She had meant to ask Elizabeth about Billie at dinner, but the Wakefields had had company and she hadn't gotten a chance.

Elizabeth sat down on Jessica's bed and folded her legs under her. "She seemed a little down, especially after her mom and dad got home from the doctor. It's too bad you couldn't have been there, Jess."

"I know," Jessica said sadly. "I would have come, but the Unicorns would have been angry if I'd missed the meeting. I've been thinking about Billie a lot, though, and I know that we just *have* to help her."

"We already are helping her," Elizabeth pointed out. "What she needs is friends she can talk to, do things with. In fact, she's agreed to go shopping with us on Thursday."

"Well, that's good. But that's not what I meant. I meant that we have to help her about this Jim-and-Sally business." Jessica laid her hand on her sister's arm and said in her most serious tone, "I know what you're thinking, Lizzie, but I'm not doing this to be a tattletale. I really want to help Billie. And I've got an idea. All we have to do is write a letter."

Elizabeth sat up straight. "A letter?"

"Yes. You can type it so she won't recognize the handwriting. Just say that Jim is hanging around with Sally. That's all," she said. "Just the truth."

Elizabeth folded her arms over her chest. "I refuse," she said firmly, shutting her eyes. "I positively, absolutely, and for the last time *refuse* to have anything to do with this nasty scheme of yours."

"But we have to help her!" Jessica wailed. "How about this? We could find out when Jim and Sally are going to be together, and then we could lure Billie there so she could see with her own eyes what's going on behind her back. That way, we'll be showing her, not telling her! She really should know that she can't count on Jim Sturbridge."

Elizabeth stood up. "Jessica," she said, in a threatening voice.

"Or," Jessica said pleadingly, "maybe I

could plant something in *The Sweet Valley Sixers* gossip column. You know, just a little clue. Like, 'Guess who we saw walking down the hall together, *again*.' And all you have to do is OK the column."

Elizabeth turned and strode to the door. "Jessica, the best way for you to help Billie Layton is to go shopping with us on Thursday and help her buy something really pretty to wear to Julie's party." She paused, and a reflective note crept into her voice. "When I was over there today, I looked in her closet, and you know what?"

"What?" Jessica asked, pouting.

"There wasn't one single dress in her closet."

"Wow!" Jessica said in a whisper.

"That's why, on Thursday, *we* are going to help Billie buy herself a dress."

Jessica was quiet for a moment. Why, of course! Why hadn't she thought of it sooner? First they would help Billie buy a dress, and then they'd give her a complete makeover. By the end of the party Jim Sturbridge would be knocked right off his feet. And Billie, herself, even though she was sort of a tomboy, would be able to see that being a girl was pretty neat after all. It was a wonderful plan!

"Oh, Lizzie!" Jessica cried, jumping up and down. "You have the best ideas in the whole world!"

After school on Wednesday, Billie rushed home to change into her Rangers uniform. She loved baseball practice, but even more she loved her walks home with Jim afterward. She quickly slipped into her uniform, pulled her hair back, and shoved on her Rangers cap. Then, grabbing her glove and her batting helmet, she raced to the park as fast as she could.

When Billie arrived, Jim Sturbridge and the other guys were already in batting practice and there were a dozen or so parents in the bleachers. Billie smiled as she approached the field and heard the crack of the bat against the ball. It was a sound she loved—as long as it wasn't *her* pitch that got hit!

Coach Andrews raised his arms and motioned the team over to the bench. "OK, everybody," he began. "Today's a scrimmage game so we're going to rotate. Everyone will get a chance at the plate." He raised his voice. "OK, gang, let's see your stuff!"

The team ran out on the field and Coach Andrews turned to Billie. "How's your arm today, kid?"

"Fine, Coach," she answered enthusiastically. "Never been better."

"Then take the mound. And don't forget, you're starting on Saturday."

He didn't have to remind her. Of course she was starting on Saturday! Who else had a fastball as good as hers? She was the only one who could keep the Rebels from hitting.

Billie trotted out to the mound and turned to face Aaron Dallas. Suddenly she began to feel painfully self-conscious. For the first time, she noticed that all the other players on the team were *boys*. Billie wondered if there was any way that the guys could possibly know that she had gotten her period.

Instantly, her mouth felt dust-dry and her breath was coming hard. When she wound up for the special overhand delivery her father had taught her, something unexpected happened. The ball sailed over the plate, fast and low, right where Aaron liked it, and he put his bat squarely on it. With a hard, clean *swoosh*, the ball sailed over the center fielder's head and smacked the fence in the farthest corner of the park.

"Hey, thanks, Billie," Aaron called, giving her the thumbs-up sign as he trotted from second to third. He was safely home long before the throw came from second base.

Billie managed to strike out the second batter, but when the count was three balls and two strikes on the third batter, Jim snatched off his face mask and trotted out to the mound for a conference.

"What's up, Billie?" he asked in a worried voice. "You coming down with something?"

Billie looked down at the ground. "Just give me a minute, huh? I'm still getting warmed up."

"You've had a minute," Jim pointed out. "This is the third batter, and your curveball hasn't broken right once."

"Don't worry," Billie said, her voice rising in spite of her efforts to stay calm.

"OK, OK," Jim muttered. "Don't get all shook up." He walked back to the plate, shaking his head.

Billie did break it, finally. She threw some nice curveballs, but she still wasn't throwing with her usual spark. When the inning was over, Billie trotted off the field, wondering whether her period had anything to do with the way she had pitched today.

Coach Andrews didn't help matters. "Billie," he said, motioning her over to the bench while the others packed up their gear, "looks like you were having a little trouble out there."

Billie shrugged. "It came out OK," she said defensively. "I got those last three batters, didn't I?"

"Sure, you did," the coach said, putting a friendly hand on her shoulder. "And it'll come out all right on Saturday, too. You just have to loosen up a little and give that fastball more steam."

Coach Andrews gave her bicep a critical squeeze. "You need some more muscle behind that ball. Maybe it'd help if you'd try a little weight lifting at home. Get your dad to show you how."

Without a word, Billie turned and walked away. *Weight lifting?* Was he saying that her fastball wasn't working anymore? Furiously, she slammed her glove on the ground.

"Hey, Billie, see you tomorrow at school," Jim called to her as he was leaving.

"Wait!" Billie scooped up her glove and ran to catch up with him. "Aren't we walking home together?"

"Sorry, I can't today," Jim said. "I've got something I have to do. See you tomorrow, OK?"

"Sure," Billie said, trying to hide her disappointment. She turned and walked away. A dull, unhappy feeling settled in the pit of her stomach. Was it because the coach had questioned her pitching ability or was it because she didn't get to walk home with Jim?

She was so busy with her thoughts that she almost didn't see Sally Holcomb hurrying down the other side of the street toward the ballpark. But when Billie looked up and spotted her—she felt even worse.

Six

◇

After school on Thursday, Mrs. Wakefield dropped Elizabeth, Jessica, and Billie off outside of Valley Fashions, a shop in the mall that specialized in teen and preteen clothing. Billie felt a little uncomfortable. She wasn't used to shopping for dresses.

Jessica didn't seem to be having any difficulty, though. "Wow," she said happily. "Look at all the new sweaters they got in!"

"But we're not here to buy sweaters," Elizabeth reminded her. "We're here to buy dresses for Julie's party—all three of us."

"I know," Jessica sighed. "But that doesn't mean I can't look, does it?" She wandered off, humming happily to herself.

Elizabeth turned to Billie with a grin. "When she comes back, she'll have half a dozen outfits over her arm. Choosing one of them will take at least a half hour. Why don't we get started? What did you have in mind?"

Billie bit her lip. Some skirts on a rack caught her eye. "Well," she said slowly, "maybe I could get a blue denim skirt and—"

"I don't think blue denim is quite right for this party," Elizabeth said. She went over to a dress rack and picked out a pink dress with ruffles at the neck and sleeves.

Billie watched Elizabeth with horror. She hated pink. And ruffles. "No," she said quickly. "That's not what I want."

Elizabeth pulled something else off the rack, a white dress with a full skirt. "How about this?" she asked.

Billie shook her head. "It's pretty, but I'd get it dirty too quickly. With my luck, I'd spill chocolate on it."

In the end, Billie found a pretty blue dress with a tiny flower print. She didn't mind that it had a narrow lace collar, because the lace was soft, not starchy or prickly. And the blue velvet ribbon that looped around the waist was a nice touch. She looked at the dress and suddenly found herself wondering whether Jim would like it. Then she shook her head at the thought. What a dumb thing to wonder. She turned back to the rack and took another dress, dark blue and very plain, with narrow sleeves and a high collar.

"Have you found something, Billie?" Jessica asked, coming over with her arms full of clothes. "Why don't we all go into the dressing room together?"

Hesitantly, Billie followed the girls as they searched for a dressing room big enough for all three of them. Jessica insisted on being first, while Elizabeth and Billie watched her model different outfits, one at a time.

"Well," she said, turning around in front of the mirror, wearing the last one, "which do you like?"

"Definitely the pink-and-white," Elizabeth said. "It's you." Billie nodded. "The pink looks nice on you," she said.

Then it was Billie's turn. Self-consciously, she slipped into the first blue dress she had chosen.

"Wait, Billie," Jessica objected impatiently.

"You can't tell much about a dress if you leave your jeans on under it!"

With an embarrassed giggle, Billie shed her jeans, too. Then she stood in front of the mirror, not looking at her reflection, while Jessica zipped the dress up the back and Elizabeth tied the blue velvet ribbon at the waist.

Jessica nodded in satisfaction. "This is the one," she said. "It's perfect."

Billie looked in the mirror. It didn't look at all like *her*. The image was all wrong and it made her uncomfortable.

"I think I'd better try on the other dress," she said slowly, turning her back to the mirror. "The dark blue one. I think I like it better."

"Oh, no!" Jessica exclaimed. "This one looks great on you, Billie. Don't you think so, Elizabeth? Why, it'll make Ji—" She put her hand over her mouth. "It'll make every boy at the party look at you!"

Elizabeth's eyes bore through her sister, but Billie didn't notice. She wasn't at all sure she liked the idea of *every* boy looking at her—unless they were admiring her fastball, that is. She turned around in front of the mirror, and the thought of Jim crept back into her mind. If she had barely recognized herself, what would Jim say when he saw her all dressed up? The thought made her cheeks flush pink.

"I agree with Jessica," Elizabeth said, and that settled it. Jessica and Billie paid for their purchases and the three girls stopped in the shoe store next door so Billie could buy a pair of sneakers.

"Wait, Billie," Jessica said, as the shoe salesman was headed for the cash register. "Don't you need a pair of shoes to go with your dress?" She sat down beside Billie and handed her a pair. "These would be perfect with it."

Billie looked at the shoes. They were shiny white with a strap. They *were* very nice. She tried to imagine how they would look with the dress, but then she pushed the thought out of her mind. "I don't need party shoes," she objected. "I've got a perfectly good pair of school shoes I can wear."

Elizabeth turned to face Billie. "Do you have enough money with you?" she whispered.

Billie nodded. Her mother had given her more than enough.

"Well, then," Elizabeth said, "I vote for the shoes. They're really pretty. And they do go with the dress."

So in the end, Billie bought two pairs of shoes after all—the sneakers for the game and the white ones for the party.

As they walked out into the mall, Elizabeth looked at her watch. "Mom said she'd pick us up out front at five," she said. "We'd better hurry."

Billie followed along happily. Shopping with the twins had been much more fun than she had expected. "Listen, Billie," Jessica was saying. "I've got a great idea. Why don't you come home with us after the game on Saturday and we'll all get dressed for the party together?"

"That's a terrific plan, Jess," Elizabeth agreed.

Billie hesitated. "Well, I don't know. My father promised to come to the game and we might go for ice cream or something afterward. He always critiques my game."

"You can talk to him later about the game. This way, we can all go to the party together," Elizabeth said determinedly.

"I guess you're right," Billie said. The more

she thought about it, the better the idea seemed. After all, she might feel a little funny walking into the party all by herself. It would definitely be better to arrive with the twins.

"Great!" Jessica exclaimed. "We'll have a get-ready-for-the-party party!"

Billie giggled along with Jessica. The twins were turning out to be pretty great friends.

Just then, they rounded a corner in the mall. Billie looked up and her heart sank to the pit of her stomach. Coming out of Casey's Place, directly in front of them, was Jim Sturbridge. And hanging onto his arm and laughing flirtatiously, was Sally Holcomb!

Billie couldn't believe what she saw. Jim— with Sally! Then the truth hit her. Sally had come to the ballpark the day before to meet Jim. That was the reason he couldn't walk home with her. He'd made plans to be with Sally! Then she remembered seeing them together in the hallway the week before. Suddenly, it was all very clear, and Billie felt sick.

From the look on Jim's face, it was obvious that he wasn't too happy about bumping into Billie, either. The only happy face was Sally's as she clung to Jim's arm.

"Hi, Jessica," she cooed sweetly. "Hi, Elizabeth." Her glance swiveled to Billie and her voice became a little cooler. "Hello, Billie."

Jessica and Elizabeth returned her greeting. But Billie mumbled a barely audible hello. Jim was too embarrassed to say anything.

"Jim," Sally said giving him a little nudge, "we have to go. See you guys later, OK?"

The three girls just watched as Jim and Sally walked away.

"I'm really sorry," Jessica said quietly, with a sympathetic glance at Billie. "I wanted to tell you about Jim and Sally, but—"

"It's OK," Billie cut in. "I guess I'm just as glad I didn't know." She looked down at the shopping bags she was carrying and started to walk toward the exit. The whole idea of the blue dress seemed very silly now.

Once outside the mall, Billie took a deep breath and tried desperately to push down the misery that was welling up inside her. But she just couldn't hold it in any longer.

"Why couldn't things go on the way they were?" she burst out suddenly. "Why did everything in my life have to change?" She made her way to a nearby bench and plopped down disgustedly.

"I guess," Elizabeth said quietly, sitting down beside her, "that that's the way life is."

"Yes," Jessica added. "Remember what Mr. Nydick said about the dinosaurs? He said the reason they all became extinct was because they couldn't adapt. Well, I guess we have to adapt."

Just at that moment, the Wakefields' maroon van pulled up at the curb and the three girls climbed in. Elizabeth and Jessica tried to make conversation, but Billie was silent all the way home. When they got to the end of Billie's block, she leaned forward. "Could you let me out here, Mrs. Wakefield?" she asked. "There's something I want to do."

"But your house is at the other end of the street," Elizabeth objected.

"That's OK," Billie said. "I feel like walking."

Mrs. Wakefield pulled over to the curb and Billie hopped out. "Thanks for helping me pick out a dress," she said to Jessica and Elizabeth before shutting the car door.

"Are you sure you don't want us to walk with you?" Elizabeth asked anxiously. Billie looked so sad.

"Thanks, but I need some time to be alone." Billie closed the door gently and started down the block.

"I don't understand," Mrs. Wakefield said. "Did something happen at the mall? Did you girls have a disagreement?"

"No," Jessica said, with a worried look. "Billie just found out the truth about someone, that's all."

It was almost five-thirty, but the sun was still above the horizon. Angrily, Billie wiped the tears from her eyes. It was silly to cry over Jim Sturbridge! she told herself. She was going to stop it this instant. She cut across a vacant lot down the block from her house, and then, on an impulse, took the overgrown path that led down to the creek. When she reached it, she sat down on the familiar willow stump and stared down into the dark water. Then she broke into uncontrollable sobs.

For the next five minutes, she just cried hopelessly. She cried because everything familiar and certain was changing. There was nobody left in the world whom she could count on anymore.

Behind her there was a rustle in the grass, and Billie turned to see her mother making her way slowly down the path. She quickly looked back at the water and rubbed the tears off her cheeks with the back of her hand.

"I saw you heading down here," her mother said, leaning against the willow behind Billie. She was out of breath from climbing down the path. "Is everything all right?"

Billie sat numbly. Now was the time to talk to her mother about getting her period, about her poor performance on the pitcher's mound yesterday. She could even tell her about Jim and Sally, and how hopeless she felt about everything. But as much as she longed to break the silence, she couldn't.

"I know," her mother said softly. "Sometimes there's just too much to tell, isn't there, honey? It all must feel overwhelming." She put her hands lightly on Billie's shoulders and then leaned over and hugged her.

Billie was glad her mother didn't insist that she talk. She gave her mother a big hug. Then she stood up, took her mother's hand, and together they walked back home in silence.

Seven

◇

Saturday finally arrived. Billie went to the ballpark early to warm up. She felt tense and jittery. There was so much riding on this game. Her father was going to be here, and she wanted to shine for him. Jessica had told her that she and Elizabeth and several of their friends would be in the stands, cheering for her, and she didn't want to disappoint them either. Of course she had to show Jim Sturbridge and Sally Holcomb that she didn't care *what* they did! But most of all, Billie wanted to prove that all these changes weren't going to affect the way she played baseball.

In spite of the pep talk she gave herself, the pre-game warm-up wasn't very promising. Her arm felt stiff and the ball seemed to have a mind of its own, skittering into the dust or sailing wildly over Jim's head.

Since it was a home game, the Rangers took the field first and the Rebels, their opponents, were first up to bat. Out on the mound, digging her new sneakers into the dirt to loosen them up a little, Billie scanned the packed bleachers. She caught a glimpse of Sally in the second row, and quickly looked away. She searched the stands for her father but couldn't spot him. Was he going to be late, she wondered, on this all-important day? Then she saw Jessica, Elizabeth, and their friends, sitting together on the highest row, waving pom-poms and chanting her name. This made her feel a little better. It was nice to have her own cheering section.

Once the game started, though, Billie began to wish Jessica and the others hadn't come. There wasn't very much to cheer about. She managed to get the first batter to foul-tip the ball to Jim behind the plate for an automatic out. But the second batter hit a sizzling line drive off her curveball. Luckily, the shortstop got a glove on it and threw the batter out at first. Two outs. But then, the sky darkened and thunder growled and she *walked* the next two batters!

Jim made a time-out sign to the umpire and trudged out to the mound. "So what do you think?" he asked casually, not really looking at her. "Think you can get this next guy?"

"Sure, no problem," Billie said, trying to keep the nervousness out of her voice.

Jim met her eyes. For a moment he didn't say anything. Then he asked, "How about a fastball, then? Catch the outside corner, maybe. And a little high?"

Billie nodded. "Outside, high," she repeated. "Gotcha."

Jim grinned. "Go get him!" He turned and trotted back. Behind Billie, the runner on second began to chant. "How about a hit! Let's have a hit!" In the stands, Jessica and her friends were jumping up and down, flinging their pom-poms into the air. "Come on, Billie!" they screamed. "Get him out!"

Pumping hard, her eyes fixed on the plate, Billie began her windup. High and outside, Jim had said, and that's what she aimed for. But the second the ball left her fingers, she knew it was low. Low and across the middle of the plate. The batter connected with it solidly—a smoking line drive flew past her and smashed into the right-field fence. Billie turned to watch, her heart sinking right down into the toes of her brand-new sneakers. It was an easy triple.

The two Rebels already on base scored runs, their fans cheering wildly. The batter raced toward third and sensing a chance for a home run, poured on the speed, heading for the plate.

The right fielder's throw came at Billie. She caught the ball, whirled and threw as hard as she could, aiming for the mitt Jim held out as he crouched on top of home plate. Her throw got to the plate a split second before the runner did.

"Out!" the umpire yelled, jerking his thumb over his shoulder. The Ranger fans went crazy, shouting her name louder than ever.

Billie was relieved for a moment as she trotted back to the bench, but she knew she was still in trouble. She had been lucky to get out of that jam with only two runs—not exactly a great performance. She'd have to do better than that in the next inning. The rest of the Rangers didn't seem worried, though. Batting well, they scored two runs in their half of the inning, much to the fans' delight.

When Billie took the field again for the top of the second, she was *glad* that her father hadn't come yet. The game was tied at two-all and Dennis Cookman, the team's relief pitcher was warming up along the first-base line. She walked the first batter. The second batter slammed the ball deep into center field for a double. The great pitching arm that Billie could always depend on had failed her completely. The people in the stands stirred uneasily. Even Jessica and the others were silent. And now it was starting to drizzle.

As Billie turned back to the plate to face the third batter, she saw Jim take his face mask off. On the sidelines, Coach Andrews stood up from the bench and motioned for time out. He gestured to Dennis to take his place on the pitcher's mound.

Billie's shoulders slumped and she blinked away the tears. She was being pulled from the game.

It was all over.

Eight

◇

It was raining harder now. Big drops splattered on the wooden bleachers noisily. Elizabeth opened her yellow umbrella and Jessica joined her beneath it.

"What's happening down there, Liz?" Jessica asked in a worried voice.

"It looks like they're bringing in a relief pitcher," Elizabeth said sadly, as Billie walked toward the bench.

"Does that mean Billie's finished?" Amy Sutton asked, pushing her damp hair out of her eyes. "Aren't they going to give her another chance?" Amy was one of Elizabeth's closest friends.

"It looks like she's through for today," Elizabeth replied, watching Billie pull her cap off.

"This is a *dumb* game," Lila said. "There's

no excitement at all." She pulled the hood of her red raincoat over her head and frowned up at the dark sky.

Suddenly a big clap of thunder crashed across the sky and everybody jumped.

"That's it," Lila announced, standing up. "I'm not hanging around here to get rained on. I don't want my hair to be all stringy for Julie's party."

"Me, either," Ellen agreed, and all the other girls began to gather their things.

Amy looked at Elizabeth. "Are you leaving?" she asked.

Elizabeth shook her head. How would Billie feel if she looked up into the bleachers and saw that everybody had gone? "I've got an umbrella," she said. She grinned at Amy. "There's room for three under it," she added. Eagerly, Amy moved in toward Elizabeth's other side.

Lila stuck her nose up in the air. "Come on, Jessica," she ordered. "The *Unicorns* are leaving."

Elizabeth glanced at her sister. When Lila used that tone of voice, Jessica always gave in. But not today. Jessica looked up at Lila and said firmly, "You guys can go. I'm staying."

"But Jessica—" Ellen began.

Lila stopped her. "Jessica can stay if she wants to," she said haughtily. "I don't have the time to argue with her." With a loud harrumph, she marched down the bleacher steps, leading the others away.

Elizabeth reached for Jessica's hand and gave it a happy squeeze. "Thanks, Jess," she said.

Jessica looked up. "Do you think I could have a little more of that umbrella? It's wet on this side."

Amy pointed down below, where a small overhang off to the side sheltered part of one bench. "Maybe we could move down there," she suggested. "It might be drier."

"Good idea," Jessica said, and they all scuttled down to the second row.

Down on the bench, Billie glanced up toward the bleachers for the third or fourth time. Her father still wasn't there. With a sharp pang she realized that he must have changed his mind about coming after all. She wasn't sure whether to be glad that he hadn't witnessed her humiliation or to be angry that he had failed to keep his promise.

Then, out of the corner of her eye, she saw Sally Holcomb making her way down the bleachers. Jessica, Elizabeth, and Amy Sutton were leaving their seats.

Gloomily, Billie turned her attention to the field again. She couldn't count on *anybody,* she thought. Not her father, not Jim. And not even Jessica and Elizabeth, who she'd thought were her friends. She felt very alone just then.

But the next time she turned around, she saw that Elizabeth, Jessica, and Amy had just moved down to stay dry. The three girls waved and smiled at her and she waved back.

It was raining harder now, and the base paths were getting muddy. Coach Andrews stood up and strode to the plate for a conference with the opposing coach and the umpire. A moment later, the umpire held up his arms to signal that the game had been called off.

Coach Andrews came back to the bench. "OK, everybody," he said, pulling his cap down over his eyes. "That's it for today. We're rescheduling for tomorrow, weather permitting. I'll see you at one for warm-up." He turned and looked directly at Billie. "I'll decide on a starting pitcher tomorrow."

Billie sucked in her breath. At least there was one consolation out of all this rainy, muddy mess. If the coach started her tomorrow (a *big* if), maybe she could redeem herself. She turned to say goodbye to Jim. He was searching the stands for Sally, and Billie couldn't resist grinning. She wasn't the only one who'd been deserted by a bunch of fair-weather fans.

Jessica and Amy had come down to the field to get Billie and the duffle bag that had her party dress and her shoes in it. Elizabeth had gone to the concession stand to call Mr. Wakefield for a ride.

"I don't feel much like a party right now," Billie said with a sigh, as the car headed toward the Wakefields'. Her hair hung in limp, wet strands around her shoulders. "I sure don't look ready for a party," she added glumly. "Besides, my dress is probably ruined from being stuffed in that duffle bag. Maybe I'd just better call my mom when we get to your house and have her come and get me."

"Don't be silly," Jessica said with breezy confidence, as Mr. Wakefield parked the maroon van in the driveway. "We know how to fix messy hair and wrinkled dresses, don't we,

Elizabeth?" They got out and went upstairs to Elizabeth's room.

"I'll take care of your dress," Elizabeth said, reaching for Billie's duffle bag. She opened it and pulled out the dress, the shoes, and the present that Billie's mom had wrapped for Julie. "Why don't you take a hot shower?" she suggested to Billie.

Billie sighed and sat down to peel off her wet socks. The twins were determined to take her to Julie's party. After all, they'd helped her buy her dress. And Jessica had organized the girls to cheer at the game.

A few minutes later, wrapped in a fluffy pink towel, Billie was sitting in front of the mirror in Elizabeth's room, while Jessica rolled her hair up on curlers.

"What are you doing to my hair?" Billie asked. The curlers made her scalp feel tight and itchy.

"Oh, just wait and see," Jessica replied airily. "It's a surprise."

Just as Jessica was finishing Billie's hair, Elizabeth came back in and hung the freshly pressed dress on the closet door. "There, you see?" she said proudly, straightening the velvet ribbons. "Good as new."

Billie had to admit it, the dress looked even prettier than it had in the store. One thing was for sure: she never would have bought *this* dress if it hadn't been for Jessica and Elizabeth.

While Jessica was taking out Billie's curlers and combing Billie's hair, Elizabeth was putting on a red dress with a matching scarf.

"Can I look in the mirror now?" Billie asked nervously.

Jessica pretended to give the matter serious thought. "Do you think we should let her look?" she asked Elizabeth.

"I don't think she's ready yet," Elizabeth said. "She needs to put her dress and shoes on."

Billie put on her dress and white pantyhose. Then she slipped her shoes on and turned to the twins. With great anticipation she asked, "Now can I look?"

But Jessica shook her head no, and picked up a tube of lip gloss.

"Wait a minute," Billie objected, raising her hand. "You guys are going too far. I mean, curling my hair is one thing, but I've *never* worn makeup."

Jessica brushed Billie's objection aside. "There's a first time for everything. And anyway, it's just a little lip gloss. After all, you *are* twelve, you know."

"I think it's OK, Billie," Elizabeth added reassuringly. "Jessica won't put on too much."

Billie sighed and sat down on the bed to submit to Jessica's makeup artistry.

"There," Jessica announced, when she was finished. She pulled Billie up to her feet. "We're ready for the great moment!"

"Wait," Elizabeth said, hurrying to her dresser. "I've got something I want Billie to wear." She took a pearl bracelet out of her jewelry box and slipped it on Billie's arm. "This is for luck," she said.

"Hey, that makes me think of something too," Jessica said. She disappeared and came back carrying a pair of tiny pearl earrings that she clipped onto Billie's earlobes.

Billie looked down at the bracelet on her arm. "Hey, you guys," she said softly, "this is really nice of you." She looked at the two of them. They were the greatest friends she'd ever had.

"*Now* do you think we're ready?" Jessica asked Elizabeth.

Elizabeth turned the mirror to face Billie. "Presenting the new Billie!" she said, with a smile.

Billie gasped. The last time she'd seen her reflection, a bedraggled baseball pitcher with limp, straggly hair had stared back at her. But now, in her place, stood a dressed-up girl with light brown curls tumbling around her face, her cheeks glowing, and her eyes shining like stars.

"Billie," Jessica and Elizabeth said in unison, "you look beautiful!"

Billie, appraising herself in the mirror, could only agree. She touched the tiny earrings and then turned to Elizabeth's bracelet on her arm, admiring its soft pearly glow.

She felt strange and wonderful at the same time, and almost as good as if she had pitched a no-hitter.

Nine

◇

"See? I *told* you she'd look great!" Jessica whispered to Elizabeth as they followed Billie down the stairs. "Just wait until Jim Sturbridge sees her! He'll drop Sally so fast that—"

Elizabeth stopped in the middle of the stairs. "Jessica, you promised," she said accusingly. "You swore you wouldn't interfere."

"I'm not going to interfere," she said. "I'm just making a prediction, that's all. Billie Layton is much cuter than Sally Holcomb, and Jim is sure to notice at the party."

At the foot of the stairs, Mr. Wakefield was waiting. "Ready, girls?" he said. Billie saw his expression change as she reached the bottom step. His eyes widened, and then he whistled, slowly, under his breath.

"Is *this* the same Billie Layton who drove

home with us a little while ago?" he asked. "The Little League pitcher?"

Billie felt herself blushing. She stole a shy glance at Jessica and Elizabeth. They were smiling proudly. "The very same one," Elizabeth said, putting her arm around Billie.

Mr. Wakefield opened the door for them, grinning from ear to ear. "I just hope that Sweet Valley is ready for you three beautiful girls." With that, they went out to the van and climbed in.

As they rode to Julie's house, Billie realized she hadn't really thought about the party yet. She had no idea what to expect.

When the girls arrived, they gave Julie their presents and were led to a large game room at the back of the house. One of the boys was playing DJ with Julie's stereo and some kids were dancing. A group was gathered around a Ping-Pong table, and toward the back of the room there was a table piled high with sandwiches, chips, cookies, and soda.

Billie hung back shyly. "Come on," Elizabeth coaxed. "You know everybody here. Let's go watch the Ping-Pong tournament."

After a few minutes, somebody thrust a

Ping-Pong paddle into Billie's hand, and before she realized what had happened, she had won three straight games. Her fastball might have evaporated on her, but she was still a pretty mean Ping-Pong player!

In a short while, Billie had forgotten all about her new dress and her curls and her lipstick, and she'd almost stopped looking around to see whether Jim was there. So when Aaron Dallas came up and asked her to dance, she accepted immediately. After that, it was Tom McKay, and then Pete Stone. None of the boys, who were all fellow Rangers, said a word about the game. They seemed to be happy just dancing with her, and Billie was having more fun than she could possibly have imagined.

In the corner by the food table, the Unicorns were all standing together. "Is that *really* Billie Layton over there?" Ellen Riteman asked Jessica, pointing to where Billie was dancing with Pete Stone.

Jessica nodded happily, munching on a chocolate-chip cookie. "It certainly is," she said. "Doesn't she look great?" She looked over at Sally Holcomb, who was wearing a peasant-style dress. Jim was with her, and they were talking.

"Billie looks *terrific!*" Mary Wallace exclaimed.

Even Lila had to concede that Billie looked nice. "It's certainly a change from the way she looked this afternoon," she admitted.

"And look at all the guys she's dancing with," Ellen remarked enviously. "Half the boys in this room are waiting in line. Even Colin Harmon wants a turn."

Mary smiled a little. "You know, maybe the Unicorns are missing out on something."

Lila looked at her suspiciously. "Missing out?" she asked. She sounded a little worried. "What could we possibly be missing out on?"

"Well," Mary began, "we have lots of talented people in the club, but Jessica is our only athlete and athletes *are* pretty special. Maybe we ought to invite Billie to become a Unicorn."

Ellen Riteman looked thoughtful. "I see what you mean," she said. "And it was sort of fun cheering at the ball game—at least, until it started to rain. Maybe it would have been even more fun if we'd been cheering for a fellow Unicorn."

But Lila wasn't so sure. "Let's not be too hasty," she cautioned. "I think we should wait and see how Billie does at the game tomorrow. I, for one, really don't care all that much about baseball." She smiled at Jessica. "I just went to the game as a favor to Jessica."

Jessica sighed. It was clear that the Unicorns really weren't interested in doing nice things for other people—not yet, anyway. She glanced over toward the spot where she had seen Jim and Sally a minute before. They were still there. It didn't look as if Jim even knew that Billie was in the room.

She had to figure out some way to get Jim and Billie together.

Out on the dance floor, Billie breathlessly turned down Tommy Parks' request for another dance and made her way to a seat in the corner to rest. Tommy followed her, insisting on getting her a soft drink.

She looked around the room at all of the familiar people. She still couldn't get over how differently the boys were treating her! She played ball with some of them at least twice a week, and although they were always friendly on the field, they had never been so attentive! The thought of Tommy Parks rushing off to get her an orange drink made her want to giggle with delight. She could feel her cheeks getting pink.

Just then, Billie heard Sally Holcomb's unmistakable laugh. She looked up and saw her over in the corner talking to Jim. Sally's bright red-and-yellow peasant dress revealed her shoulders and made her look at least fourteen. All of a sudden Billie's own dress, which had seemed so grown-up and beautiful a moment ago, seemed babyish in comparison.

Jim looked up just then, and stared straight at her. Forcing herself to smile, Billie waved. But Jim didn't wave back. He just stared at her with a kind of curious look, as if he were looking at a stranger. Then, he turned his back to say something to Jessica, who had just come up beside him.

The excitement Billie had been feeling turned to instant gloom. It was nice that all the boys paid attention to her. But she had to admit it was Jim's attention she wanted. And it was very clear he was too busy to even say hello to her.

Without waiting to tell Tommy she didn't want the orange drink, Billie crossed the room and went into the hallway, blinking back the tears. She was trying so hard not to cry she didn't pay any attention when Jim looked at her with a shock of recognition on his face. She didn't even see him take two steps toward her, with his hand out.

Billie just kept on walking down the hallway, heading for the front door.

"You're not leaving so soon, are you, Billie?" It was Mrs. Porter, standing beside the stairs. She sounded concerned.

Billie took a deep breath. "I . . . I have to," she said. "I have to go home. Thank you for the lovely party."

At that moment, the doorbell rang. Mrs. Porter opened the door.

"I'm Commander Layton. Is my daughter here?"

Mrs. Porter stepped back. "Yes, she's right here," she said.

Billie blinked in surprise. "Daddy!" she exclaimed. "What are *you* doing here?"

There was a worried crease between her father's eyes. "I've come to get you," he said.

"To get me?" Billie's heart was beginning to pound. "Is there something wrong?"

"No," he said. "At least, I hope not. I've just taken your mother to the hospital. Your little brother is on his way!"

Ten

◇

Billie's mother had decided to have her baby in a special area of the hospital called "The Stork Club." It was on a floor adjacent to the regular maternity rooms and the delivery room, but "The Stork Club" was completely different. Instead of the stark white walls and ceilings that she had imagined, her mother's two-room suite was more like a hotel room. There was a sofa, a TV set, and photos of babies on the wall. There was even a little refrigerator and a hot plate in the corner.

"The Stork Club" was different in another way, too, as Commander Layton explained to Billie. In this part of the hospital, she would get to hold her baby brother as soon as he was born.

"Me? *Hold* the baby?" Billie asked in alarm. "If it's all the same to you, Dad, I don't think I want to hold him right away."

Her father didn't respond. "Margaret?" he called, opening a door to another room. "Billie's here." He opened the door wider and ushered Billie in. "I'm going down to the snack bar for a few minutes," he announced. Then he left and Billie found herself alone with her mother. She had expected her to look sick or worried, but she didn't at all. Her cheeks were pink and she seemed excited and expectant, lying in a bed that was made with pretty, pink-flowered sheets. She was wearing her favorite pink night-gown, and there was a bouquet of flowers on the bedside table. Beside the bed stood a little wicker bassinet, already made up with blue sheets and a blue blanket.

Happily, Billie's mother held out her arms. "There you are," she said, "my favorite daughter!" And then her eyes lit up with surprise and admiration as she gazed at Billie.

"Oh, Belinda!" she exclaimed. "You look so pretty! Your dress is simply beautiful—and your *hair!*"

Billie couldn't help smiling at her mother's surprise. "Jessica curled it," she said, patting the light brown ringlets on her shoulders. "And Elizabeth helped, too."

"What fun!" her mother exclaimed. "And how was the game? Did you win? I'm awfully sorry that Dad didn't make it, honey. He wanted to wait and hear what the doctor had to say."

"Oh, that's OK," Billie said, waving her hand. "We got rained out, anyway." She gave her mother a close look. "We got rescheduled for tomorrow. Do you think he can come then?" She wasn't quite sure why she asked. Things had been so bad today that maybe Coach Andrews wouldn't even want to start her tomorrow.

"I'm sure he can come," her mother said. She sighed and patted her tummy under the sheet. Billie saw that there were little tears— tears of happiness—in the corners of her eyes. "I can't *imagine* a nicer time than being here with my grown-up daughter, waiting for her little brother to arrive!"

Suddenly, neither could Billie. It seemed like the most exciting moment in the whole world. And somehow, it also seemed like the perfect moment to tell her mother about getting her period.

When she finished the whole story, her

mother squeezed her hand. "My *very* grown-up daughter," she murmured with a big smile.

At that moment, Billie's father came back, with hot coffee for himself and an orange drink and a magazine for Billie. Commander Layton started talking about the things all four of them would do together, but Billie's mind kept wandering.

"And when he gets a little older," Billie's father continued, "you can show him your famous fastball."

Billie made a face. "My not-so-famous fastball," she mumbled, thinking about that afternoon.

But suddenly it didn't seem very important. She had pitched a couple of bad innings. So what? After all, even the best pitchers in the world had a bad day once in a while. And as for Jim Sturbridge and Sally Holcomb—well, that was something she could probably get used to, as long as she and Jim could still talk about baseball once in a while.

A little while later, the doctor arrived with two nurses, all dressed in green pants and green smocks. Billie kissed her mom and took her orange drink into the other room. She sat

down on the sofa with her favorite magazine—
Sports Illustrated—open on her lap. There was a
great story about one of her all-time favorite
baseball heroes.

Billie had a hard time keeping her mind on
the article, though. She was exhausted from the
events of the day. Sleepily, she curled up in a
corner of the sofa. Maybe she could take a quick
nap. She dreamed she heard a baby crying,
sweet and far away, and she curled up tighter,
feeling warm and happy. It was a nice sound.

Then she felt her father gently shaking her
shoulder, and realized she hadn't dreamed it
after all!

"Wake up, honey," he said, "your brother's
here!" He was beaming from ear to ear. "Big
and healthy and ready for anything!"

Billie sat up straight and rubbed her eyes.

Her father held out his hand. "Come and
see," he invited.

Tiptoeing gingerly, Billie went into the other
room. Her mother was sitting up in the bed,
looking a little tired but very happy. In the crook
of her arm, she was holding a tiny baby,
wrapped in a soft blue blanket.

Billie sat down on the edge of the bed, a

new and very strange feeling flooding through her. She stared at the baby, her new little brother, as he waved one tiny fist and made a sucking noise with his lips. He was the most helpless little creature she had ever seen, and her heart was filled with love for him.

"Would you like to hold him?" her mother asked softly.

Billie looked up at her father with a worried frown. "Do you think it's OK?" she asked. "I mean, I won't hurt him or anything, will I?"

"I'm *sure* you won't hurt him," her father said. "Babies are tougher than you think." He smiled. "You certainly were. You were one tough little kid." He looked at her. "Cute, too."

Billie couldn't help laughing. But she stopped laughing when her father picked up the baby from her mother and put him in Billie's arms.

"Here you are," he said. "Meet your brother, William Arthur Layton."

Billie leaned over the baby, cuddling him close and making comforting noises. All the jealous thoughts she'd had about him were forgotten. He was her very own baby brother. It seemed like a miracle.

Eleven

◇

As Billie sat on the bed, her father stepped back, looking at the two of them together. He smiled for a moment, and then his expression suddenly changed to surprise. He whistled softly. "Hey," he said, "who's this beautiful, dressed-up young lady?"

Billie looked up, startled. "What?" she asked. She looked around the room.

"He means *you*, honey," Mrs. Layton said, laughing. "I guess he hasn't seen you in a dress lately."

Commander Layton shook his head in surprise. "I know I've had a lot on my mind this afternoon," he said, "but how could I have missed . . . ?" He grinned and touched Billie's curls. "Margaret, she has your hair, and your complexion, too." He whistled again, in admiration. "She's going to be a beauty when she grows up, just like you."

"She *is* grown up," her mother said, very softly, with a special look at Billie. "She's a young lady now."

"You're right," her father said. "She is, indeed. And a very beautiful young lady, at that!"

As Billie held the baby, her father bent over and hugged and kissed her. She realized that this was the very first time she'd ever gotten his attention as a *girl*. He'd always complimented her on her athletic abilities, but none of those compliments had ever been as sweet as the one he paid her just now.

"I think," her mother said, "that if you two don't mind, the baby and I would like to have a little nap now." She smiled at Billie. "Would you put him in his basket for me, honey?"

Carefully, as if she were holding an armful of robin's eggs, Billie put the baby into the basket and loosened his blanket. Just at that moment, a blissful smile crossed his face and he opened his eyes.

"He smiled at me!" Billie exclaimed excitedly. "And he's got blue eyes!"

Her mother laughed as she snuggled into

the pillows. "I expect that that smile is here to stay."

Billie's father held out his hand. "Come on, Billie. Let's let these guys get some rest, huh?"

Billie pulled herself up straighter as they left the room. "Actually," she said, "I think I'm getting a little too old for a nickname like that. Can you call me Belinda? Besides, we've got a real little Billy in the family now. It would be pretty confusing if there were two of us."

Commander Layton laughed huskily and put his hand on her shoulder. "You sure about that, Bil—Belinda?" he asked.

"I'm sure," Belinda said. And she was.

As they got into the car to go home, her father suddenly looked stricken.

"You know," he said, "in all the excitement this afternoon, I forgot all about the baseball game! I'm really sorry I missed it, Belinda."

"You don't have to be sorry," she told him. "You didn't miss a thing. We got rained out so we'll be playing tomorrow. That means we can't go fishing, but I guess we'd have postponed the trip anyway since Billy arrived early. Mom said you could probably make the game, though."

Commander Layton nodded as he started

the car. "I'm sure I can. Are you pitching again?"

Belinda shrugged. "I don't know," she said. "I had a couple of bad innings this afternoon. Maybe Coach Andrews will decide to start Dennis instead."

"Well, I'll be there," her father promised. "I'll be cheering for you." He stole a sideways glance at her. "Hey," he said, "I'm really hungry. In fact, I'm starving. What do you say we stop for a pizza? With a double order of anchovies?"

Belinda giggled. She and her father both loved anchovies. "That would be great," she said happily. "A double order of anchovies."

On Sunday, there was a not a single cloud in the sky and the sun shone brightly in Sweet Valley. Belinda was at the field at one o'clock sharp. Her newly-washed uniform was clean and white and she'd pulled her still-curled hair back into her usual ponytail. She hadn't been able to resist using just a little dab of lip gloss that she'd found on her mother's dressing table, and one tiny squirt of perfume.

As she got out of the car and began to trot

toward the home side of the park, she ran into Pete Stone, who played center field.

"Hi," Pete said. He was staring at her.

"Hi," Belinda said, suddenly feeling shy.

Pete cleared his throat. "Listen," he said, "I was wondering . . . Uh, maybe you'd like to go over to Casey's after the game for some ice cream?"

"Hey, thanks," Belinda replied. "Can I take a rain check? My dad and I are going to the hospital to see my new little brother."

Pete grinned. "A new brother, huh?" He gave her an admiring look. "Well, he's got a heck of a lot to live up to."

Belinda shot the grin back. "Thanks," she said. Pete's compliment made her feel good all over.

Coach Andrews was standing by the bench when she came up, her glove in one hand and a ball in the other. "Well," he asked, squinting at her, "how does that arm feel today, Billie?"

Belinda looked up at him. "Would you mind," she said sweetly, "calling me Belinda? That's my real name, after all. And I've got a new brother—we're calling *him* Billy."

The coach blinked. "Yeah, sure," he said. "Well, what do you think, Belinda? How's the arm? Feel like you can start for us today?"

Belinda grinned confidently. "Sure, I can start," she said, smacking the ball into her glove, hard. "The arm feels great! Better than ever, in fact."

The coach slapped her on the back. "OK, then, you're on. You and Jim warm up, huh?"

As Belinda spun around to start warming up, she spotted Jessica and Elizabeth in the stands. Her father was sitting on the same bench, eating a hot dog. He waved at her with a proud grin on his face and held up two fingers in a V, for victory.

Jim was buckling on his face mask when Belinda found him. "Coach says for us to warm up," she said briefly. "I'm starting this afternoon."

Jim's face broke into a broad grin. "Hey, that's great!" he said. Then his grin turned sheepish and his ears began to grow pink. "Uh, about yesterday—" he began.

Belinda took a deep breath. *Why did he have to bring that up?* "I know I didn't do so well yesterday," she admitted. "But today's going to be a lot better." She rubbed her arm, feeling the strength and power in it. "I can *feel* it."

"No, no," Jim said, flushing deep red. "I don't mean about what happened at the game. I'm talking about the party."

Then Belinda remembered. Jim and Sally. The look on Jim's face when he looked at her, as if he were looking at a stranger.

"Oh, that," she said flatly. He didn't need to bring *that* up, either. It was over with, and best forgotten.

But Jim was insistent. "I just wanted to say that I didn't recognize you yesterday afternoon at the party, that's all. I mean, you were so pretty in that blue dress, with your hair all curled. You looked so *different*. I didn't even know it was you until Jessica told me. I went looking for you then, but I couldn't find you anywhere. Then somebody said you'd left." He looked down at the dirt and drew a circle in it with the toe of his sneaker. "I was sorry you'd gone," he said. "I wanted to ask you to dance."

"You did?" Belinda asked delightedly. "You really did? Honest?"

Jim looked at her, his eyes very serious.

"Yeah," he replied. "I really did. Honest." He flashed her a grin.

"Thanks for telling me, Sturbridge," Belinda said. She took a dozen running steps backward and tossed the ball at Jim. He caught it and plopped it a couple of times in his mitt, getting the feel of it. Behind his mask, he was grinning.

"OK, Layton," he challenged, lobbing the ball back to her. "Let's see what you've got on the ball today!"

What Belinda had on the ball today was *lots* of steam. Her fastball sizzled and her curve dropped as if it had a magnetic attraction to home plate. Hardly anyone got to first base. And when the game was all over, the score was Rangers eight, Rebels nothing. It was a solid shutout!

Behind the plate, Jim yanked off his mask and rushed out to hug Belinda. "Great game!" he shouted. Tom McKay dashed in from second base, and Pete Stone from center field, and they all did an impromptu dance on the pitcher's mound. Up in the bleachers, Jessica was leading the Ranger fans in a victory cheer.

But Belinda was happiest when she saw her father. He had borrowed a pom-pom and was waving it wildly, and she could hear his voice over all the others.

"Hooray, *Belinda!*" he shouted. "Way to go, Belinda!"

Twelve

◇

The next day, Jessica and Belinda carried their lunch trays to a table where several of the Unicorns were talking about Ellen Riteman's new idea.

"A birthday-party service?" Jessica asked, opening her milk carton.

Ellen nodded. "Sure. Mothers who want to give a birthday party for their kids could call us, and we'd do the whole thing. Balloons, games, refreshments, decorations. They'd pay us, and we'd donate the money to Sweet Valley Middle School. That way we'd be *sure* to win the Service Award!"

Jessica put her milk down and clapped delightedly. "Ellen," she crowed, "that's a fabulous idea! Parties are *exactly* what the Unicorns do best. We'd make tons of money—and it would be great for our image!"

"Just think what a glorious new image we'd have!" Lila chimed in.

Janet looked up from her plate of spaghetti. "Let's put Ellen's suggestion at the top of the agenda for our next meeting," she said. She turned to Belinda. "Right now, we've got something else we need to take care of."

Belinda looked around the table, feeling a little uncomfortable. She wasn't sure why Jessica had invited her to eat with the Unicorns.

Janet cleared her throat and sat up straight. "Belinda Layton," she said, in an authoritative voice, "you've been asked here for a very important reason. In view of your extra-special accomplishments, the Unicorns have chosen *you* to become a member of the club."

Belinda stared at Janet. "A . . . a member?" she squeaked. "Of the *Unicorns*?"

Jessica nudged her. "Say yes," she whispered. "That way we can spend more time together."

Janet began talking about what a privilege and honor it was to become a member of the Unicorns, and how the Unicorns were all unique and special. She went on and on, but Belinda scarcely heard her. Then Janet paused and looked at Belinda. It was obvious that she was waiting for an answer.

Belinda looked around the table. The other girls were watching her expectantly, and she felt a flush of pride. Belinda Layton, a Unicorn!

"Yes," she said happily. "Yes, I'd *love* to be a Unicorn."

Jessica threw her arms around her. "Oh, Belinda," she said ecstatically, "this is *wonderful!*"

After lunch, Jessica and Belinda put their dishes on the conveyer belt. "Are you going to the concert next week?" Belinda asked. "My mom said she already has a list of books she plans to order for the school library." Sweet Valley Middle School had organized a rock concert featuring a very popular high school band, The Wild Ones, in order to raise money for new library books.

Jessica nodded. "The concert's going to be a lot of fun," she said. "I can't wait to see that gorgeous lead singer up close. I've already planned what I'm going to wear."

Behind them, Ellen Riteman spoke up. "And Secca Lake is a perfect setting for a concert. *Everybody* will be there."

"Everybody but me," a gloomy voice said behind them. With a noisy crash, a boy dumped a load of dishes on the conveyor belt.

Jessica spun around. "Patrick Morris," she exclaimed, "why won't *you* be there? It's one of the biggest events of the year. Everyone's looking forward to it."

Patrick looked down at his feet. "I guess I shouldn't have said anything," he mumbled.

Jessica studied him. "But you have to come," she insisted.

Patrick threw her a miserable glance. "My folks won't let me go," he said. "They say the concert will go on past my curfew."

"Curfew?" Jessica could hardly believe her ears. "Curfews went out with the Dark Ages!"

"Not at *my* house they didn't," Patrick said. "Curfews, rules, regulations—you name it, my parents have a rule for it, with *no* exceptions." He turned and walked away with his hands deep in his pockets, his head bowed.

"Ugh," Belinda breathed, "how awful! Can you imagine having such *strict* parents?"

Jessica thought of her wonderful parents, always so understanding, always ready to listen when she had a problem. She stared after Patrick's retreating figure.

"No," she said, "I can't imagine it." *Poor Patrick*, she thought. *Living in his house must be like living in a prison. There ought to be a law against parents like that!*

We hope you enjoyed reading this book. If you would like to receive further information about available titles in the Bantam series, just write to the address below, with your name and address: Kim Prior, Bantam Books, 61–63 Uxbridge Road, Ealing, London W5 5SA

If you live in Australia or New Zealand and would like more information about the series, please write to:

Sally Porter
Transworld Publishers
(Australia) Pty Ltd
15–23 Helles Avenue
Moorebank
NSW 2170
AUSTRALIA

Kiri Martin
Transworld Publishers (NZ) Ltd
Cnr. Moselle and Waipareira Avenues
Henderson
Auckland
NEW ZEALAND

All Bantam and Young Adult books are available at your bookshop or newsagent, or can be ordered at the following address: Corgi/Bantam Books, Cash Sales Department, PO Box 11, Falmouth, Cornwall, TR10 9EN.

Please list the title(s) you would like, and send together with a cheque or postal order. You should allow for the cost of book(s) plus postage and packing charges as follows:

80p for one book
£1.00 for two books
£1.20 for three books
£1.40 for four books
Five or more books free.

Please note that payment must be made in pounds sterling; other currencies are unacceptable.

(The above applies to readers in the UK and Republic of Ireland only)

BFPO customers, please allow for the cost of the book(s) plus the following for postage and packing: 80p for the first book, and 20p per copy for each additional book.

Overseas customers, please allow £1.50 for postage and packing for the first book, £1.00 for the second book, and 30p for each subsequent title ordered.